SON OF WOLVES

Fictive Kin book five

SON of WOLVES

Nico Silver

WHITE RAVEN PRESS

Second Edition, 2024.
ISBN: 978-1-998212-26-2
This book was previously published as by Nicole Silver.

White Raven Press,
North Cowichan, British Columbia, Canada

Cover design and digital alterations by Nik Sylvan
Model stock © Neo-Stock via www.neostock.com
Animal stock © Ramon Carretero via Dreamstime.com
Background stock (road and moon) © Dary423 via Dreamstime.com
Background stock (city) © Songquan Deng via Dreamstime.com
Background stock (forest) © Shukaylova Zinaida via Shutterstock.com
Fog brushes © Krist A via brusheezy.com
Title typefaces: Eva Antiqua Heavy by Spiece Graphics, and Snell Roundhand by Linotype

Content warning: This book contains material that is not suitable for all audiences. It is recommended for readers 18+. Some content that may be triggering for readers includes explicit sex, violence, and sexual violence.

For Mark, who has to put up with me.

Chapter One

THE SMELL WHEN I open the door to Magne's apartment is almost overwhelming.

Bleach and fabric softener and carpet cleaner seem to hover and mingle in the air like a noxious fog and I have to take a step back into the relatively clear air of the hallway to take a breath.

"Magne?" I know he can hear me. He'll have heard the grinding of the industrial elevator as I took the one floor up. And no, I'm not lazy; I could take the stairs but we always use the elevator so those of use who live here know when the others come and go. It's a courtesy and a comfort.

I take a deep breath and plunge into the loft, grab a kitchen stool on my way by, and climb up to reach the lever that cracks open one of the upper windows. The old once-industrial building has huge panes of glass on one wall but, except for the window that leads to the fire escape, they only have small panels at the top and bottom that angle open a few inches.

I pause to suck in a breath when I get the bottom window cracked, then move on to the next.

Magne doesn't make an appearance until I've got the last one open and a trickle of fresh air has started to clear out the fumes. He looks like hell.

His eyes are red and watery from the cleaning products, and his hair is lank and flat. Unwashed-looking. I mean, his hair is never really *styled*, per se, but its shaggy unkemptness – looking like he just rolled out of bed and ran his fingers through it – is dead sexy on him. Right now, he looks the opposite of sexy.

"Hey Su," he says, and tries a smile. It looks forced, and this is a man who grins as carelessly as breathing. And he's the only person I've ever met who looks so comfortable in his body that a casual lean looks actually casual and not like he's posing. Now, he looks like he doesn't know what to do with his limbs.

"You look like crap, Mags," I say. No point in being subtle with him. He can probably smell what I'm thinking.

So yeah, I'm Su, and my best friend is a werewolf. A big, hairy man who can take the shape of something more-or-less wolflike, who looks dumb as a truck, but is actually one of the smartest people I know.

He shrugs and puts down the contraption he's hauled with him out of the depths of his apartment. It's a rental carpet cleaner. I'm pretty sure there are no actual carpets in here.

"No one to look hot for," he says.

"And here I thought you went around looking hot just in case." That provokes something like the grin I'm used to. The dimple in his cheek even makes a brief appearance.

He gestures to the living area, with its low sofas and chairs and way more cushions – in all shapes and sizes – than any normal person could ever possibly want. "Just tidying up a bit." Now that I look, I can see lines where he's used the carpet cleaner to steam clean the furniture. I study his face again. I mean, Magne's tidy – way more organized than I am – but I've never known him to be a clean freak.

"When was the last time *you* tidied up?" I say. "Yourself, I mean." Like I said, no point in being subtle.

He shrugs again. "I can't smell myself."

"I don't know how you can smell anything in here." The bleach has dulled my own nose, and mine's even more sensitive than Magne's, because I'm not exactly human either. The air is beginning to clear a bit, at least, as a breeze finds its way in the windows.

"I can smell *her*," he says. He meets my eyes finally. I don't think the redness is from tears, just from cleaning products. Magne is far too macho to cry, even alone, which is too bad, because honestly, a man who's not afraid to cry is deeply sexy. But werewolf culture is pretty focused on men being manly, apparently.

Her. His recently departed girlfriend – now ex-girlfriend – Cara, a beautiful, powerful, witch woman who decided our friend group was too weird, scary, and dangerous to stay close to.

Who discovered she was pregnant with Magne's offspring and decided she really needed to go home.

"Come on," I say. I take Magne's hand and pull him towards the door. "You're spending entirely too much time feeling sorry for yourself. You need to run. And this place needs to air out."

"Yeah," he says. "Back atcha."

Because, oh yeah, my beautiful vampire boyfriend, love of my life, is now *my* ex. It's a long story, and there are reasons, and it's not that he fell out of love, but it still sucks in every possible way that we can't be together.

Me and Magne, a perfect matched pair of newly-dumped non-humans. Well, matched except that he looks like a brown-haired Viking, and I look like what resulted when a Viking took the Silk Road to China and decided to leave a baby behind.

I barely pause to let him put shoes on before dragging him outside and down the street towards the park. We live in a light industrial area of small factories, buildings converted to loft apartments, and abandoned storefronts. It's popular with *other* kind, because normal humans don't come here too often. We like it because it's only a few minutes brisk walk to a big park that borders the river.

Under the trees, we stop at a huge oak – a mother tree if I ever saw one – so Magne can undress and stash his clothes. I step around the tree to give him privacy – not that he cares; he's the least shy person I know and always seems as comfortable naked as clothed. But I move out of sight also because – once I finally got the hang of it – shifting for me is as simple as walking through a door, and I don't even have to undress.

Between one heartbeat and the next, I go from being a mid-height Euro-Asian woman with absurdly long hair to being a rusty-red fox with an absurdly bushy tail.

Yeah, how that came about is a story for another day.

I wait until the creaking of joints and snapping of tendons stops and all I hear is Magne breathing. Werewolves aren't really supernatural; they're made when a symbiotic organism takes over the running of a human body and transforms it. New joints form and old joints move in different ways until a perfectly human-looking person can transform – like those cartoon robots – into a creature you might mistake for a wolf in a dark forest.

In full daylight, what Magne looks like is harder to describe. One of those old-school movie werewolves that seems to be caught somewhere more than halfway between human and canine is probably the closest thing I can think of, but Magne has a wild, terrifying beauty that those movie monsters lack.

"Shall we?" he says, his voice rough and slurred around his massive teeth. It's hard to talk when your mouth has turned into a muzzle, I guess.

I turn and let my legs carry me. I could answer, but even I find it weird to hear my perfectly human-Su voice coming out of my completely fox body.

Magne follows and for a long time we just run. Under and around trees, in and out of dappled sun. The trees here aren't as big as they are farther north, but they're big enough and leafy enough that they keep a lot of the smaller plants from getting much light, so it's easy to weave a path around and over the undergrowth. It's been too long since I had a good run, and judging by the way Magne's lungs are working, it's been too long for him, too.

When we reach the river, I find a nice mossy spot to bask in the last of the afternoon sun while Magne wades right out into the water. I'm not sure how were physiology works, but I do know he won't feel the cold much until he's back in human shape, and anyway, it's nearly summer. Once he's back in human form, though, he'll be wanting a hot drink and a warm blanket. Too bad our lofts aren't equipped with fireplaces.

At first he just splashes in the shallows, but then he spies something under the water and goes still, and stalks, and pounces.

In human shape, Magne's pretty nice to look at, even if he is a bit too hairy for my taste. Or so I keep telling myself. In wolf shape he moves like liquid, smoother than the river he's hunting in, and watching him is like listening to the finest poetry.

There was a time when we might have been lovers – the attraction was there on both sides – but then I met Evgeny and fell head over heels despite my best efforts not to. I mean, vampires kept trying to kill me; why would I even want to have sex with one, let alone *love* one? And Magne met Cara. And that was that.   But watching him emerge from the water with a gleaming silver trout in his mouth, I wonder if we're better as friends or if we should see if we can build something more.

I mean, I do love him. I have for ages, but he was always relegated to the "friend who is not for snogging" part of my brain. And he always acted like an older brother. Now with both of us single again, and him hurting – okay, *both* of us hurting – I just want to make everything better.

Well, not in these shapes we're wearing now. I'm not into bestiality, thanks ever so much. Besides, in our *otherly* shapes, Magne's like ten times my size. Or several times, anyway.

We share the fish he's caught. My fox nature makes me much less squeamish than I might be, and anyway I've always like sashimi. Then we curl up side by side on the moss and watch the sky fade from bright blue to a deeper shade and then to black, and lights appear on the shore of Wonder Island, just visible poking out around the end of a bend in the river.

"I thought this end of Wonder Island was all wild," I say, curling in closer to Magne's body heat.

He lifts his head to look, then relaxes back onto the moss. "It is," he says, sounding sleepy. We should head back soon and see if I can convince him to take a bath and get some sleep. I could probably use both of those things myself.

"I see lights there," I say.

"Maybe someone's camping." I can hear his lips sliding over his teeth as he speaks, trying to keep the words clear.

"That's a lot of light for camping." It looks like a couple of floodlights, maybe, and little points of hand-held flashlights moving here and there. There's no way to tell, but I'd bet something's happening over there. The people who actually live on the island are extremely private, though, so we'll probably never know.

I stir again when I feel Magne shiver. I guess his wolf shape isn't entirely immune to the cold, and since it isn't even – strictly speaking – an actual wolf shape, he doesn't have a full coat of fur like I do. The promise of an early summer has faded with the sunlight and the air has become crisp.

"Yeah," he says, when I stand. "Time to face my empty apartment."

"I'm sorry," I say, as if it's my fault Cara chose to leave. It isn't; I wasn't even in the country. But if I'd been home to deal with Evgeny's… situation… maybe she'd have stayed.

Magne butts his head against mine and then we're racing back through the trees towards the mother oak. I could, if I wanted to, leave him far behind. Werewolves have better night vision than humans, but nothing near as good as a fox's, so he has to run slow enough to let his other senses keep him from running into trees. And whatever variety of fox woman it is that I am is crazy fast anyway, whether that comes from my dad's *hexenfuchs* ancestry or from whatever powers the old Asian fox ladies who once saved my life gave me. But that's another story for another time. What it means is that I'm never quite sure what I'm capable of.

But anyway, I'm some kind of magic fox hybrid shifter, and I can be very, very fast. So I could leave Magne far behind, if I wanted to. But he's my friend and I don't want to bruise his manly ego too badly, so I just run fast enough that we arrive back at the tree at the same time. I mean, I may be soft-hearted, but that doesn't mean I have to let him *win*.

I take his hand – once it's hand-shaped again – as we walk home. His fingers are freezing.

"One of these days you're going to get hypothermia," I say.

"I've got a nice bottle of Scotch waiting for me," he replies, and pulls his hand away so he can drape his arm across my shoulders. It's a friendly gesture, not a come-on, and I wonder if I want it to be him making a move. Back in our human shapes, I remember how it felt when we were newly neighbors and I desperately wanted to get him naked.

I like sex. A lot. And with Ev gone, maybe I don't really want Magne. Maybe I just want someone to fuck. Except I don't think that's the case. I mean, I don't go out a lot, but I haven't found myself drooling over every hot man or woman I run into when I *do* go out.

"You know that doesn't actually work, right?" I say. "The booze just makes you *think* you're warm."

He pulls me closer and kisses the top of my head. Only the fact that he smells like he hasn't showered recently and like he just ate a fish raw, guts and all, keeps me from reacting to the kiss like it's more than he meant it to be.

"I'll put it in hot chocolate," he says. "Want some?"

"Only if you take a bath first."

"You know you love my manly scent." He growls into my hair, then tilts his chin towards his armpit. "Okay, maybe I smell a little *too* manly."

Without even saying anything, we decide to leave Magne's place to its airing out, and keep going up to the third floor, where my loft is.

My place is much less homey than Magne's, really. It's mostly open space. Handy for practicing kung fu, but not really inviting. But I've got a reasonably comfortable collection of mis-matched couches and easy chairs, a kitchen area to which I recently added an actual stove, and a huge bed with curtains that pull around it for the days when I want to hide in a dark, enclosed space.

The bathroom is the only part of the loft that's got walls and that's where Magne heads as soon as he's got his shoes off. Even before I knew him very well he had a tendency to treat my place as an extension of his own.

I put the kettle on as the shower starts up. I try not to think of him in there, naked. He's in the shower a long time – he must have been even colder than I thought – and when he comes out he's just got a towel wrapped around his waist. Because he couldn't make it easier, could he?

"I should have stopped at my place for clean clothes," he says.

I try very hard not to look at his chest, broad and furry and covered, like the rest of his body, with a tracery of thin white scars. They're the result of the brutal process of being made a werewolf and the only place nearly free of their map-like lines is his face. Only one thin scar bisects his right eyebrow and another follows the line of his left cheekbone.

"I don't mind," I finally say, aiming for a cheeky grin, and then hand him a cup of tea with a healthy dollop of whisky – not as top-shelf as what he usually drinks, but still decent. I go to step around him for my turn in the shower and he stops me by moving between me and the bathroom.

"Are you okay?" he says. "Really?" I rest my forehead on his chest and feel the solidness of him.

"Not really," I say. "But I will be."

"Yeah," he says, and I feel the movement of his lips against my hair. "Me too." He gathers me close in a gentle hug, like he's afraid of breaking me. I hear him sip his tea, feel the bunching of his muscles. Evgeny was my true love, but Magne is my rock, solid and immoveable and always there to anchor me.

"It's funny," he says. "When I started seeing Cara we agreed we didn't want anything serious. It was a fling for both of us. Fun, good sex, a bit of companionship." He sips his tea again, and I turn my head to listen to his heartbeat, slow and strong.

"Then all that shit happened with Ev." Yeah, another story for another time. "And she was there, helping. I don't think I could have got him to Wonder Island without her. And I started to think maybe we could be more than short-term bedpartners." He pauses again, sips his tea, then puts the mug on the counter. His hand, when it puts it on my back, is extra-warm from the heat of the mug.

"And then we found out she was pregnant," he says. His smoked-whisky voice is soft but steady, like he's just stating facts, but I can feel the tension in the way he holds me.

"I'm so sorry, Mags."

"Yeah," he says. "Me, too. I never thought I'd want to be a father. I mean, I figured someday, but not yet." I feel his sigh, deep like it's moving through his whole body.

"I mean, she wasn't even far enough along to show. It was just two little clumps of cells inside her, barely big enough to see. But the *idea*...." He pauses, takes a deep breath. "I suddenly wanted that more than anything. I think I might have wanted those babies more than I wanted Cara."

"Magne..." I start to say, but he pulls away far enough to press a finger to my lips.

"She texted this morning," he says. "To let me know the... the appointment went well. She's fine and the pregnancy was terminated." His voice breaks a little on the last word and his arms tighten. "She *texted*," he says. "She couldn't even *call* me."

I can't help it. I don't want him to be hurting. So I stretch up to put my arms around his neck, stand on tiptoes, and kiss him.

I feel him hesitate, like he's going to pull away, but then his muscles soften, his body relaxes against mine, and he kisses me back.

And there's the sudden loud buzzing of the building intercom and we pull apart to stare at each other. I can't remember the last time someone buzzed either of us. Anyone who comes here usually calls, or texts, or has a key.

I let go of Magne reluctantly, feeling the absence of his warmth like a cold wind, and go to the wall by the door, press the button.

"Yeah?" I say. My voice comes out shaky.

"Miss Fuchs?" The voice is vaguely familiar, pronouncing my last name like the speaker knows German, and I sense Magne go still behind me. Very still.

"Yes?"

"It's Detective O'Malley. Magne's friend. I… may have some news about your sister."

Chapter Two

I BUZZ THE DETECTIVE in and I guess Magne realizes he's not dressed because he suddenly whips the towel off, hands it to me, and heads out the door, striding down the hall towards the stairs.

I don't try to pretend to myself that I don't enjoy the sight of his naked backside.

"You're welcome to use my place, if you'd rather," he says as he reaches the stairway door.

"He's coming up here," I reply, pulling my gaze away from Magne to check the elevator lights. The ancient industrial device begins its grind upwards. "But come back when you're decent." I have to assume his werewolf hearing will catch that last bit, because when I glance back the stairway door has closed behind him.

I look around the loft, thinking I should tidy, but there's not really much to clean other than the wet towel in my hand and Magne's discarded clothes on the bathroom floor. I stuff it all into the laundry hamper and make it back to the door as a short – compared to Magne, anyway – middle-aged man with unremarkable greying brown hair and pale blue eyes gets off the elevator.

I spoke to Detective O'Malley in the phone once, but never in person, so I wasn't sure what to expect. I definitely *didn't* expect someone so ordinary looking. He looks a little bit like a TV cop in jeans and a dark blue button-down shirt, but otherwise he could be anybody, and I have to remind myself that he's one of Magne's family's extended pack members and therefore a werewolf. Which means he's probably a lot older and a good deal more dangerous than he looks.

"Miss Fuchs," he says, holding out his hand. I shake it and can tell he's moderating his grip, letting me feel just a little of his real strength.

"Call me Su," I say.

"Su," he repeats. "Nobody ever calls me anything but O'Malley."

"Hey, Seamus. How are you?" says Magne, slapping the detective on the back so hard the other man winces. He didn't take the elevator up, and he didn't make a sound as he came along the hall. I get out of the way so they can both come in. They clasp forearms and smack shoulders as manly men do. I can tell Magne is genuinely pleased to see O'Malley, and I think it's mutual.

"You dad says 'hi'," the detective says and something flickers in Magne's eyes, but he doesn't react otherwise. "You know I'm supposed to be keeping an eye on you, kid."

Magne snorts at that. "I called home last week."

"And talked to your mother, your sister, and no one else." O'Malley doesn't press the issue, but turns back to me, instead.

"You have news?" I say. I try to make my voice even and strong, but I guess I don't succeed, because Magne's there right beside me suddenly. Not touching me, just *there*.

"Can we sit?" O'Malley gestures toward the couches.

"Tea?" I ask. "Or coffee?"

"I'll make coffee," Magne says, and plants himself in the kitchen, as at home as he is in his own place, except he has a lot more stuff for cooking food in his kitchen. And since Evgeny introduced him to the difference between good coffee and merely strong coffee, he has at least three different devices for making it. Here, he has to make do with a kettle and a French press. At least I have several jars of very good beans and a coffee grinder, even if my selection isn't nearly as extensive as my collection of teas.

I sit in one of the big chairs and pull a blanket across my knees. I really want to sit where Magne can sit next to me, but I don't want to seem too needy. So I curl into my chair and wait as the detective chooses the couch along the back wall where he has a view of my entire nearly-empty loft.

He puts two folders on the coffee table. "I'm not officially on this investigation," he says. "But since Magne's a mutual friend, the detective who is on the case asked me to liaise."

I nod.

"Since there haven't been any developments in nearly seven years, it's more or less considered a cold case, even though it's officially still open."

I nod again, and take the coffee Magne hands me and automatically take a sip. Lots of sugar, no milk. I want to take the files off the table and look at whatever's in them, but cops make me nervous even if this one is a werewolf and knows my backstory. It wasn't all that long ago that I was paying the bills by pickpocketing.

"I take it some private citizen finally found something and reported it, since your lot don't seem to have gone looking recently." Magne's voice is teasing, but not entirely unserious, and O'Malley looks at him sharply. He sits on the other couch, on the end closest to me, where he can reach me if he needs to. I used to hate people trying to look after me – still do, really – but it's also nice to have a big, burly dude in protective mode hanging around nearby when you're feeling vulnerable. Even if the vulnerability is emotional and not physical.

O'Malley ignores the jab except to say, "I saw you born, kid, and you're still a brat."

Magne snorts. "I was never a brat."

O'Malley considers Magne. "You know," he says, "you're right, you always were more of a mama's boy. A nice kid. Your poor old dad kept *wishing* you'd be more of a brat. Your older brothers were total shits."

"They still are total shits," says Magne, then he takes a sip of his coffee.

"I won't tell them you said that," O'Malley says, and follows with a sip from his own cup, as if to end the topic.

But Magne says, "Please do tell them."

O'Malley looks like maybe he wants to say more, and if I weren't chewing my fingernails to stubs worrying about what news he has about my sister, I'd be dying of curiosity to hear more of Magne's childhood. He doesn't talk much about his family.

O'Malley sets the coffee cup aside and picks up one of the folders. He taps the other one with an index finger. "Copies for you," he says. "And you didn't get them from me." Then he opens the first folder and lays the contents out on the table – a set of black and white eight by ten photographs.

I don't look at them, afraid of what they might show. Instead, I stare at his hands as he pulls a notebook and pen from his pockets.

"I've been sent to ask if you can identify any of these items," he says. "They were found in a garbage bag on the south end of Wonder Island yesterday and reported to us earlier today. We have a team over there now looking for more evidence, but considering how long it's been, they don't expect to find much."

Was that the lights we saw? I glance at Magne, but he's looking at the pictures spread out on the coffee table.

"You think these might be her things?" he says.

"We're hoping Miss Fuchs – Su – can tell us that."

Not a dead body then. I finally make myself look down at the table and the photographs spread out there. Nope, no images of bloated corpses. I suck in a breath and let it out slowly. I had to go with my mom to the morgue to identify Dad when his body washed up on the river bank. Mum had to be IDed from dental records when they found her a few weeks later. The fish hadn't left enough of her face intact. My sister, who had disappeared with Dad, was never found at all.

"Su?" Magne's voice, soft, low, like someone trying not to startle a wild animal.

"Sorry," I say. I sound surprisingly calm. "I was just afraid of what I might see." I focus my mind away from my worst memories and look back at the photos in front of me.

"We're hoping you can tell us if these are the possessions of your sister, Kristine Mei Fuchs." Detective O'Malley says the words in an official cop tone, but there is sympathy there, too. I remember how kind he seemed on the phone, when Magne called him because I had started to remember I had a family and a past, but could only remember that something terrible had happened to them.

I pick up one of the photos. It shows a plastic trash bag half buried in river bank debris, with holes torn in it, like a wild animal scratched at it with long claws. Some fabric is visible through the holes, and what look's like a child's t-shirt has been pulled partway out. There are smallish animal prints in the sand, but it's too coarse to tell what made them.

I set the photo down and pick up the next. A wider shot of the scene, showing more river debris and scuffed sand and gravel. Then there is a series of images of things laid out on a big white table. A small pair of jeans, socks, underwear. A My Little Pony backpack. A journal that looks like it has sparkly stickers all over the cover. An animal-chewed package of beef jerky snacks and a bag of sour candy.

And a child's t-shirt. It has a unicorn on it, and a rainbow, and it says "smile" in big puffy letters. There was a ridiculous amount of sparkly ink used in its design, that catches the light as I grabbed my little sister and tickled her sides until tears of laughter were running down her face.

"Stop," she gasped, so I stopped. "No fair," she said. "You're bigger than me." Her hair was reddish-brown, like Dad's, and her eyes were dark as dark can be, like Mum's.

Magne's hand on my arms brings me back to now and I realize I have tears streaming down my face just like my sister did, only mine are not tears of laughter.

"This t-shirt is pink," I say. "Mum gave it to Kit for her birthday that year, and she wore it almost every day for months."

"Was she wearing it the day she disappeared?" The detective's voice is as soft as Magne's, almost.

I shake my head. "I don't know. I was away at university. Mum made me stay until…." I have to stop to pull in air. I feel like I can't breathe. I want to get up, to pace around the room, but I can't make my legs move. "Until I had to help identify Dad's… until I had to identify Dad." I look up at Magne. His eyes are gentle and deep and I wish I could lose myself in them. Then I look at the detective. His pen is poised over his notepad.

"It is hers, though," I say. "And she wore it all the time."

"And you're sure it's hers?"

I nod. "There's a little stain near the hem where she spilled some blackberry syrup." She'd put too much on her ice cream and it ran over the side of the bowl. I point to the spot on the photo.

The detective asks a few more questions and I answer mechanically. It seems like forever, and like no time at all, when he gets up to go.

"Thank you," he says. "I'll let you know if we find anything else."

I try to get up from the chair, to see him out, but Magne's hand on my shoulder keeps me in place. I stare at the other folder on the table – copies of the photos for me, the detective said. If I turn my head, I'll be able to see another folder sticking out from between some books on the bookshelf. It holds the rest of the case files – also not officially provided by Detective O'Malley. But I still can't make myself move.

I hear the door close and the elevator grind as the detective leaves. I don't hear Magne until he's crouched next to my chair. I muster enough energy to look at him. He doesn't say anything, he just waits.

"She's probably dead," I say. I don't want to hope. Hope hurts too much when everything goes to shit.

His shrug is almost imperceptible. "She could be alive," he says.

"That was her clothes," I say. "Even her socks and underwear. Whatever happened to her, it wasn't good."

Magne nods, and instead of reaching out to hug me, maybe thinking I won't want to be comforted, he lays his head on the arm of my chair, just touching my shoulder. I lean over and bury my face in his messy hair. He smells clean now, but somehow still wild. A little musky. He smells like Magne, like comfort.

"She'd be fourteen now," I say.

"She might still be."

I make myself keep breathing, practice the techniques my long-ago kung fu teacher drummed into my stubborn, angry, adolescent brain.

"She might," I say finally, without lifting my face from Magne's hair.

Then I sit up, look over at the bookcase where the files about my parents' deaths poke out, one beige folder corner exposed.

"My parents were murdered," I say.

Magne gets up and I hear rummaging in my fridge. One of his solutions for feeling crappy is to feed whoever is unhappy. Ev used to do that, too.

"My sister vanished. Probably also murdered." My voice is weirdly devoid of emotion, even to me. I feel like I'm on the edge of a cliff, about to fall over and not sure how to stop myself. I try to keep breathing evenly. "And nobody can tell me why, or by whom."

Magne's rummaging gets louder, which is a bit of a feat, since there's hardly anything in my fridge.

"Don't you have any actual food?" he says.

I'm up and poking my finger into his chest before I can even think about what I'm doing, while his hands are still occupied with the fridge door. The edge of that cliff looms closer.

"My family was *murdered*," I say.

He takes my hand in his, so I poke him with the other one until he holds that one, too.

"We have more clues, now," he says, and traps both my hands by tucking them between us and pulling me close, holding me so tight I can't move.

"That," I point my chin at the folder on the coffee table, since I can't point with a finger, "is hardly more clues."

"We know someone tried to hide her things," he says. "If she was killed, it wasn't the same way your parents were."

He's right, and I'm glad he isn't trying to tiptoe around the issue. My parents had their throats and wrists cut and their bodies dumped in the river. Their clothes and their belongings were still intact.

I bang my head against Magne until he puts one big hand on it and holds me still.

"Breathe, love," he says. I can feel his breath on the top of my head, feel his ribs move in and out, regularly, strongly.

"I just feel so helpless," I say.

"You have my help," he says, releasing my head so he can stroke my hair. "And maybe, since Wonder Island is involved, we can ask Wolfram Gottfried for help."

Wolfram Gottfried, self-styled "Illustrated Manikin, the world's only fully-tattooed dwarf," who runs the Wonder Island Carnival and leads the people – mostly non-human – who live there. According to Magne, Wolfram is as far beyond *other*-kind as *others* are beyond human. Maybe more so.

"And," he says, "maybe it's time you introduced me to your memory-meddling friend whose business card was found in your dad's wallet. What was his name? Your former poli sci prof who tried to make you remember things that might not have happened?"

"John Pradip," I say, my words muffled against Magne's giant pecs. "He was my lover once, too." I tilt my head to look up into his face, not even sure what reaction I hope to provoke, let alone what will actually happen.

Magne blinks at me, then eases his grip so I can free my arms. I wrap them around his waist.

"I promise I won't get jealous," he says, and grins such a big cheeky grin that his dimple appears, and a second dimple I didn't even know he had makes a brief appearance on his other cheek.

Then he bends his neck to bring his mouth close to mine and I'm just parting my lips to let in his tongue when his phone starts vibrating.

He pulls away. I can feel his reluctance, but he must have been waiting for a call or a text. Without letting go of me, he pulls out his phone and glances at the screen.

"Shit," he says. Then he does step away.

"Is everything okay?" I try not to sound pouty. I guess I succeed in keeping my voice normal, because when Magne studies my face, he seems content with whatever he sees.

"I've gotta go," he says. "Make sure you eat something. Real food. Raid my fridge if you want." Then he's off to the door where he grabs his shoes and is out before I can say anything.

"Take away curry, then," I say, and I try to remember where I left my phone.

Chapter Three

I GUESS A LOT of *other* folk like curry, or don't like cooking, because our weird little neighborhood has three takeaways within a reasonable walking distance, plus a pizza place, a sushi place, and a Chinese/Korean/ Thai restaurant.

I mean, they're not actually *in* the neighborhood of old factories, but they're just on the outskirts, where proper stores and low-rise apartment buildings start to proliferate.

I'm in the mood for papadums, so I pick the place with the best, even though it's not the place with the best vindaloo. Or the best rice. I order enough for two – in case I want leftovers – and by the time I get back from picking it up, Magne's truck is parked in the street again, so he's back from wherever he had to hurry off to.

The big elevator smells not-quite-right, and then I notice the droplets of blood on the peeling linoleum, and a smudgy reddish fingerprint on the second floor button.

And yeah, I was already thinking about stopping by Magne's to see if he's had a chance to eat and might want to share my curry, but the blood decides it.

The door isn't ajar when I get off the elevator as it usually is when he hears me coming, but when I knock he calls, "It's open," so I walk in. I hear splashing from the direction of the bathroom, and he says, "In here." He sounds tired.

I put the takeaway bags on the counter and leave my jacket draped over the back of the couch and move towards the bathroom, trying not to hesitate with each step. I mean, Mags is not the least bit embarrassed about being naked in front of… well anyone, really, but he's usually pretty careful of other people's feelings about being around naked people.

And it's not that I *mind* seeing him naked, I just don't know how I feel about it yet, or what it means. Does he *want* me to look at him, or does he even care one way or the other?

Unlike the apartment door, the bathroom door is open. Or mostly open. I hear water slosh, and the clink of glass. When I poke my head around the door frame I see a bottle of Scotch on the floor next to an absurdly fluffy grey towel and an empty pair of boxers with a howling wolf print on them.

Magne's shaggy head pokes over the top of the tub – an immense clawfoot that's almost as big as the one upstairs in my bathroom – and there's a glass mostly empty of amber liquid in the soap dish. The size of the tub almost makes Magne look small. Ish.

There's a big dark bruise coming up on his cheekbone and his eye is starting to swell shut. It'll be mostly healed by tomorrow – werewolf symbiont, you know – but right now it looks painful.

The rest of Magne – and I'm not sure if I'm disappointed or relieved – is hidden by an abundance of cedar-scented bath bubbles. Trust Magne to make a bubble bath smell macho.

One hand appears from beneath the bubbles, revealing a swirl of pink-tinged water, to lift the glass to his lips. He hisses as the alcohol touches what looks like a pretty badly split lip. Then he drains the glass and puts it back in the soap dish.

"Do I smell curry?" he asks.

"I got enough for two," I say. "You look…"

"Like hell?"

"I was going to say, 'Like shit.' I hope the other guy looks worse."

"Other *guys*," he says. "They look much worse."

"Everything okay?"

"Just had to settle a wolf dispute."

"Ah," I say. I don't ask about werewolf business. Magne doesn't seem close to his family, which is what a wolf pack is after all, and I don't want to pry. But I do want to *know*. I didn't think Magne was any sort of leader in his community, even though he seems to know every were and *other* within – and probably some ways without – city limits.

"It's all settled?" is all I ask.

"Yeah," he says. "I hope so."

He looks way more tired than a minor squabble should make him look, I think, and the blood in the elevator – and the pink-tinged bathwater – makes me think he's more injured than he's letting on.

"You look tired," I say.

He glances at me and sits up in the tub. The bubbles, starting to pop and disintegrate now, slide down over his chest, revealing a nasty-looking gash that's sluggishly seeping blood, but is already starting to scab over.

"I'll recover," he says, and starts to stand.

"Mags," I say, wanting to ask about his injuries, but not quite daring to. He'll tell me if he wants to share, I tell myself firmly. No prying.

"I'll recover," he says again, and I retreat hastily as the bubbles slide away, threatening to reveal the rest of his nudity.

"I'll go unpack the food," I say as I turn away.

"Coward," he says.

I don't deny it.

When he comes out of the bathroom he's wearing loose sweatpants and a t-shirt that sticks to his chest. It's peach colored and has a drawing of an elf sitting on a wolf and it says, "To Hunt, To Howl, To Live Free," in big fancy letters. I can see where he's wrapped a bandage around his torso to cover the gash.

And did I mention that my werewolf best friend loves wolf-related merch and I have no idea if it's supposed to be ironic? Though to be fair, the art on this t-shirt is a lot better than his airbrushed howling wolf computer wallpaper.

He's moving stiffly, so I suspect he's more hurt than the bruised face, split lip, and gashed chest. From the way he favors his left side, and the ridge of bandages under his t-shirt, I'd guess he's got another injury on his ribcage. If he was facing another werewolf – were*wolves*, plural – it could be anything from broken bones to bite wounds.

"Are you sure you're okay?" I don't think that whatever's happened to his ribs is going to heal as fast as his face.

He goes to the freezer and pulls out an ice pack and presses it to his cheek. I know from past experience that there are several more ice packs in there, and they all get regular use. Werewolves tend to settle their differences physically, especially when they're away from their pack.

"I'm fine," he says, and there's his smile again, finally. Not a two-dimple grin, but still pretty cheeky. "Actually, I feel pretty good." But then he winces when he reaches for the plate I've filled for him. "Okay, not great, but I've been worse."

"Just a dispute?" I say.

"Mmm," is all he answers, his mouth full of curry. He ignores the kitchen island with its hard stools where we usually eat, in favor of the sprawling sectional couch. I'm always nervous about sitting there with food, because if you drop something, you might never find it again in all the cushions he's got scattered everywhere.

"I was thinking we should either go to Wonder Island tomorrow, or go find your professor friend," he says, when he's polished off his plate and filched a popadom from mine.

"Wonder Island," I say, trying not to talk with my mouth full. I swallow and set my plate on the coffee table. "I'll call John and set up a meeting for later in the week."

"John, is it?" he says. The dimple creeps back.

"We did sleep together for almost a year. It would be weird to call him Professor Pradip."

"That's longer than –" He snaps his mouth shut.

Longer than I was with Evgeny, he means.

"Yeah," I say.

"I miss him." I know he's not talking about John Pradip. Obviously.

I'm sitting at the other end of the couch, but he's a large man, with arms of proportionate length, and he only has to lean a little ways towards me to brush his fingers over the side of my face. I turn my head towards his touch.

"Yeah." My voice is barely audible. I nuzzle his hand and he strokes my cheekbone with his thumb. "Me, too."

When he pulls his hand away I follow it, moving closer so I can lean against his shoulder. He tilts his head to rest on top of mine.

"Fuck," he says.

"He's not coming back."

"He'd be stupid not to."

"He's got a new boyfriend now," I say. "A new love." I almost choke on the last word.

"Luke," says Magne, settling his arm around me. "There's something about that guy that just seems off."

"You just think that because you think Ev should've stayed with me," I say. "But as long as he makes Ev happy." I haven't met Luke, Evgeny's new love. My replacement.

"If he hurts Ev, I'll…." He doesn't finish the sentence.

"Me, too."

"We make a good team," he says, and kisses the top of my head.

That's *not* where I want him to kiss me, so I shift position and get a glimpse of his eyes widening in surprise before my mouth meets his.

Like last time, he hesitates. But also like last time, it's brief and then he relaxes, turns so he can pull me closer, and kisses me back. And then, after a long and delicious snog that leaves me breathless, he pulls away. Not just his mouth, but his whole body.

"Su," he says.

I get up, grab our plates, and take them into the kitchen.

"Sorry," I say. "I don't know what came over me." And how lame does *that* sound? I keep my back turned, run water in the sink, add soap, and then he's there, warm at my back, reaching past me to turn off the tap.

His kiss on my cheek is gentle. I don't want gentle. I want fierce.

"I can't tell you how much I want this," he says. "How much I want *you*."

"But," I say. I can feel the "but" coming.

He grasps my shoulders and gently turns me to face him. You wouldn't think such a big man could be so gentle, but he is. A big marshmallow. Except to whomever hit him in the face hard enough to split his lip and swell his eye nearly shut. Though both of those injuries look a little less bad than they did before supper.

"But," he says, a smile tugging up one corner of his mouth, not enough to reveal a dimple. "I don't want you to want me because you miss Evgeny." His voice is deep and rumbly, as smooth and smoky as his favorite whisky.

"That's not –" His lips on mine stop my words. It must hurt him, what with the werewolf-related split lip, but there's no hesitation this time.

"You miss him," he says. "*I* miss him, and I wasn't the one having loud, obnoxious, and probably glorious sex with him every night."

"I –" This time it's his fingers, just the barest touch, that quiet me.

"I'd rather wait until I'm sure it's really me you want. Because...." Now he looks away, staring down at our feet, his bare and mine covered in deep purple wool socks. I'd rather be barefoot, too, but I had shoes on earlier, and I can't stand shoes without socks.

"Fine," I say, wondering how it's possible to be both touched and hurt at the same time. "Okay. You look like you need sleep anyway."

"Su...."

I pull away and head for the door. I'm not upset. Not really. In fact, it might be better for our friendship if we didn't sleep together. But if I don't sleep with *somebody*, I might lose my shit. Those old fox women might have taught me how to dampen my overactive sex drive, but obviously being celibate doesn't agree with me. And Magne's right. It's not fair to use him like that. Maybe I should just buy some sex toys.

Magne sighs. "Wonder Island tomorrow?" he says as I scoop up my shoes and jacket and open the door.

"Wonder Island tomorrow," I say. I risk a glance back as I pull the door shut behind me. He's leaning against the counter, watching me leave, and I almost go back in.

"Sleep well, Mags," I say.

"Sleep well, love," he answers as the door closes.

And then I realize he was about to say something else, something that started with "because." Something, from the look on his face, that would make him extremely vulnerable.

Back in my loft, I contemplate a bubble bath of my own, think about my skin slippery with soap, between my legs slippery with desire. It would go a long way towards relieving some tension, maybe even help clear my head.

But, as much as I hate to admit it, Magne's right: I don't know if I really want him as much as I think I do, or if I'm just missing Evgeny so much any good-looking well-built person will do, and Magne just happens to be close by.

And it's kind of weird – and has never stopped me before – but I don't want to think about either of them while I pleasure myself until I can figure out what, or rather *who* I'm actually longing for.

I mean, of *course* I still want Evgeny, but if he showed up at my door right now, I'd send him away. I told him last time I saw him that I wouldn't wait, and now he's got someone new.

Or at least I don't *think* I'd let him in and drag him off to bed. I hope I have more class than that.

So I settle for a shower – a *cold* shower – and then try to settle down with a book and a cup of tea. But my eyes keep sliding away from *The Trees in My Forest* to the book case across the room, where the beige folder pokes out, so I finally set my book aside and fetch the folder back to my chair.

I spread the contents out on the coffee table, along with the photos in the new folder. Missing person's reports, autopsy reports, photos. I shove the photos of my parents' remains to the bottom of the pile. Magne told me Detective O'Malley didn't want to include them, but he did so reluctantly when Magne said I needed all the information he could give me.

I sort through the documents until I find the photos of the contents of Dad's wallet. Driver's license, cash, credit and debit cards, and one lone business card. Dr John Pradip, Professor of Political Science.

I copy the info into my phone contacts, but I don't dial. Maybe I'll try texting him tomorrow. Right now, I don't want to think that deeply about any more ex-lovers.

The photos of Mum's things don't give me any more clues. She was in the water longer, and any bits of paper in her pockets were reduced to unrecognizable pulp. And neither do the photos of Kit's things turn up any new information. Until I find that the last photo – the one of her backpack and its contents – is stuck to another that I didn't see before. The laser-toner-coated pages aren't as crisp as the photos the detective had showed me, but I can make out all the smaller objects that had been in Kit's backpack. A report card from school that she was especially proud of because her art teacher had praised her "boundless imagination;" a pen with a fluffy, feathery end that waved and wafted as she wrote; a ticket stub from the movie we took her to on her birthday; and a business card. A twin to the one that was found in Dad's wallet.

"Motherfucker," I say. It's not my favorite swear – that would be "shit" in German – but the situation seems to warrant something much filthier than my usual curse vocabulary.

"That fucking weasel," I say. I make myself breathe calmly. After all, there could be a perfectly normal, ordinary, not at all nefarious reason why John Pradip's business card had been found with my dead father's belongings *and* my missing sister's things. I'd almost be willing to bet that one of the clumps of paper pulp found in Mum's pockets had once been just such a business card, too.

If I hadn't already been suspicious of him before – he had tried to work some kind of memory magic on me when I saw him a couple months ago, before I left for Germany with Alex – I sure am now. As far as I could tell, he'd been trying to make me think that our sex life had been better than it really was (and honestly, it hadn't been bad at all, even without the false memories), and that we'd been madly in love, and that he'd met my family and they adored him.

Had he been trying to manufacture a certainty in my mind that he could never have harmed my family? Did that mean he *had* been involved in their murders? The man I remembered – in my real memories, not the ones he tried to implant – had been kind and *nice*, even if he had taken advantage of my grief to get into my pants. But he had never met my family, at least not when I was around, because we hadn't become lovers until *after* Dad and Mum were found dead and Kit missing.

My phone is in my hand, and I'm starting to dial, but I make myself take several deep breaths and cancel the call, set the phone on the table with the number uncompleted. No, he can wait. He can wait until I'm calm and rational. Until I can think of the best way to bring up the tricky subject of his meddling with my memories and his suspiciously-located business cards.

Until I have a large, solid, very intimidating werewolf at my back to help drive home the importance of answering my questions honestly.

It's very hard to lie to a werewolf.

Chapter Four

WONDER ISLAND IS not the sort of place I would normally choose to go. It's bright and noisy and entirely full of people. I did go once with Alex, and yeah, I had a pretty good time, but it's not somewhere I ever thought I'd willingly return to.

Magne, on the other hand, looks like he loves it. His grin is so wide, I'm pretty sure his big teeth showing is the reason we aren't having any trouble moving through the crowd. People just seem to get out of his way. The bright sun, promising summer, has really brought people out in force and it doesn't help that it's Saturday. Why did either of us not remember that Saturday is the worst day to go to a carnival?

"So where do we find this Wolfram?" I ask. Magne has been here before – in more than the tourist capacity that I visited. It's where he brought Evgeny when the demon he had trapped is his head got too much to bear. And sure, I've *seen* Wolfram Gottfried, but only from a distance, and in a photo in the local newspaper.

Magne's paused to buy a huge cone of blue candy floss and stuffs a big chunk in his mouth before offering me some.

I take a tuft and pull it to bits, watching it turn back into colored sugar in my damp fingers.

"You're supposed to eat it," he says. Then he points at a big tent up ahead and enough people move out of the way that I can see the sign on it. It's garish and bright, with thick hand-lettering. "The Illustrated Manikin."

"I wonder how many people get the reference," Magne says. I must look confused because he adds, "*The Illustrated Man*? Ray Bradbury?" I still don't get it. "Don't you read?" he says, and stuffs another piece of sugar fluff into his mouth.

"I read," I say. To be honest, I mostly read non-fiction. "Ray Bradbury wrote *Something Wicked This Way Comes*. It gave me nightmares as a kid." I pause a moment to savor the fact that I've remembered something from my childhood. My memories are slowing returning, but a lot of my life is still a blank.

"A Bradbury reference probably *should* give people nightmares. It at least should warn them about what sort of place this is, and that they shouldn't linger after closing time."

"Do you think it's dangerous?" There *was* something about the carnival that gave me the willies, but I assumed it was just all the people. And there's also something deeply comforting about it, like if you belong here, it's a place that looks after its own. I'm going to have to do some thinking about that, once I have time to think about less immediate things.

Magne shrugs and tosses the now-empty floss cone into a garbage can as we head towards the tent. The bright sign also promises a cabinet of curiosities. I wonder if that means two-headed calves in jars.

"I know they're very careful to make sure no outsiders wander away from the public areas," he says, wiping his fingers on a paper napkin and stuffing it in his pocket. "And they didn't want us lingering once Ev came out of... wherever it was they took him when..."

"Yeah." I heard the story of Evgeny's fight with the demon, both from Ev and from Magne. I know there was no way I could have been here, but I still feel guilty for leaving Ev to deal with it on his own. I can't help thinking that if I was here for him, the demon wouldn't have been able to implant those terrible images in his head. That we'd still be together.

But Ev wasn't on his own, was he? He had Magne, and Cara, and even the mysterious Wolfram Gottfried. He just hadn't had me.

Magne's hand on my shoulder pulls me out of my dismal thoughts. We're standing at the entrance of the tent. "Can we walk right in?" I say.

Just then, a giggling pair of teenage girls emerges from the tent flap and almost walks into us. Their eyes widen when they see Magne, immovable as a cliff face, and they skitter around him, giggling again. I watch as they pass, and one of them turns to glance back. I'm pretty sure she's checking out his ass. And I'm pretty sure she likes what she sees. She covers her smile with her hand and turns back to her friend. Oh, to be so young. 'Cause yeah, I'm almost 27 and obviously ancient.

Magne holds the tent flap aside for me, and I duck inside. The dimness within is punctuated by spotlights, and yes, there is a two-headed calf in a jar, and a whole lot weirder. But I only glance at the display, because beyond that is a bigger spotlight, and a stage, and on the stage, standing on a revolving platform, is a tiny perfect man.

I mean, he's obviously a dwarf, or Little Person, or whatever the PC term is these days. It's hard to tell from here, but he probably doesn't even come up to Magne's chest. And he's beautiful. Handsome, dark-haired, perfectly muscled – and it's easy to tell, because he's wearing almost nothing. And every part of him save his face is covered in tattoos.

As if he feels us watching, he suddenly opens his eyes as the platform turns him towards us. His eyes are a startling, clear grey, like that uncanny color the sky turns right before a storm, and almost seem to glow. I feel his gaze meet mine, then shift to Magne's. He nods, once, then closes his eyes again and the revolving platform turns him away from us.

A moment later, a tall, rangy woman who looks so like the little man save her height that she must be a relative, steps out of the shadows.

"Magne Thorvaldson," she says in a voice that makes me shiver. It's light but husky, and somehow ice cold.

"Thea Gottfried," he says. So she must be Wolfram's sister. She's beautiful. Sexy. Frigid and hot at the same time.

"You are well?" she asks, and the coldness of her bearing seems to warm a touch. I think she likes Magne.

"Well enough," he says. "You?"

"As you say," she says. "Well enough."

She beckons and we follow her out of the tent. Somehow, it feels like following her is the only option and I wonder if she's using a subtle magic, or if she just seems so regal that doing her bidding feels like the right and natural order of things. I hope it's not magic. I hate being magicked. Also, ignoring her gesture would be rude, and rudeness, I suspect, is simply not a thing you do here.

"My brother will speak to you after his show," she says. "In the meantime —" She stops suddenly and turns to me. "We have not been introduced."

"My apologies," says Magne. "This is my friend, Su."

"Ah, the fox girl," she says, and holds out her hand for me to shake. "Your friend?" She emphasizes "friend" and I feel a sudden rush of warmth as I take her hand. She is *very* attractive and I wonder why I thought she was cold.

"Very pleased to meet you." Her smile is touched with something predatory and now I want to step behind Magne so she'll stop looking at me.

He reaches out and gently takes my hand out of hers, and keeps holding it while he steps closer to me, so we're shoulder to shoulder. Or shoulder to arm, since he's too tall for our shoulders to be level.

"Ah," she says, a different kind of smile on her lips. I'm usually really good at reading people, even vampires who don't show enough emotion to be easily deciphered, but I can't tell what she's thinking. At all.

"Friend," she says and the way she emphasizes it this time is entirely different. I wonder if Magne has any idea what this conversation is about, because I'm totally lost.

"Your witch *friend?*" she says, yet another kind of emphasis on the word.

"She left." Magne's tone of voice says he's not interested in explaining.

"I'm sorry," she says. "I liked her." She looks like she wants to say more, and I wonder if she knew Cara was pregnant, but she stops and tilts her head slightly.

"I wanted to thank you," Magne says. "The people of Wonder Island. For your help with Evgeny."

She accepts the change of subject with grace. "My brother felt the welfare of Evgeny Alexeyevich was… important. To us as well as the world at large. How is he, anyway?"

"He's…" Magne hesitates. This woman is asking all the hard

questions. "I haven't seen him much lately."

She glances at me, and I suspect she knows Ev and I were together, and now we're not. "Too bad," Thea says. "He was interesting. I rather liked him." She looks briefly at our clasped hands and a smile quirks the corner of her lips. I wonder how *much* she knows about our past relationships.

She turns back to me and her look is sympathetic, I think. "It will take him some time to figure out how his ordeal has changed him. He may act in ways that do not seem like him, like the boy you knew. Some of the changes are temporary, some will not be. I hope he will realize how much he needs his true friends."

Then she gestures towards a bench in the shade of a small, gnarly tree that's just starting to put out pale blossoms. We've left the busy areas of the carnival, and there are no other people around. "If you wait here, Wolfram will be along soon."

"So she was scary," I say, as Thea walks away and we settle on the bench to wait.

Magne has let go of my hand, and he drapes his arm along the back of the bench behind me, but doesn't put it around my shoulders. He sits close enough I can feel the heat coming off his skin, but not touching me. I want to move closer, to press our legs together, but after our talk last night, I don't dare. It wouldn't be fair, but hell, it's not going to be easy, just being friends.

"She is," he says, closing his eyes and tilting his head back to let the fractured sunlight bathe his face. "I'm pretty sure she could kill me with her bare hands before I realized what was happening. I like her."

I look at him sharply, thinking maybe he's putting me on, but there's no hint of teasing on his face. He hasn't even opened his eyes. "Really?"

Now a smile does quirk the corner of his mouth. "Yes. I like dangerous women." I jab him in the shoulder and the smile grows, but he still doesn't open his eyes.

"Gottfried, brother and sister both, are a lot more than they appear." Then he does open his eyes and they're serious. "This whole place is more than it seems, and I'm pretty sure we haven't been allowed to see even a fraction of its secrets."

"You would be correct," says a voice, and we both manage not to startle, somehow.

The small man – Wolfram Gottfried – is standing on the path right next to our bench, and neither of us heard him approaching. His voice is as deep as Magne's, deeper even, but gentle somehow.

For a moment we all just stare, then Magne and Wolfram break into a smile at the same moment.

"Magne." Wolfram holds out his hand and they do the forearm-clasp, shoulder-slap manly greeting thing. "We don't trust easily," Wolfram says.

"Mr Gottfried," Magne says, and the other man laughs.

"Please," he says. "Just Wolfram. No one uses my surname except the government, and I deal with them as little as possible."

"This is Su," Magne says, putting his hand on my shoulder.

"Hey," I say, wishing I had some more intelligent greeting. There's something about this man that feels as ancient as that old vampire Karasu who was around even before vamps and weres split into two different creatures. Ancient and *powerful*. And I think he could be as terrifying as Karasu, except he chooses not to be.

"I've heard about you," he says. "You may not have been here during young Evgeny's ordeal, but I believe you were a large part of what kept him sane." His storm-colored eyes shift from me to Magne. "Both of you." Then he seems to notice our unease. "I see relationships have shifted since we last spoke."

"A bit," says Magne. "Ev's… not around."

"Ah." Wolfram examines both of us, a slight frown creasing his mouth and forehead. "I would suggest that it isn't the best idea for his mental health, but I suspect his not being around much isn't what either of you would have chosen."

I don't know what to say to that, so I opt to keep my mouth shut. Magne just says, "No, it's not what we would have chosen."

"Well," Wolfram says. "That isn't why you came to see me today."

"No," says Magne again.

Wolfram turns his attention back to me. "There isn't much I can tell you that your detective friend hasn't already. Troll found a garbage bag near the south end of the island that appeared to have been ripped open by an animal. A fox, he thinks, though I don't suppose that matters. When he saw what was in the bag, he came to me, and I notified the police."

My brain sticks on the word "fox." I mean of course there are wild foxes here. Most of the island is wilderness, so there's all kinds of wildlife. But I guess my own fox nature has made me want to think anything to do with foxes can't be coincidence. And I wonder who Troll is. There's a building labelled "Troll's Menagerie" in the carnival, and when Alex and I visited it turned out to be full of animals – two-headed snakes, albino raccoons, and various other things that could probably not survive in the wild. I don't remember seeing the person who ran the place, though.

Wolfram reaches out and touches my shoulder. "I could show you the place, but it's a bit of a hike and the police haven't left much to look at."

I shake my head. "I guess I was hoping you'd know something. Or maybe someone had seen something. I mean, my parents were found nearby, too, and…" I trail off.

His voice is soft and he squeezes my shoulder gently. Magne does the same to my other shoulder and I feel protected in a way I haven't since, well, ever. "Your mother was found here, yes. But your father was upstream, on the east bank of the river."

"So… nobody saw any suspicious people? How did the bag get there?" I know my voice sounds desperate and I make myself breathe slowly, evenly.

"I would know if anyone had been here who shouldn't. Troll believes the bag washed ashore from upriver, just as your mother did."

"So my sister was never here? We need to look upstream?"

"She was not here. Not unless one of the… one of those who dwell in the wild parts of the island decided to conceal her." He sounds thoughtful. "It is very unlikely, but I'll ask around. And some of the residents do venture upstream from time to time. Perhaps someone might know something and not even realize they know it. But the passage of time will not have helped."

"Thanks," I say.

"What kind of… people live in the wilds of Wonder Island?" Magne asks, and Wolfram turns to look at him, dropping his arm back to his side.

I miss the warmth of his hand. It was comforting.

"That is their own business, son." He sounds amused.

Then, between one breath and the next, his attitude changes and I get a hint of the power he could wield. It's vast and frightening, and I remind myself never to underestimate him, or this place.

He steps closer to Magne, grabs his chin, and tilts his face toward the light to see more clearly into his eyes.

"What –?" says Magne. He looks startled but holds himself very still.

"Quiet a moment." Wolfram stares intently into Magne's eyes and I can tell Mags wants to look away but doesn't dare.

After a long moment, Wolfram releases Magne's face and steps back. "Curious," he says.

"What?" says Magne.

"There's something there, something about you, that wasn't there last time I saw you."

"What?" Now Magne sounds nervous, and Wolfram smiles.

"Nothing to fear, son," he says. "But you seem to be growing some new power. This place can have that effect sometimes." He studies Magne's face again. "What do you remember of your birth?"

"Um, nothing. Does anyone remember being born?"

"Surely your parents spoke of it?"

Magne shrugs one shoulder and rubs both hands through his hair, leaving it sticking up in a very appealing way. "I was a quiet baby. Dad thought I was mute because I never cried. He didn't believe Mum when she said I babbled just like any infant when I was with her alone."

"How old were you when you were made a werewolf?"

"Thirteen. Why?"

"I'm not sure." Wolfram looks thoughtful. Really thoughtful, like he's just been presented with an intriguing puzzle. "Thirteen is rather young for being changed, isn't it?"

Now Magne looks away. He's gone subdued. "Eighteen or nineteen is more usual. When the person has a better chance of surviving the process."

"Why so young then?"

Magne's nostrils flare and he doesn't say anything for a long moment. "Is it important?" he finally says, still staring off into the distance. I get the idea that this isn't something he wants to talk about. Something about the memory hurts him.

"It might be, son. It might not be. Whatever magic is waking in you… Knowing your history might help me figure out what it is. I don't think it's something negative, but I can't know for sure."

"Magic?" Magne turns his eyes to stare at Wolfram. "I'm just a regular, entirely non-magical wolf. Infected with the werewolf symbiont so young I shouldn't have lived, because my old man thought I was too soft. 'If it doesn't kill him,' he told Mum, 'maybe it'll make him a son I can be proud of.' The old fucker's never been proud of a single thing I've ever done. Not even surviving being torn apart by my own family when I was barely starting puberty." His breathing has gone harsh and ragged, and his big canines flash with every word. He stops talking with a snap of teeth.

Then, "Fuck. Sorry."

Wolfram grips his arm. His nostrils flare and when Magne turns his head away and stares down at the ground, Wolfram puts his other hand on Magne's head briefly, like a father stroking his kid's hair in comfort.

"I'm sorry, son," he says, and the regret is evident in his deep voice. "We all have memories that bring out our worst."

"Mags," I say softly, but I don't know how to follow that up, so I just put my hand on his thigh. He doesn't look like he'd welcome a hug just now.

"Are you sure," says Wolfram, gently, "that you weren't born a werewolf? It's extremely rare, but it wouldn't be the first time a pregnant mother infected her unborn child. And it might explain why the Island has taken an interest in you."

Magne shakes his head. I desperately want to interrupt and ask what Wolfram means about the island taking an interest, but I clamp my mouth shut.

"Your mother is human?" asks Wolfram.

"No, she's a wolf, but…" Magne looks up again, confusion on his face. "I've always thought being a werewolf is something I've always been, but I *remember*. I was thirteen." He holds out both arms, turning them so the tracery of scars shines in the dappled sunlight. "I got these scars when Dad and Thorstein and Bjarni tore me to shreds and left me to die in the woods.

I *would* have died, except..." He trails off and shakes his head. "I..." He looks at Wolfram. "I don't think I've ever actually tried to *remember* that before. Not consciously. It's all fuzzy and unclear."

He slumps back against the bench and covers my hand with his. I don't think he's aware he's done it, especially when he laces his fingers between mine and strokes the side of my hand with his thumb. Warmth floods through me and I try not to react, try to stuff all thoughts of him back into the "not for snogging" part of my brain.

Wolfram shifts his weight and breaths out a noisy breath. "It would be nice if I knew someone who was good with memories," he says. "I might be able to jog them, but it would be a crude attempt, and might just result in a headache. Even with assistance from —" He ends his sentence abruptly and rubs one upper arm absently. Both arms have Norse-style blue-black tattoos from wrist to elbow. The ones I can see looks like animals, wolves maybe. His sleeve covers most of whatever designs are higher up except what might be a beak, and I don't remember from my brief glimpse in the tent.

Magne sits up. "Su knows those fox women," he says. "They helped with her memory."

I shake my head. "I don't think they specialize in memory," I say. "They accidentally erased my whole past when they tried to remove one traumatic event. And they weren't able to fix it when they returned that one." But I reach into my pocket and pull out a folded piece of paper. It's the photo of the contents of my father's wallet, including a certain business card. "But I know someone who does."

Chapter Five

I DISENTANGLE my hand from Magne's and unfold the paper, holding it out for them to see.

"If he's been messing with your memories, love," Magne says, "I don't think I want him anywhere near my head."

"We're going to question him about my parents anyway," I say. "And I think I could tell if he was messing with your brain."

Wolfram takes the paper from me and studies it. "John Pradip," he says thoughtfully. "I have heard of a family in India who were known for their skill with helping people recover lost memories or deal with painful ones. Perhaps he is a descendant."

"Are they *other*?" Magne takes the paper when Wolfram offers, but he doesn't look at it. He's seen it before.

Wolfram shakes his head. "In a sense, I suppose. In another sense, perhaps not. I haven't looked into them because I assumed they were humans born with a small amount of magic than can be passed to their descendants."

"So kind of like witches," I say. Except *otherly* witches have no true magic. And those witches who do have true magic are in another category entirely. I think. I've been suspecting for a while that the world is both more and less complicated than we've been assuming, and that magic is more common. And witches have always been rare, so no one seems to really understand them, not even other witches.

"Something like," Wolfram says. "As I said, they didn't seem any sort of threat to my people, so I didn't look into them any further. Perhaps I was wrong to dismiss them so quickly. You say this man meddled with your memory?" He moves off the path, finally sitting down on the bench on the other side of Magne. I have to lean forward to see him around my bulky friend.

"Yeah," I say. "I knew him in university. He was one of my professors. When my parents died, he was kind and comforting."

I pause and Magne says, "He was a predator."

I shake my head. "He *was* kind. But yeah, he took advantage of my grief."

"You became lovers," says Wolfram. His voice holds no judgement.

"For almost a year. Then he just stopped talking to me. I didn't even run in to him by accident on campus."

I glance up at Magne and he's watching me, his eyes soft but his mouth in a hard line. No dimples.

"Anyway, just before I went to Germany in the spring, I ran into him on the street. He seemed super happy to see me. Worried, like *I* was the one who ghosted him."

"This was just a few months ago? When Evgeny was here?"

"Just before that, yeah. And he… We were having coffee and I had told him about losing my memory and he said he could help. He sort of touched my head –" I put my fingertip between my eyebrows, just where John had done "– and suddenly I'm in the middle of an intense memory of us together. One I had forgotten along with the rest of my past." I can feel the heat on my cheeks, creeping up my neck.

"And was this a real memory?"

"I'm pretty sure that it was. Later, I started to dream about him, about our past together. Some of the dreams were real and some had a sort of unfocussed quality. But also like they were too bright. Like an old movie."

"Those memories, those dreams, you believe he created?"

"Created, altered, something like that. They weren't quite *true*." I realize I'm clenching my hands together in my lap, so I relax them carefully.

Magne shifts over a little so his arm is pressed against my shoulder. Moral support, I guess.

"To what end?"

"I wish I knew. As far as I can tell, he was trying to make our love life seem better, and like he knew my family, like they accepted him like a son. But they never even met him."

"Like your relationship was much more meaningful than it really was?" Wolfram asks.

"Yeah, but I don't know why. I thought maybe so I wouldn't suspect he was involved somehow in my parents' deaths."

"But you think he was." This time it's not a question.

"His business card was in my dad's wallet and my sister's backpack. I'd bet anything there was one in Mum's stuff, too, but it disintegrated in the water."

"I can see why you wish to speak to him." Wolfram leans back so I can't see him behind Magne. I hear him sigh.

"I know you're not my people," he says. "But I feel a certain connection with the two of you. And young Evgeny. I think the Island would be happy to have you, should you ever wish to shelter here." He stands up from the bench and paces a few steps, then back again.

"If you're willing, I would like it if you brought this man, this Dr Pradip, here to question him. It would allow me to learn more about who and what he is, what his family is, to assess if he is a threat or an asset. And it would allow me to extend my protection to you. He would not be able to meddle with your memory here."

I nod. "I hate to ask for help, but … yeah, I'd be okay with that."

"And you don't entirely trust me yet." Wolfram smiles at my discomfort. He's right. He *feels* okay. Safe, even. But I don't know him, even if he did help Ev when I couldn't.

"Good," he says. "Some people trust too easily." He looks sidelong at Magne, who doesn't seem to notice.

"I'd also like," he continues, "before you interrogate him, to see if he can remove whatever block this young wolf has put on his own memory."

Magne looks up at that. "You think I blocked my own memory of being made a wolf? Why? It was – it was supposed to be – the proudest moment of my life."

"Perhaps it turned out to be the most traumatic."

"I don't know," says Magne. "I don't like people poking around in my brain."

"Nor should you," Wolfram replies. "But I can guarantee he won't be able to meddle."

"But memory isn't your thing."

"No, but I do have an… associate who can monitor the process. Nothing of that sort can get by her."

"Not Thea?" Magne shivers. "I mean, I like her, but…"

Wolfram laughs. "My sister lacks the patience to probe anyone's mind, even if she had the ability. No, this is someone you haven't met yet. I think you'll get on fine."

Magne still looks doubtful, but just then his phone vibrates in his pocket. "Yeah, okay," he says. "I'm game." He checks his phone screen. "Looks like something's come up at work." He touches my knee. "You can get home okay?"

I poke his chest, hard. "Of course I can. Don't make me kick your ass."

He holds his hands up in mock surrender. "Let me know what your professor friend says about meeting here. See you at home." And then he walks off before I can say any more.

Wolfram and I watch him leave and then Wolfram says in a low voice, "I'm going to assume you know he was lying to you."

"That wasn't his work," I say. "I know." I'm not even sure how I know, exactly. I sure as hell don't know why he didn't tell me the truth.

Wolfram sits back down. "Do you know where he's going?"

"Nope."

He pats my knee. "If it helps, I think he hates lying to you. I suspect he's doing something he thinks could get you hurt."

"Last time he said it was a wolf dispute. And he came back with a black eye, a split lip, and some kind of wound on his ribs that was leaking blood all over the place."

"Curious." He hasn't moved his hand from my knee and I can feel heat creeping up my leg heading right for my crotch.

Not for snogging, I tell myself. *Not for bloody snogging.*

Out loud, I say, "I wish he'd let me help. With whatever it is."

"It probably is werewolf business of some kind. His father is pack leader. Do you know what kind of relationship he has with his pack?"

I shake my head. "Before today I'd have said good, but not super close. Now I don't know." I think about how he called his father an "old fucker."

Wolfram sighs and leans back, closing his eyes. His hand is still on my knee and I don't think he's even aware of it. I don't think he's making a move, but my hormones have gone into overdrive and I find myself staring at his lips. They look *very* nice for kissing.

"Evgeny has left you," he says softly, not quite a question.

"The demon gave him terrible visions of what it wanted to do to me. When we… well all those images came flooding back when we tried to… you know. Get intimate."

I'm blushing so hot I feel like I must be glowing, but Wolfram's eyes are still closed.

"And Magne's lovely Cara has gone as well. I liked her." He sighs. "Is everyone falling out of love this year?" He sits up and looks at me. "Aren't you young people supposed to be forever falling in love?"

And that's when I do something really, really stupid. I lean over and plant my stupid lips right on Wolfram's beautiful, wistful smile.

I realize how stupid I've been as soon as I do it, of course. I'm not sure what came over me. No, I lie, I know *exactly* what came over me. My sex-hungry fox woman hormones just decided they were done waiting for me to stop missing Ev and took over my brain.

To my surprise, Wolfram doesn't pull away. He's surprised, I think, but he allows me to kiss him, even kisses me back, before putting a hand on my face and gently disengaging.

"Shit," I say. "I'm sorry. That was inappropriate."

A smile pulls up one corner of his mouth. "I am," he says, his voice breathy, "very, *very* flattered. And if I were a great many years younger, I would be delighted to oblige." The hand on my face strokes my cheek gently, then tucks a stray lock of hair behind my ear and drops away.

"But," I say, pulling myself back into a normal, not leaning over to kiss a guy I've just met position. There's always a *but*, and even though I shouldn't have kissed him in the first place, it's disappointing.

"Truthfully, even at my advanced age, I'm sorely tempted." I could point out that he *looks* like he could be anything from thirty-five to sixty-five. He's almost certainly a lot older than that.

"But," I say again, and he smiles wider.

"But I'm not the one you really want."

I stare off in the direction Magne went and lick my lips. They suddenly feel very dry. I'm suddenly thirsty.

"Magne thinks I only want him because I miss Evgeny."

"And?"

"And I do miss Ev. He was the love of my life. But I *do* want Magne. For *himself*. He keeps me grounded. He's like a big fucking mountain. My anchor."

Wolfram laughs, but not in a mocking way. "He is a large man."

"I just... I worry that he could be right. After the fox women saved me... They gave me some of their own nature, and I guess part of that is a kind of... sex magic. Like super sex pheromones that let you cloud someone's mind so they do what you want. Except *my* sex powers seem impossible to turn off. And they affect my own brain, too. Make me want to have sex a lot. A *lot* a lot."

I take a deep breath and dare to meet his eyes. There's no judgement there. He reminds me of Magne that way. And maybe that's why I kissed him.

"I don't think I ever realized how bad it was until now." I look down at my hands. "I love Magne, I know that. He's my best friend. But what if me wanting him is just the fox women's sex thing taking over my brain and he's the nearest attractive person I can fuck?"

"Like I was," he says. I dare to look at him and a smile quirks the corner of his mouth again, makes his eyes crinkle.

"Yeah," I say, and stare back at my hands. "And what if he only wants *me* because I can't turn the sex powers off?" By the end of the sentence, my voice has dropped to a whisper.

"I don't think you need worry about *that* at least." When I look back up, he says, "You could not have influenced *me* with those powers, and I find you quite attractive."

"Oh."

"As for the rest, I think I know someone who can help you."

"The fox women? They think I should just be able to automatically turn all my powers on and off. They don't know how *they* do it, so they can't tell me how I can do it."

"I met your fox women once," he says. "If they're the trio who live at Chesterly Garden."

I nod.

"We spent several… very diverting evenings together."

"Did they use their pheromones on you?"

"I think it was magic rather than anything biological. And yes they did, or they tried to. But it didn't work, and I was already a willing participant, so they stopped trying. And decided not to kill me afterwards."

I'm blushing again, and I think it amuses him, but he doesn't laugh at me.

"Could they have killed you?"

"I don't think so. Individually, definitely not. Together… I'd have been in trouble, at least."

"Hunh." I can't think of anything more intelligent to say.

"No," he finally says. "I know a woman who lives to the east." He gestures towards the wild side of the island. "She has similar abilities and might be able to help you control yours."

I'm twisting my fingers together so I make myself stop. "I'd like that," I say. "I want to at least find out if it's just my hormones or pheromones or fox magic or whatever, or if…"

"If you really want to be with your giant werewolf friend." He smiles again. Like Magne, he smiles easily, but unlike Magne, his is tinged with sadness. "I can tell you he very much wants to be with you."

"He told you?"

"No. He doesn't know me that well yet, even if he trusts me more than caution dictates. But he's very easy to read. Unless he concentrates on stillness, every emotion is on full display with that boy."

Wolfram keeps calling Magne "boy" and "son" and "young" and I realize I don't actually know how old he is. He *looks* – and mostly acts –

thirtyish, but he's a were so he's probably older. A *lot* older. Like fifty or sixty, even. It only takes me a second to realize I really don't care.

"You like him," I say, daring to tease him a little.

His smile grows. Shit, he's got a dimple, too. I'm surrounded by gorgeous men with dimples. Did I mention I have a serious weakness for dimples?

"He reminds me of myself," he says. "I was a lot angrier, but like your Magne, I was always trying to do the right thing, to help others, to be selfless and *good*. And I did not have a healthy relationship with my father." He pauses to watch a small brown bird peck between the blades of grass on the side of the path. "Of course, I was a lot shorter."

The laugh bursts out of me like a snort as I try to keep it in. You're not supposed to make fun of people for their height. Especially not people with dwarfism.

He bumps his shoulder against mine. "You're allowed to laugh," he says.

I settle for a grin. "Thanks," I say, and I'm pretty sure he'll know it's not for giving me permission to laugh, that it's for looking out for Magne. And Ev. And everything he's done for a bunch of misfit *others* who don't even belong on his island or in his carnival. His sanctuary?

"So shall I contact the Leanan Sidhe?"

"The who?"

"Leanan Sidhe. The woman who might be able to help you with your… issues."

I smile again, this time at my own expense. Yeah, I'm Su, and I'm a magic nympho. "Yes, please," I say.

He nods and tilts his head and if I didn't see him do it, I'd swear there was a crow sitting next to me, cawing.

From the trees comes an answering caw, and then a big black bird appears between the branches, sees us, and tilts its wings in our direction. It lands at Wolfram's feet but gives me a keen look. It's big for a crow, I think, but not so big as a raven, and it has a single white feather in its left wing.

Wolfram gestures at the bird. "This is Sgian," he says, pronouncing the name something like "skeen."

"I give a little wave. "Hey," I say.

The bird looks at me, then at Wolfram. "Who's the babe, old man?" it says, in a perfectly human-sounding Scottish accent.

Chapter Six

I KNOW, I'm a woman who turns into a fox; I shouldn't be surprised to meet a crow that speaks with a Scottish accent. But there it is.

"Do I need to remind you to be polite?" Wolfram says to the bird, but I can see from the dimple on his cheek that he's trying not to smile.

"What can I say," says the crow. "You found me in the gutter." Then he or maybe she turns to me and bows. "Pleased to make your acquaintance, lovely lady," in a perfect Received Pronunciation English accent that slips back to Scottish by the end of the sentence.

"It's just Su," I say.

Wolfram shakes his head. "Would you mind, if you can spare the time from your busy schedule of scavenging in the carnival garbage bins, flying over to ask Máiréad if she is willing to meet a friend who is in need of assistance?"

"What's in it for me?"

"I don't send you back to the gutter you came from."

"Fine," says the crow. "Back in a jif," and launches into the air and flies away.

I must still be goggle-eyed, because Wolfram says, "I take it you haven't met a talking crow before."

"I really shouldn't be surprised by anything any more."

"I've lived a lot longer than you, child, and I'm happy to say the world has not ceased to astonish me."

"Is that a good thing?"

"Absolutely. A predicable world would get boring very quickly." He stares contemplatively into the distance and then says, "She wasn't always a crow."

"Oh?" I admit, I'm dead curious, but I don't want to seem too eager to learn the secrets of Wonder Island. Show too much interest, and he might stop talking.

"She was *sith*, from a good family. She could take the form of a crow at will, and she was a trouble maker from a young age, or so she tells me."

"*Sith* is like a fairy, right? Or an elf? Another thing I didn't know existed for real." But I think of the Jinny Greenteeth I saw captive in Charleston's research facility.

"It is, more or less. Unfortunately for Sgian, she was also a thief and a pickpocket, and she decided to lift the wrong god's wallet."

"She picked a *god's* pocket?" I take a breath. "Wait, gods are real? And they carry wallets?"

"As I think you have come to suspect, a great many more things are real than you realized. If you're going to spend much time here, you might want to get used to it."

He flashes a dimple at me again and I resist the urging of my magic fox hormones to lean over and kiss it.

"And yes, many of us carry wallets. They're convenient for holding identification and money and other things needed to exist in the world as it is today."

"So whose pocket did she pick?" I try not to think about how I spent a year making a living that way myself, until very recently. And I might have to take it up again, if I don't find a mundane job soon.

"Wotan."

"She picked *Odin's* pocket. Holy shit."

"Holy shit, indeed. Our Sgian found herself deep in it."

"So she was cursed to be a crow permanently?"

"And sent to live in the human realms."

"Where you found her scavenging garbage in a ditch."

"Precisely." He stretches and gets to his feet.

"And now she scavenges garbage on Wonder Island. Is that any better?"

Wolfram smiles. "She's well fed, like all our staff. Scavenging garbage is a cover, because her job is to keep an eye on the carnival visitors. Of course, she's not above eating what she finds. She's especially fond of candy floss and caramel apples. And those tiny donuts."

Further questions have to wait as the crow returns. She looks at me with one beady eye and I can't help thinking she looks like she's leering at me. But crows don't really have facial expressions, so how could I tell?

"She says she'll meet you at the old man's statue."

"When?"

I swear the crow actually shrugs. "Now."

"Your service is appreciated, Sgian." I notice Wolfram doesn't thank her, and I remember from my folklore reading that fairies really don't like being thanked. I file the information away a little closer to the front of my brain so maybe I'll remember when I need it.

"Just don't send me back to the cursed city."

"Keep your beak clean, and we'll see."

The bird makes a snorting noise I think might be laughter, then launches again and is gone.

"Would you really send her back?" I ask.

"I would not," says Wolfram. "And she knows it. But it doesn't hurt to remind her that she's here because she's allowed to be. Of course, she is also paid for her duties, aside from being well fed."

"She gets paid?"

"In very shiny silver." He emphasizes "shiny" and chuckles.

We've been walking as we talked and come around a bend in the path to see a bustling market area. Most of the browsers don't really look like tourists, but I suppose the Islanders need a place to shop, too.

We pass through to a huge stone building and stop at a wooden door.

"Is this the old asylum? Or prison, or whatever it was?"

Wolfram shakes his head. "This building was used, but soon abandoned. Most of the institution was there." He points off to the left, where a concrete wall forms one side of the market. "We renovated it as apartments for carnival staff."

"Do you live there?"

He raises an eyebrow at that – another damn person who can raise just one; I can't do it despite hours of trying in the mirror. Both my eyebrows go up together.

"You *are* full of questions," he says. "Good thing I believe you to be trustworthy. And yes, I do live there. I don't place myself above my people." Then he snorts a laugh startlingly like the crow's. "Except I live on the top floor, so I guess I *am* literally above them."

I try not to stare at the folk running the booths while I wait for him to open the door. A lot of them are tall and thin and very pale. They look like they might be siblings. Or maybe they're more fairy folk who just happen to all look alike.

Wolfram pulls a ring of keys out of his pocket and unlocks the door. All I can see on the other side when it opens is darkness. He stands another moment, like he's hesitant to enter, but then he shakes his head and says, "I don't know why Máiréad wanted to meet in the House and not in the forest, but it is her right to ask."

"The House?" I can practically hear the caps when he says it, but this building does not look like a house. It looks like something that has a dungeon. And a garret. Several of each, probably.

"The House is… not something I can explain. Not yet. Perhaps, if you return to the Island often, you will one day understand. It is not a place outsiders are permitted to go, normally. Even Islanders seldom come here."

"If it's locked, how can the woman we're meeting get in?"

"Only the door nearest the public spaces is kept locked, as extra security. The other entrances can take care of themselves."

That's too cryptic, and too *spooky* for me. I decide maybe I better just shut up and follow. And hope this "house" doesn't swallow me whole.

"This is where I brought Evgeny Alexeyevich, when Karasu delivered him to me."

"Here?" I peer in the door again, wishing I could have been there for Ev.

As if he knows what I'm thinking, Wolfram says, "You would not have been allowed inside, then."

"Did Magne go with him? This far at least?" I hate to think Ev was left with only strangers to help him and I know Mags would go to the ends of the earth if he had to.

"Magne did not come even as far as the market. I requested he and Cara wait in the carnival proper. Evgeny was only allowed because he was becoming – perhaps had already become – something more than *other*."

"Oh." Does that mean *I'm* something more than *other* now? I suppose it does.

He still seems hesitant to enter. "I think Máiréad is testing you. Testing *me*, perhaps. She will decide you are worth helping if I think you can be trusted inside the House, and if the House allows you to pass through."

"You trusted Evgeny."

"It was necessity. And the House accepted him. There is a room here that was probably the only safe place for him to face the being haunting him."

"Oh." Yeah, I'm just full of intelligent commentary today.

"Besides," and his smile is back, the hesitation gone. "I like him."

Then he gestures at the dark doorway. "Come, but follow me closely. Even if the House allows you in, there are dangers for the unwary." As he steps through the door, lights come on in the walls, glowing patterns like Viking knotwork, shining pale blue-white. The light reflects in Wolfram's eyes, making him look uncanny. And very old, very powerful, and very, very scary.

Hell, what have I got myself into this time? But I follow, and the door closes behind us on its own. The path through the halls to the courtyard we emerge in is mercifully quick, but I can't keep from looking behind me with every few steps the whole time.

There's never anything there, just the stone corridor with distantly-spaced doors. There isn't even any dust or cobwebs.

The courtyard is a relief, open to the sun as it is, though only in comparison to the halls. It's paved in stone flags and there's a cracked and non-functional fountain in the middle with a statue. An old man, just as the crow said. Odin, I think, with a raven on each shoulder and wolves crouching by his feet. One eye is in shadow, maybe missing, but his face looks an awful lot like Wolfram's. I decide not to think about that too closely. Not right now.

A slender, dark-haired woman in a blue-green wool dress over creamy white linen stands next to the fountain. Her feet are bare and her toes dirty. When she turns to us, I'm pretty sure my mouth falls open. She's beautiful. Like unearthly lovely. And since she's a fairy – *sidhe*, I should say – I guess that makes sense. In all the stories, the *sidhe* are either extremely gorgeous, or horrifyingly ugly. Or both, by turns.

"Wolfram," she says. Her voice has faint traces of an Irish lilt, but she pronounces the "w" as a "v," the German way.

He takes her outheld hand and brushes a kiss on the backs of her fingers.

"Máiréad," he says. "You look well."

"You look tired," she says. "And you never visit anymore."

"I've been busy."

"Too busy for poetry?"

"Too busy for many things."

Then she turns to me and I can feel the heat of her regard. "And this is she who needs my help."

"Su," I say. "My name, I mean." And then I remember that names are supposed to give fairies power over you, and I wonder if I've made a mistake. I feel like an awkward teenager talking to their crush for the first time.

Her smile is kind. "Is it inspiration you seek? You know there is a price?" She withdraws her hand from Wolfram's and takes mine instead. "No," she says. "I think it is something else."

"I'll leave you," says Wolfram. "Thea is waiting for me so she can throw knives at me." He sees my look and adds, "Her carnival act is knife-throwing. I'm the usual target." Then he turns back to the fairy woman and bows slightly. "If you could escort our guest to the market, I think she can find her way from there."

"Of course," she says.

"Um," I say. "That's fine."

"Keep me informed about your professor," he says. "Magne has my contact info." Then he leaves me with this frighteningly beautiful woman.

She leads me to the fountain and we sit on the edge, and to be honest, I'm not really sure what happens after that. I mean, I know I tell her – stammering and blushing the whole time – about the sex magic thing, but I don't remember any of my words, nor any of hers. I tell her I don't know how to turn it on or off, and worse, it's working backwards and muddying *my* thoughts.

I think she leads me through some thought exercises, sort of meditations or guided visions, but that's where things gets *really* hazy. But I guess whatever it is she's taught me works, because somewhere along the line, I stop feeling the flush of heat under my skin that sitting so close to her was causing. And I stop thinking about Wolfram's dimple and his cute ass and what he looks like in only the gold lamé g-string he wears for his tattooed man act. I stop desperately wanting to get laid.

My mind clears and after that I remember what happens as well as I remember any other day's events.

"There," she says, slapping her knees with her palms. "You're a quick study. I think you won't have any more trouble with your ability to make people desire you or not, exactly as you please."

And I know I can use those powers at will, though like the fox women, I can't tell you *how*.

"And your own desires should no longer overwhelm you."

Tentatively, I think about Magne. And get hot between the legs. I don't have to say anything; somehow she can tell. "Whomever you're thinking of now is someone you truly desire, not a person you merely find somewhat attractive," she says.

I very carefully do *not* think about Evgeny.

I'm about to thank her when I remember how Wolfram pointedly did not thank Sgian. Instead, I say, "I appreciate your help."

She nods graciously.

And I remember that fairy gifts always have a price.

"Do I… do I owe you anything in return?"

She smiles. "Were you an ordinary mortal, seeking to create desire in others, you would owe me a great deal."

My heart sinks.

"But you are not human, and you already had that ability; you merely needed help in controlling it. And we are not so different, almost sisters in a way. Perhaps one day I will ask for *your* help, but there is no obligation between us."

I nod and it's *really* hard not to say, "Thank you." I wonder if she knows that, too, because she's got a funny smile, but she only holds out a hand to pull me to my feet. This time, when our hands touch, there's no overwhelming rush of heat, just the normal feeling of grasping another person's hand. Another *attractive* person, it's true, but it's okay. I feel normal. I feel lighter.

She takes me back through the house to the market, and I barely glance at the tables, even though I'm curious about what things are sold here.

Now that I know it really *is* Magne I want, I can't wait to get home, to tell him.

To kiss him.

I swear, every time I get back to our building lately, something's wrong. I mean, I don't notice anything at first. I take the elevator up to my place, to change into yoga pants and let my tail out. I give it a good swish and almost knock myself off balance. It feels so good to have a tail again after keeping it hidden most of the day.

Then I send a quick text to John Pradip. Just, *Hey, do you have time to meet? Tomorrow, maybe? I'll be @ Wonder I carnival.* He'll say yes or he won't. After that I take to elevator back down to Magne's floor so he'll know I'm coming. His truck was out front, so unless he's gone for a run, he's home.

His door is ajar, the way he leaves it when he hears me come home and is open to company – not that he's ever *not* open. But when I go to close it behind me, I find his keys still in the lock, the rest of the keys hanging from the ring. And I hear swearing and thumping.

I drop the keys on the coffee table and head – cautiously – for the noises.

Thump! "Fuck." Whack! "Fucking fuck," and so on. The cursing isn't loud but it's fierce, angry. It sounds like he's beating the crap out of something.

There's a room on the right wall I've never been in. Actually, I've only been in the kitchen, living room, and bathroom, and since Magne's apartment actually has walls and separate rooms – unlike my open space – that leaves a handful of places I haven't seen. The door to this room is also ajar, and it's where the sounds are coming from.

Magne's breathing is harsh, like he's been punching whatever it is for a long time. Or like he's crying. But it can't be that; Magne doesn't cry.

I poke my head around the door, and to my relief I see he's hitting one of those big punching bags that boxers use, or martial artists. I've hit a few of them myself, when I used to go to kung fu class. But then I notice he's been hitting it so hard, and so long, that he's split his knuckles open on both hands and blood is dripping on the floor.

"Fuck fuck goddammit fuck," he says, his voice more growl than words. Every muscle is standing out so much I can see most of them bulging through his clothes. "God fucking dammit."

"Magne?" My voice comes out tiny. I've never seen him so angry, so… He *is* crying. Tears and snot both run unchecked down his face and he just keeps hitting the bag over and over, leaving dark red splotches on its surface.

"Mags…" I force my voice a little louder. At the best of times I have difficulty taking loud, and this is definitely not the best of times. "Sweetheart, you have to stop." I've never called anyone sweetheart in my life. Not even Ev. But right now his name doesn't seem intimate enough.

He stops abruptly, hands still up like he wants to keep swinging, but suddenly lacks the will. He rubs the back of one hand over his face, smearing the tears and blood and mucous all together. His shoulders shake and his knees seem to give out, like he's lost the will to stay standing.

"Magne?" Now I'm scared, cold gripping my guts.

He looks at me finally, and he seems devastatingly young. The look in his eyes makes *me* want to cry. Anger, shame, sorrow.

"I fucked up, Su," he says, his voice rough. "I failed."

I step closer and pull his head against me and he buries his face in my belly. I have no idea what's hurt him, but I want to fight something to make it better.

"Tell me what happened," I say, keeping my voice soft like you do with a frightened animal.

"I didn't get there in time," he says. "Now that poor kid's going to die."

Chapter Seven

MAGNE LETS ME hold him for a few minutes, then he pulls away and sits with his back to the wall. He looks miserable, angry, defeated. I don't think I've ever loved him so much.

For a long time, he just stares into space, then he scrubs at his face with both hands. "There's this kid," he says.

"A werewolf?"

He nods. "Just made this year, which makes him around eighteen, I guess. He's thin, delicate. Pretty. I don't know how he survived being made a werewolf, but he did. Stronger than he looks, I guess."

I crouch down close to him, but not touching. I get the feeling he doesn't want to be touched. His anger feels like heat to my fox nature, but it's directed inward, at himself.

"Who is he?" I keep my voice soft.

"One of my cousin's kids," he says. "Distant cousin. I see him sometimes when the whole pack gathers. Real piece of work. Homophobic fucker."

I think I see where this is going, and I feel cold. "He hurt the kid?"

He shrugs one shoulder, then rubs it absently with his other hand. I think he's beginning to feel the effects of beating the crap out of that bag. "He might. Probably. I don't know."

"The kid's gay?"

He looks up at me, then away. "Werewolf culture has laws against sexual deviancy," he says. "But it's the local Elders who get to decide what that means. All wolf packs have zero tolerance for rape, incest, pedophilia…"

"Punishable by death."

"Usually."

"But…" I know there's more. Worse.

"The Elders of my pack include homosexuality, transsexuality, anything that falls under the LGBTQ alphabet soup."

"So gay werewolves get killed by their own families." It's very hard not to sound angry, but I manage to keep my voice even and low.

He looks up at me again. "As far as I know, most of them stay as far in the closet as they can. But some of them…"

"Can't hide who they are."

"Yeah."

"This kid was too pretty."

"Too pretty, too sweet, too non-violent. They'd probably have given him a hard time, sent him before the Elders, even if he *wasn't* gay."

"How did you find out?"

"I've… I've been helping closeted wolves for a while. I guess this kid's mom heard about it."

I think about all the times phone calls and texts called him away, about him coming home injured, but not unhappy.

"Won't you get fallout from this? You can't help people if you're a target."

He gives me half smile, but it doesn't go past his lips. "I'm not quite *that* dumb. I use an alias, go-betweens, non-were contacts, and no one I have to fight ever sees my face."

"So you were going to help this kid?"

"Someone found out and got to him before I could get him to safety."

"What were you going to do with him?"

"There are packs to the north and west that take runaways and help them find safe places to go. I'm in touch with a few of them."

"And now?"

"The kid'll be hauled in front of the Elders, they'll pass sentence, and his own family will rip him to shreds." He looks at me again, and there are tears in the corners of his eyes. One swells and pulls free to roll down the side of his nose and he scrubs it away. "If that doesn't kill him, they'll break his neck."

I don't know what to say at that, so I move closer, put my arms around him, and nuzzle his hair. He smells like sweat and anger.

For a moment he's still, and then he starts to shake. "Don't," he says, pulling away, curling his body away from mine. "Just leave me alone for a bit."

Reluctantly, I leave him there and close the door behind me. I look around for something to hit, and have to settle for beating up a couch cushion. Magne's jacket is draped over the couch nearby and while I'm assaulting the upholstery it slides to the floor and something falls out of his pocket with a clatter.

His phone. I stare at it for a moment, then pick it up to put it on the coffee table. But I pause before setting it down. I touch the screen and it lights up. His lock screen is a photo of the three of us – him, me, and Ev – with a tv showing a black and white monster movie behind us. That was the night he made us watch *Godzilla Raids Again*. I have to blink away tears of my own.

To my surprise, the phone unlocks with my face. I don't remember him adding me to his phone, but I guess he must have, in case of emergency.

Is there someone I can call? Someone who can help Magne's cousin's kid? How long before the boy is killed? The problem is, I don't know anyone. There's no way I'll call Evgeny, even if I thought he could help. Wolfram? He's been very willing to help us so far, but I don't want to push my luck. We're not his people, and even if we're welcome on Wonder Island, he has no obligation to us.

But there's no one else. So I open Magne's contacts and scroll through them. Wolfram's there, phone, email, website, and cell. I hesitate, but then I hear the punching start up in the other room again. No swearing this time, which seems somehow worse.

I hit "dial" and listen to the ringing on the other end.

"Hi Magne! What can I do for you?" Wolfram sounds glad.

"It's Su," I say. "I borrowed Magne's phone because I left mine upstairs and I don't want to go get it." I realize I'm dangerously close to babbling nonsensically, but he must hear something in my voice.

"Is he okay?"

"No," I say. "Well, yes. Kind of." I try to explain what's happened, but I can't seem to get events in the right order or lay things out in a way that makes sense. Wolfram makes me stop and start over slowly, asking small questions until I get the whole story out. Finally I stop talking because I don't know what else to say.

He's quiet for a moment, and I hear classical music in the background, something soft, with flutes. "I don't know what I can do to help," he says. "Werewolves – *others* in general – are out of my jurisdiction. Technically, anyone not from Wonder Island isn't mine to help or hinder."

"Oh." I'm not sure any sound even comes out of my mouth. I knew it was a long shot, but I still hoped. Maybe I can go find the kid myself, somehow.

"However," he says after a long pause, "Werewolves and vampires both *are* under Karasu's charge. And Karasu owes me a very large favor."

"I… I don't want you to lose any leverage," I say. "You might need it later." Karasu is a very scary and ancient old vampire with motives and concerns all his own.

Wolfram makes a dismissive sound. "I don't enjoy holding debts and I will not be unhappy to discharge this one. Let me make a call."

"Okay," I say. "I… thank you."

"Anything from your professor?"

"I left my phone upstairs."

"Right, so you said. Let me know. If Karasu will help, you'll know soon."

"Thank you," I say again.

"Think nothing of it," he says. "Just look after that overly noble wolf of yours, and make sure he knows he doesn't have to do everything alone."

"Yessir," I say, and he barks a short laugh and hangs up.

When I go back to check on Magne, he's sitting on the floor with his back to the wall, almost like he never moved, but there are more dark red spatters. He's staring at the blood dripping off his knuckles, but he looks up when I come in.

"Sorry I'm acting like such an ass," he says. "This isn't your shit to deal with."

I've brought a wet washcloth with me, and the first aid kit. I kneel in front of him and wipe his face. "You're not an ass, Mags. You're…" I pause while I get the last of the blood and mucous off his upper lip, and then start on his knuckles. I can't look at him when I say, "You're the finest man I know."

"I wish that was true," he says, his voice just above a whisper.

"It *is* true." I tape a bandage in place and make myself look up at his face.

His brown eyes are bottomless. There's self-recrimination there, but most of the anger is gone. And there's something else, something raw and open. Vulnerable. I don't think I ever thought to see Magne look vulnerable.

"Listen Mags," I say, and I tell him about what happened when he left Wonder Island, talking crow, beautiful *sidhe* woman, and all.

"That's great," he says. "I'm glad you're getting more control. You're amazing when you can use your fox abilities." He blushes. "You're amazing anyway."

And holy shit. I mean, Magne's fair skinned enough to show pink, but he's always been so shameless I didn't know he *could* blush. It makes him look younger.

"And I was thinking," I say.

"Mmm?" He tugs at the bandages on his hands, tests them to make sure they're not going to fall off. They won't. Having a very physical werewolf for a best friend means I'm really good at patching up all manner of injuries.

When I don't say any more, he looks at me again. "You were thinking?"

I don't know what to say, how to tell him I figured out what he means to me, now that I don't have magic sex hormones influencing every thought in my head. So I just lean over and kiss him.

He pulls away so quickly he snacks his head on the wall behind him. "Su…"

"I know," I say. "You don't want to start anything until you're sure I'm not just missing Ev." I sit back. "I know."

"We both miss him," he says. "But he was the love of –"

"Look," I say, interrupting, suddenly very irritated. Annoyed at him for being so noble. Ticked off at myself for not figuring things out sooner. And flat out *pissed* at Evgeny for dumping me in the first place. "I'm never *not* going to miss him, but that doesn't mean I can't move on. He could dance naked through that door right now –" I gesture violently towards the white-painted wooden door into the rest of his apartment "– and I would tell him, 'Hi, nice to see you, please put some clothes on.' And then I would kiss *you*."

I realize I'm poking him in the sternum to punctuate every word, so I clasp my hands together in my lap.

Magne just stares at me for a minute, and then he starts to laugh.

"What? Did I say something funny?"

He's laughing so hard he's holding his ribs and breathing in gasps, and I can't help but smile.

"Seriously, Mags, what did I say?"

He forces himself to stop laughing, and says, "You've got me picturing Ev doing a naked can-can through the doorway." His shoulders shake with the effort of stifling his merriment. At least they're not shaking with grief anymore, even if it is at my expense.

"Oh, stop it," I say, smacking his shoulder. "Will you listen to me?"

He clamps his lips together and tries to hold still. I smack him again.

"Ow," he says, but grins. Two dimples. "Okay, what?"

"I love you," I say. And there it is. So incredibly simple, and so very hard to say.

He stares at me. "Su…" he finally says, breathy, his voice almost a growl.

"Okay?" I say, tilting my head up defiantly. "I love you, you big dumb hairy werewolf, so please say something."

He doesn't. He just looks at me until I want to smack him again. Then he touches my cheek with two fingers, tracing the side of my face. A smile quirks his lips, crinkles the corners of his eyes. Not a grin, but a slow smile of wonder. He touches my lower lip with a fingertip.

"Say that again," he finally says.

"You big dumb hairy werewolf," I say pretending to snap at his fingers.

"Not that part." But his smile grows.

"I love you."

His breath goes out in a rush and I realize he's been holding it, as if he was afraid he'd misheard me.

I poke him. "I love you, Magne, and if you don't kiss me soon I will expire right here on your floor."

He shakes his head, not in denial but in wonder. "Su," he says, almost whispering. "I think I've loved you since that first time you showed up at my door, apparently human and boldly asking dangerous questions about werewolves."

Then, *finally*, he kisses me. Every time we've kissed till now – recently, anyway – it's been me surprising him, and even when he responded, he let me take the lead. This time, he leans forward, slides his hand behind my neck, and covers my mouth with his.

He starts gentle, nibbling my lower lip, parting my lips with his, but then he grows more insistent, more demanding, until he's kneeling over me, pressing our mouths together like he wants to devour me. His tongue is sliding across mine and his breath is coming in gasps, and I can't get enough of him. I grab his hair in both hands and try to make him kiss me harder, deeper.

Finally he pulls away and we're both panting.

"Gods," he breathes. "I've wanted to do that for so long."

"Do it again," I say, and he does, though not quite so forcefully. Then he removes his lips from mine, and applies them to my earlobe, my neck, across my collarbones to my other earlobe.

The next time he pulls away to catch his breath, I say, "If you were so in love with me, why did you always make suggestive comments? Icky ones?"

"Was I icky?" he says. "Sorry, love. I didn't want you to get hurt."

"That doesn't make any sense."

"I thought you were human. I mean, it's common for werewolves and humans to have relationships. My dad's first wife was human, and never wanted to be made a wolf." Mention of his father makes him pause and his nostrils flare, but he shakes his head. "But you seemed so naive, so unprepared. And way out of my league. So I figured if you thought I was a dog, you'd stay away and be safe."

"A noble dog," I say, head-butting him gently.

"Except it didn't work," he says. "On at least one occasion, I distinctly recall you trying to climb me like a tree."

I feel a blush creeping up my neck at that. "I was, unbeknownst to me, suffering from an overabundance of magic fox lady sex hormones."

"Like. A. Tree." He kisses the end of my nose.

"Well, you *are* about as tall as a tree."

He laughs and touches my face again, the look of wonder back in his eyes. "You're still way out of my league," he says.

"I'm very not," I say. "I'm just a woman trying to get by in the world as best she can without hurting anyone else in the process. *You* are a kind, generous, selfless…"

"Big, dumb, hairy werewolf," he finishes.

"I was going to say stone cold hottie," I inform him. "And I don't really think you're dumb."

"I know."

"You're probably the smartest person I know."

"Nah."

"Yeah, you are. And *you're* way out of *my* league. Especially brain-wise. But there is one thing you're dumb at, and Wolfram specifically asked me to tell you this."

"Did he?"

"And if I recall correctly, which I absolutely do, you were always saying this exact thing to a certain Russian-born vampire of our acquaintance."

"What dumb thing have I done that I used to call Ev on?"

I tilt my head so our foreheads touch. "You don't have to do everything by yourself."

He's quiet for a moment. "You know, our Evgeny *could* be pretty dumb sometimes."

"He really could."

He shifts on the floor so he can pull me closer. "I'm sorry, love," he says. "I should have told you what I was doing."

"Mags, you're running a fucking underground railroad for queer werewolves."

He snorts. "Yeah, I guess I am."

"You're amazing, and I want to help."

He looks sad again. "I just fucking wish I got that kid safely away. He doesn't deserve what they're going to do to him and there's no way I'll be able to get anywhere near him now. And his mother shouldn't have to lose her son because of some old fucks' prejudices."

I hear the sound before he does. Footsteps, moving rapidly up the stairs and along the hall. The building is practically sound-proof and the feet belong to someone used to moving silently, so I'm not sure how I hear them at all, unless he *wants* us to hear.

I make it to the living room at the same time our visitor does.

Karasu. He's carrying a bloody bundle in his arms, and he does not look happy. He must be damping down on the aura of terror he usually wears about him like a cloak, because I barely notice it. Or maybe I've become less afraid.

"I am *not* an errand boy," he says, and lays his burden on the floor with more gentleness that I'd ever have expected of him.

"What?" says Magne behind me.

"Well, now you're not indebted to Wolfram Gottfried anymore," I say.

"I suppose I should thank you for that," he says. "The boy's mother will be along shortly. I could not carry them both." And then he's gone, literally disappearing in a swirl of dark mist.

"Show off," I mutter.

"What was that all about?" says Magne. Then he sees what Karasu deposited on his floor. And I realize what it was he was carrying.

Not a bundle, but a young man, so covered in blood and dirt it's impossible to see how injured he is.

"Oh fuck," says Magne, dropping to the floor next to the boy and feeling for a pulse. "Come on, kid," he says.

"Is he —" But I can't finish the question.

It's a moment before Magne says anything else. "He's alive. Barely, but he's alive."

Chapter Eight

W HAT DO YOU need me to do?"

Magne's running his hands over the kid, trying to figure out where the worst wounds are. He looks up and hardly seems to see me.

"If he lives through the night, he's going to be hungry."

"Okay," I say. "Food." I head to the kitchen and open the fridge. Beer. Condiments. A surprising bounty of fresh vegetables. I don't think broccoli and carrots are going to be what a newly healed, ravenous teenaged werewolf is going to need.

"I need to clean him up. I can't see anything." I hear tearing cloth as Magne takes the quick route to getting the kid's clothes off – or what the pack left of his clothes.

"Okay," I say. "Water. Cloths." I detour to the bathroom and pull out every clean washcloth I find in the cupboard and dump them in the sink. I run hot water on them, then grab a clean towel and bundle the lot up and drop in on the floor next to Magne. Good thing his towels are dark grey, because I don't think that much blood is going to wash out.

I kneel down to help and he says, "Look for anything still bleeding freely," as we work to clean away the blood and dirt. Some of the shallower cuts are already closing, but with this much to heal, the boy's symbiont will be working slowly, stretched thin.

"Bandages?" I ask, about to get up and head for the first aid kit.

"Not yet. Just keep pressure on the worst. This kid needs blood."

"Does this kid have a name?"

"Probably."

Magne rolls up the sleeve of his shirt and makes a fist.

"Wait," I say. "How are you planning to give him blood?"

He looks at me, gives me a half-smile, and says, "The old-fashioned werewolf way." Then his jaw becomes muzzle-shaped, his big canines protruding like monster movie fangs, and he bites the inside of his own forearm, hard.

"It's not so much the blood," he says, his speech slurred as his mouth re-forms into human shape, "as the symbiont *in* the blood. He's lost a lot of his own, maybe so much it can't heal him." His arm bleeds freely, dripping down his skin and onto the kid. He holds it over the worst wounds, clenching and unclenching his fist to make the dark liquid flow.

"Don't kill yourself trying to save this kid," I say, but I say it quietly.

He leans over and plants a hurried kiss on my lips. He tastes like his own blood. "I would," he said, "if it was the only way. But I really don't intend to die today."

He rolls up his other sleeve and is about to bite his arm when he pauses and nods towards a sort of alcove formed between the bathroom and the exercise room walls. "There's elk steaks in the freezer," he says. "Make lots. I'm going to be hungry, too."

I turn away as he rips open his other arm.

At least thawing meat gives me something to do besides fret and watch the man I love drain himself to save a boy whose name he doesn't even know. When I've got as many steaks thawing as I can cram in the microwave, and a sink full of more in cool water, I lean against the counter and watch.

Magne has pulled the kid into his lap and is pressing one of his bleeding arms onto the boy's abdomen, where a gaping gut wound looks like it was a fraction of an inch from spilling entrails. The boy's head is tilted back against Magne's shoulder, and he's so pretty it seems unreal, even covered in dried blood and grime. High cheekbones, fair hair falling over his eyes. Wide, full lips. He looks a lot like Evgeny, except for his coloring, pale where Ev is dark-haired and olive-skinned. Even with a full tank of blood, this kid would be pale. I wonder how such an ethereal-looking creature came to be born into a werewolf family.

I'm about to say something, I don't know what, just something to break the tension, when the crackling buzz of the building intercom goes off.

When I press the button, I barely get out, "Hello?" when a breathless, panicky female voice says, "Please, my son, is he here? The vampire said he'd be here." I don't answer, I just hit the switch to let her into the building.

Out in the hall, I listen. No elevator grinding, so she must be taking the stairs. I meet her at the door to the stairwell.

"Where is he?" she says, still breathless but more from panic and fear than from running up the stairs. "Please." She pushes her long light brown hair back out of her face and I can see where her son gets his looks. She could be an angel, a fairy woman out of a bedtime story. Who apparently married one giant asshole of a werewolf.

"He's here," I say, putting a hand on her arm. She looks wildly around, spies the half-open door, and starts towards it. Her fear makes her awkward, and she shoves me aside with her shoulder without even seeming to realize I'm still there. I hate using mind powers on people – I hate it when they're used on me – but I don't want her to hurt herself, or her son, or to fling herself headlong into Magne's way. So I push out a little of the fox woman magic to make her focus on me. To her credit, and I guess a demonstration of the depth of her concern for her son, it almost doesn't work and I have to push harder.

She calms and waits for me to lead her inside, and even knowing it's helping her, I hate having to use that power. It reminds me too much of the way the witches invaded Evgeny's mind and subjugated his will.

"He's okay," I say. "I mean, he will be. He's alive. Magne's doing what he can." I take her into the living room and all her panic returns when she sees the kid, covered in blood in Magne's arms. I have to push the fox pheromone magic on her again, harder, so she won't fling herself at Magne and tear her son away.

Magne still has the boy in his lap, but now he's got a bloody arm pressed to the boy's face. The kid has roused enough to grab Magne's arm in both hands. It takes me a moment to realize the boy is drinking Magne's blood.

I mean, weres and vamps are closely related, so I guess it stands to reason that werewolves can drink blood and derive sustenance from it, I just didn't know they ever *did*. But this is special circumstances. Maybe getting the symbiont into the kid via his digestive tract is also effective.

Magne looks up, focusses slowly on the woman. "He's doing better than when he arrived." His voice is soft, and he looks relieved, but then he sways and I realize he's given the kid more of his blood than maybe he should have.

"Mags," I say. "I think it's time to get him bandaged up now." And, I don't add, to get *Magne* bandaged up.

The boy goes limp and drops his hands from Magne's arms. His mother gives a sort of moan and flings herself to the floor next to him before I can stop her. But she's not so panicked that she doesn't take care not to jostle him. She takes one of the boy's blood-streaked hands in her own and breaths a deep breath of relief when she discovers he's just passed out again.

I join her on the floor next to Magne and press one of the washcloths to his forearm – the one that seems to be bleeding the worst. "You may have overdone it, sweetheart," I say.

He leans unsteadily over to kiss my forehead. "I'll live," he says. "And so will he."

The woman looks up, tears in her eyes. She looks to be in her forties, and definitely human. "Thank you," she says. "Thank you."

Magne rubs his face with his hands.

"Your blood won't, like, cause an immune reaction or something?" I say. I don't know that much about were physiology, and I figure you never know what information could be useful.

"It shouldn't. We're from the same pack, and most wolves have multiple makers. The process is…"

"Brutal," says the boy's mother. "Barbaric. Cruel."

Magne doesn't protest. "I was going to say, a bit of a free-for-all. If the wolf-to-be has any kind of strength, he'll fight back and any blood he sheds will end up contributing to his making. So he'll be fine. It's not like I gave him an actual blood transfusion. Our blood type doesn't have to match, just our symbiont."

"And one pack all have the same symbiont."

"Mostly. Anyone who was made in the pack will. Anyone from outside won't, which is mostly spouses who married in. It's basically a blood borne disease. If the symbionts were too different, we might have a problem. Anyway, he should have enough in him now to make it through the night. Enough to heal the worst of that mess and buy him time to heal from the rest. He survived being made a wolf in the first place; he'll survive this."

He gets up slowly, like he's exhausted – and he probably is. The woman watches him, and I see the moment she recognizes him as her eyes widen and she pulls in a sharp breath.

"I know you," she says.

Magne stretches and I watch closely to make sure he's not going to just fall over. "Your husband's a distant cousin," he says. "We've seen each other around now and then."

"Not my husband much longer," she says. "Not after this." Then she studies his face again. "You're Thorgrim's son." It comes out like an accusation, and if I wasn't watching Magne so closely, I might have missed the sight flinch.

He gives her a grim smile. "Guilty," he says.

"Why are you helping us?"

"Because I may share some of Thorgrim's DNA, but I don't share any of his opinions."

She frowns, so he goes on. "I'm the youngest of four kids, three of them boys. I was an accident, as far as my father goes; the extra kid who wasn't supposed to be born. I may not know everything your son's been through, but I *do* know what it's like to be unwanted in a culture that's all about family bonds." He looks at me, then, and smiles. "And I'll be damned if I let my old man make me into someone I can't face in the mirror every morning."

I smile back and turn to the woman. "What he's trying to say," I tell her, "is that killing people because they're gay or trans or a different color or whatever is wrong. And because, even though he looks about as thoughtful as a Mack truck, Magne here is a good man, and tries to do the right thing."

She looks back and forth between us, and finally smiles. "I hope my son meets someone who supports him the way you support each other," she says. "I've tried to raise him well, despite…"

"Yeah," Magne says. "But not all werewolf packs are as trapped in the Dark Ages as mine."

Between the three of us, we get the boy so wrapped up in bandages he looks like a B-movie mummy, then Magne scoops the kid up in his arms – he sways but recovers quickly – and carries him towards his bedroom. "Let's get him someplace more comfortable," he says. "Then we'll get some food ready for when he wakes up."

Right. I'm supposed to be cooking colossal amounts of elk steak. I yank open the microwave and start peeling butcher paper off meat. By the time Magne gets back from settling mother and son in his own bed, I've got every burner going with a fry pan full of meat. This man really has an absurd amount of cookware.

He sits on one of the stools at the island and I hand him a beer. He takes a long swig. "This is probably going to knock me out, considering how much blood I've lost." Then he points at a drawer. "There are baking sheets in there. You can put the rest of the steaks in the oven."

While I do so, he takes another gulp of beer – something very dark from a local craft brewery – and peels the wrapper off a granola bar I slide across the island to him.

"His name is Tyler," he says. "The kid." He eats the bar in two bites and lays his head down on his hands. "Wake me when the steak is ready."

"You saved his life," I say.

He pushes himself mostly upright again and looks at me seriously. "I think *you* saved his life. What strings did you have to pull to get the world's oldest, scariest vampire to condescend to rescue a… what was his word… lowly cur?"

I flip one of the steaks. "I'm pretty sure it was the demon-ghost who called you a cur," I say, sliding the steak onto a plate. "Karasu merely affected intense disappointment at the degeneracy of his so-called descendants."

"Right," he says, cutting into the steak and stuffing a much too big bite into his mouth. I'm not sure he even chews it before he swallows. He must be ravenous, because Magne usually likes to taste his food.

"I actually called Wolfram," I say. "*He* pulled the strings."

"What did he want in return?"

"Nothing. Did he expect anything when he helped Ev?"

"No," he says. "He just implied that Karasu owed him big time."

"And Karasu implied that you owed *him*?"

"No, and that worries me a bit."

I poke the steaks and turn the ones that need it. "He likes you," I say. "Wolfram. I think he sees you as the son he never had." I'm joking, but as I say it, I have to wonder.

He holds out his plate for another steak, and this one he cuts and chews more slowly. I'm not the best cook in the world – hence why I eat a lot of take away – but even I'm almost salivating at the smell of the frying meat.

"How do you know he doesn't have kids?" he says between bites.

"I don't. He's old, and he implied he was quite the ladies' man when he was younger. He probably has dozens."

He's quiet while he finishes the steak, then he slides the plate aside and rests his head on his fist. I busy myself making a stack of the rest of the steaks and dump all the pans into the sink to soak.

"Thank you," he says, and I'm not sure which part of this very long evening he's thanking me for.

I point at the couch. "Sleep," I say.

"Is that an order?" He's smiling again, anger and self-recrimination gone, and I can't say how relieved I am.

"It's not the order I'd *like* to give you," I say, reaching over to tug at a piece of hair that's fallen over his face. His hair badly needs a trim, but somehow it still looks sexy as all hell.

"Oh, and what would that be?" Both dimples have made an appearance and I feel a little wobbly in the knees.

"You're too weak to execute it anyway," I say.

"Weak, am I?" He jumps up from his stool to grab me, stumbles, and has to catch himself on the counter. "Okay, maybe a little weak."

"Sleep, werewolf of my heart," I say. "Ravishing me can come later."

"Was that what you wanted me to do?" he says, mock surprise in his voice and posture. "Am I just a sex toy to you?" He presses the back of one hand to his forehead and pretends to swoon. I notice he's still got the other hand braced on the counter.

"Not *only* that," I say, grinning. Then I take his hand and lead him to the couch. "Look, here's a nice comfy sofa, big enough for a werewolf. It's almost like someone planned for large men to nap here."

He's sprawled out with his eyes closed before I even get through all the words. His breathing evens out and I realize he's already asleep.

The early morning sun is just finding its way into the tops of the windows when I wake up. First, I'm aware of Magne's bulk at my back, his arms keeping me from sliding off the edge of the couch onto the floor. Not that it would hurt, because there are enough pillows and cushions everywhere to outfit six department stores.

Next, I hear his breathing, deep and even, and quiet. Then, slowly, I become aware of noises in the other room, where the boy – Tyler – and his mother are staying. And between one breath and the next I can tell that Magne is wide awake.

He stretches, and I slide off the edge of the couch, but somehow he catches me before I hit the floor. Or the pillows *on* the floor.

"Good morning," he says, and kisses behind my ear.

"Morning," I say, then, "I really need to brush my teeth."

"There's an extra toothbrush under the sink if you don't want to go all the way upstairs."

As I'm getting to my feet, the boy's mother – I really should ask her name – emerges from the bedroom, There are dark circles under her eyes and her makeup has run, but she's still impossibly beautiful.

"How's Tyler doing, Mrs Harkett?" Magne asks.

She looks startled. "Just Bonnie," she says. "I won't keep his last name any longer than I have to."

"Neither will I." The boy sounds weak and exhausted, but he's standing.

"I cooked steaks last night," I say, pointing to the stack still on the counter. They're cold, but you need to eat."

"I'm starving," he says. His mother helps him to a kitchen stool and I load up a plate with steak for him.

"Eat," I say.

"I feel like there isn't enough food in the world," he says, smiling shyly at me. That smile is going to shatter some other boy's heart one day.

"Well, I only cooked enough for two armies, so you're going to have to make do."

Magne hands the boy's mother – Bonnie – a cup of coffee, then draws me aside. Before I can protest, he hands me a coffee, too. "I've got to find a way to get him up north as soon as possible. Do you think our interview with Mr Professor can wait a day or two?"

I take a long sip of coffee. Once Evgeny taught him the difference between good and strong, Magne took to making coffee like a true calling. It's dark, rich, strong, sweet, and very smooth.

"I haven't even checked my phone since I texted him yesterday afternoon," I finally say. "I left it upstairs, and then, well." I gesture towards the kitchen. "We'll figure something out."

"Thanks, love." He kisses my forehead.

"However," I say, and he looks down at me. "I'm going to be pretty cranky if I don't get a better kiss soon."

"Oh, there will be many and much better kisses at the soonest available opportunity." He brushes his lips over mine softly. "And much, much more than kisses," he adds, his voice dropping to a growl.

And then, for the second time in less than a day, the building buzzer goes. We look at each other, and then over at Tyler and Bonnie. He's absorbed in working through as many steaks as he can, but she's looking at us, fear in her eyes.

"Who could it be?" she says.

"Let's find out." Magne walks over to the door and pokes the button. "Yeah?" he says.

"It's O'Malley," says the distorted voice of Magne's father's detective friend.

"Su's upstairs," Magne says. "Is her buzzer not working?"

"I'm not here to speak to Su, kid. Let me in."

Magne lets go of the button and cuts off the intercom.

Bonnie has her arms around her son and is looking like she might panic again. I feel a bit like panicking, too. I like Detective O'Malley. But he's a member of Magne's pack. Magne's dad's pack. Magne's dad's extremely homophobic pack that just had their latest victim snatched from their very jaws, aided and abetted by the pack leader's own son.

The buzzer sounds again and Magne hesitates, then pushes the button. "I'm coming down."

"Let me in, kid. I know what you're doing."

Bonnie whimpers, and when I look over Tyler is on his feet, arms around her, like he's ready to defend her with is life. Except he can barely stand.

"I'm here to help, Magne," says O'Malley.

I hold my breath as Magne releases the button again.

"Fuck," he says, then presses the switch that unlocks the building's front door.

Chapter Nine

MAGNE PUTS HIMSELF between the door and our guests and I stand beside him. And we wait.

The elevator begins its slow grind upwards and I hear the door slide open with a cheery "ding." There's a soft tap on the door.

"It's open." No one who doesn't know Magne would hear the tension in his voice. He sounds relaxed and entirely unworried. But I hear it. Is O'Malley here to drag the poor kid back to the fate his pack had planned for him, or is he here to help?

And more importantly, is he here alone? By himself, he's not much of a threat to either Magne or me. At least I don't think so. Aside from the fact that acting against him would put us on the wrong side of the law. And cut off our best source of information about the investigation of my sister's disappearance.

The handle turns and the door swings inwards. Detective O'Malley looks pretty much like he did last time I saw him. Middle aged, middle height, entirely ordinary. He really doesn't *look* like a werewolf, but I guess there really isn't any one way a werewolf could look. This time, though, he's wearing a dark jacket, and I'm pretty sure the bulge under one arm is a gun.

"Hey kid," he says.

"Seamus."

"Can I come in?"

We back away from the door and around the living area to give the detective lots of room. He takes a few steps into the apartment and shuts the door.

"Why are you here?" says Magne. His voice is cautious, but not hostile.

Bonnie's breathing has sped up and I can smell her fear, though she seems to be trying hard to control it. I push a little fox magic at her, force her calm, hating it even as I do it, but we do *not* need her freaking out.

O'Malley looks from Magne to me, then beyond us to Bonnie and Tyler. I see his eyes widen and his nostrils flare, just a tiny bit.

"You look a lot better than I expected," he says. "I thought you were dead." Then he looks back at Magne, his bandaged arms and hands, his haggard face. "And you look worse."

"It was a long night," says Magne.

"Don't take my son," says Bonnie, and Tyler says, "Mom," half exasperated teenager, and half protective son.

Magne looks at O'Malley and waits.

"I'm not here to take him back, Bonnie," O'Malley says, holding out his hands like he's calming a spooked horse or something. I feel Bonnie relax slightly, hear Tyler climb back onto a stool. He shouldn't even be out of bed yet, let alone trying to defend himself and his mom.

"Kid," O'Malley says, focusing on Magne again. "You've got yourself in a whole shitload of trouble." He rubs a hand on the back of his neck. "I don't know how he found out, but your old man knows you were trying to help this kid get away. And I think he suspects you found him in the woods after…" He sighs and takes the few steps to the couch and drops onto it. "Let's just hope he believes Tyler is dead."

"How?" says Magne, but he's not really asking O'Malley.

"Fuck if I know."

"How did you find out?" Magne rounds the couch and sits on the opposite side of the sectional from O'Malley, facing him.

"I suspected. I didn't know for sure till I got here. You're not very good at bluffing, kid."

Magne snorts. "I guess not. What made you suspect, then?"

"Twenty-five years ago," he says, "my daughter left home in the middle of the night. We never saw her again, but once in a while we get a letter." He looks up from where he's been contemplating his shoes. "She always says to say hi to you."

A little smile is quirking at the corner of Magne's mouth. "You've never mentioned that," he says.

"I figure she's probably in contact with you. Email, or something."

"I didn't help her leave," Magne says. "I just asked her why she didn't and helped her figure out where to go. She was the one who inspired me to move away from the farm, to go to school in Great Valley. She visited whenever she was in the city."

"Close enough to help anyone else who needs it, but far enough to be away from your brothers."

Magne doesn't reply.

"She never says anything about her life now or why she left. But I can guess. And she never includes a return address. She can't even trust her old man." O'Malley stares back at his feet. "I wish she knew she could trust me. And her mother. We miss her."

"At least you know she's safe," Magne says softly. "She could never be safe here, unless she wanted to live a lie." Then Magne shifts in his seat to pull his phone out of his pocket. He looks at it thoughtfully, then seems to come to a decision. He pokes the screen a few times, types something, then puts it away.

There's a bleep from O'Malley's pocket.

"You'll want to look at that," Magne says.

The detective reaches for his phone and stares at it for a long moment. All I can see from where I stand is what looks like a photo of two women and a little girl. O'Malley looks like he might cry. It makes him look softer, kinder.

"Siobhan and her wife Jess found a sperm donor," Magne says. "The girl's name is Aislinn." He pauses and his grin takes on a wicked look. "Grandpa."

"Holy shit," O'Malley says. He looks from the photo to Magne and back. "I'm a granddad." His smile grows and he looks almost handsome. Then he frowns, but I'm pretty sure it's mock anger. "This donor wouldn't happen to be you, would it?"

Magne spurts out a startled laugh. "Gods, no. I'm too closely related." He grins the sly grin again. "Uncle Seamus."

"I'm a fucking granddad."

"She wanted to tell you," Magne says. "But you're too close to the pack leader. She got away, but she's still afraid somehow he can drag her back and hand her over to the Elders."

"Holy shit," O'Malley says again. Then he leans forward. "Thank you, kid. Thank you for helping find a safe place for her."

Magne shrugs. "I tried to get her to take me with her, but she told me I had to finish college. After that, I came to Riverbend instead. Of all my cousins, Siobhan was the only one who didn't follow my brothers' lead. She always tried to include me in everything when they wanted to leave me behind. It meant a lot. So when she told me she was a lesbian and didn't want to marry… What was his name?"

"Oh gods," says O'Malley, leaning back on the couch. "That big ugly kid of Giselle's. Frank. I don't know why I even gave my blessing to that lunk."

"Frank. Right. So I asked some guys I know – vamps, not wolves. They asked around, and put me in touch with a pack that was happy to welcome her." Magne looks sidelong at me. "That was the first and only time Liam ever did anything for me without being paid."

Good old Liam. I almost miss the underhanded black-marketeer.

O'Malley smiles again. It's definitely a good look on him. "So when I hear that in the last year several wolves have up and left without a word, I began to wonder. Then this pretty boy's dad shows up to talk to Thorgrim when I was…" He pauses and looks a bit guilty.

"Reporting to the old man on the goings-on of his black-sheep, city-dwelling, entirely useless son?"

"Something like that. So he says he's got a kid that's too soft, suspects the boy's gay, and asks your dad to call a meeting of the Elders. Anyway, I put two and two together and came up with Magne. I guess your dad did the same, though he's not known for his mental agility."

"Or Bjarni did," Magne says.

"Could be. He was always the cleverest of the lot, aside from you."

"So why are you here?"

"To help. I can't do much without tipping your old man off, but at least I can get Tyler and Bonnie to whichever pack you were planning to send them to."

"No," says Magne. "I don't want to put you at risk." He pauses and adds, regretfully, "And I don't know if I can trust you."

"You can trust me."

"My *dad* trusts you." Magne gets up and paces. "I can take him."

"Not in your truck," says O'Malley. "That thing is recognizable from here to Great Valley." He stands up. "And I'm not here to help the pack leader's wayward son pull one over on his old man. I'm here to help my baby sister's *only* son keep himself from getting killed."

There's a shifting of kitchen stools behind me and I turn. Tyler has pushed himself back to his feet, and is leaning on his mom. "I think we can trust him," he says.

"I've got good reason to head up north," says O'Malley. "I have an informant I need to check on."

"Fine," says Magne. "But I'm coming."

"You're too obvious," O'Malley says. "It's not like you can hide in the car."

"You have to take me," Magne says, "even if I ride in the trunk. Siobhan won't open the door without the secret knock."

They finally decide on some excuse or another for why Magne would be driving up north with the detective, that they can use if anyone asks. It seems a bit flimsy to me, but Mags is determined to go along.

Tyler and his mom are both on the small side, so they'll hide under blankets in the immense back seat of O'Malley immense Crown Vic – it's unmarked, but still a police cruiser through and through.

That leaves me to arrange a time to meet John Pradip at the Wonder Island carnival, and to scrub all the steak pans. And to fret.

I make Magne promise to text me when they get there and he lingers behind as the others leave. He cups my face in his hands, and gives me a long, hard kiss that leaves me breathless.

I want to cling to him like a helpless maiden in a fairy story, but that's just not me. And hell, I saved my ex from a vampire cabal's lair *and* a bunch of angry witches. I can manage to entertain myself for one day.

My loft seems even more empty than usual when I push open the door. First, tea. I put the kettle on then grab my phone from the coffee table where I abandoned it yesterday. One missed call, one text, no voicemails.

The call was Alex, all the way from Germany. It's not urgent if she didn't leave a message, unless the text is her, too. But the text is John, responding to mine from yesterday.

Tmrw good. Time? & where in carnival?

Tomorrow is, of course, now today. And I don't want to do this without Magne. Even if Wolfram didn't want John to poke around in Mags' memories.

Something came up, I type. I've never been able to break the habit of mostly typing full words and sentences. *I can't make it today. Tomorrow for sure? Meet @ Peculiar tent.*

He answers almost immediately. *cu tmrw. Cabinet of Peculiarities? 2pm ok? Hv am class.*

I don't really even want to keep up this abbreviated text messaging, let alone actually talk to him, so I just send a thumbs up emoji, and get one back in reply.

The water's boiled, so I fill the teapot and have the world's fastest shower while it steeps. Or, at least, the fastest shower I can have with hair almost down to the backs of my knees.

Then, clean and dressed in fresh clothes, tail free to swish behind me, I sit on the couch with my phone in my lap.

What time is it in Germany, even? I have no idea, so I look it up. Early evening. That should be okay, assuming Alex isn't deep in the Hexenwald. I don't think there's even cell service in Shönstadt, is there? I didn't even look at my phone the whole time I was there. Not until I was waiting for my flight out and got to find out all at once that Evgeny was suffering. And that he probably wouldn't want to see me anymore when I got home.

Well, at least I can try. So I hit the button to return the call and wait as it connects and rings. And rings. I'm about to give up when a voice says,

"Su! It's Li. Alex is driving. Hang on till we can pull over."

"Driving? In Germany? She's a braver woman than I am." I admit, I was anxious to make this call. Alex, though a good friend now, was once a lover, a potential long-term partner, and I'm still not sure how to be around her. It does help that her new (or not-so-new now) beloved, Li, is really easy to get along with.

"You and me both," says Li. Then she pauses and says, "Alex told me." She sounds like she's trying to find the right words. "About how the witch resurrected me and used me to get Alex to come to Germany. How I'm a bargaining chip to keep her here."

"Ah," I say. I didn't expect this. I wasn't even sure if the witch had let Li be herself again, or if she was still a barely-animate living doll. I can't say how glad I am that she seems to be her normal self.

"Anyway, things are good. I'm me again." She laughs. "Or as normal as a hot lesbian zombie can be."

That startles an answering laugh out of me. It feels good, like a relief of pressure I didn't even know was building.

"Okay, we're parked," says Li.

"Hey, Su!" Alex sounds good. Really good. Happy.

"Hey, hey," I say. "I saw you called. Any urgent reason or can I just relax and enjoy the convo?"

"No reason. Well, not much of one. I wanted to tell you that Rose-Perle has pretty much given Li her life back. We can leave Shönstadt now, even the Oktober Mountains. So to celebrate, we're in Berlin for a week."

She tells me how her magic studies are going really well, to the point that Rose-Perle — the infamous Witch of the Wald — only requires her to visit once a week to demonstrate what she's learned.

"The rest of the time, I study on my own. And I'm helping at the toy museum. Me and Li have dragged it into the twenty first century with a website, and interactive virtual tours, and everything."

She pauses and I think I hear Li say, "Tell her."

"And I've been learning scrying," she says. "Not like telling the future, which is changeable anyway, but like seeing things that are hidden, or looking at things that are far away."

I make a noise to let her know I'm listening.

"So I was thinking about your sister, you know. And I thought I'd try looking for her."

I sit up straight on the couch, suddenly tense. "And?" I try to keep hope out of my voice.

"Well, maybe I'm too far away," she says. "I've tried a few times, and all I see is a fox running through the woods. Like you running, maybe looking for her. But I can't see *her*."

I let that sink in. "Do you think that means she's dead?" I say, trying to keep my voice normal.

"Not necessarily. After the first time it happened, I thought so, so I tried scrying for a grave or whatever. I just saw that riverbank and the garbage bag of her stuff that you texted me about."

I make myself relax back into the couch cushions. "Thanks for trying," I say.

"I haven't given up yet," she says. "I just wanted to let you know I'm working on it."

I keep hoping that one day she's going to call and tell me she's ready to come home. I really miss having a non-male, non-hairy-werewolf bestie to bounce things off of.

"So how are you?" she asks. "I'm sorry about Evgeny. I thought he'd have seen reason by now and come crawling back to you."

I tell her what's been going on, all of it, right down to stupidly kissing Wolfram, in as much detail as I can remember. Okay, maybe not *quite* as much detail. She listens, and makes affirmative noises now and then so I know I have her full attention.

"Wow," she says, when I finally stop. "Magne finally succumbed to your charm. I knew he was into you."

"You did not."

"Did. Evgeny, too."

"I mean, it was pretty obvious Evgeny was into me. Even *I* could see that."

She chuckles. "Not what I meant," she says. "So you're going to grill this Pradip guy tomorrow, hunh? I sure wish I could be there."

"Me, too" I say. Alex would be really handy to have around when "interviewing" the memory-meddling John Pradip, professor of political science. Her witch powers would know if he was trying anything underhanded, and I bet she could read him like a book, too.

"I remember when he made you dream a fake memory, about your sister eating something she's super allergic to."

"I wish I knew what his motivation was," I say. "He really doesn't feel, you know…"

"Evil?"

"Evil, bad, even the least bit malicious. But obviously he's up to something."

"Just be careful," she says. "And remember to block him, like the fox women taught you."

"Yeah." I stretch my legs out onto the coffee table, suddenly not knowing what to do with myself. "Listen," I say. "You be careful, too. That old witch isn't exactly stable. She could take back whatever she gives you at any second."

"I know. But I've almost worked out how she animated Li, how she brought her back in the first place. All of it. I'm pretty sure I can do whatever it is she did once I've figured out the last details. And then I can return Li entirely to herself."

"And then you'll come home?" I know it's too much to hope for. There are several lifetimes worth of witchy things Alex can learn from Rose-Perle. She'd be foolish not to stay and get as much as she can.

"Maybe," she says, and I can't help but grin. "I'm thinking about living part time here, part time there. We'll see how it goes."

Then we talk about inconsequentials for a while and finally hang up. My tea has gone cold, so I make a fresh pot and while I wait, a text from Magne comes in.

Here safe. O'M just met his d in law and grandkid. Think he might explode. Kid & ma are good. Tired. Heading home soon. It's followed by a string of hearts in rainbow colors.

I type something, erase it, type again. *I love you.* Erase. *Luv ya.* Erase. *Miss you*, and variations thereof. Finally, I just say, *JP good for tomorrow at 2pm @ Wonder I*, and hit send.

His answer comes back so fast he must have been typing while I was trying to figure out what to say. *Can't stop thinking about kissing you. Good thing O'M was driving or I'd have hit a tree.*

    Idiot, I type. *I can't have my way with you in a hospital bed.*

    I mean, you could.

    I laugh. Then I take a deep breath and type, *I love you Mags.*

    It seems like forever that the three little dots flicker on and off, showing that he's typing. Finally the text arrives. *Your big dumb hairy werewolf loves you too. So fucking much.*

Chapter Ten

I FINALLY GIVE UP trying to do anything useful and curl up in the middle of my bed. I have no idea what I'm going to ask John Pradip tomorrow. I just hope Magne and Wolfram will have some good questions.

I wake when my fox-sensitive ears catch the grind of the elevator. Magne comes right up to my loft, like he knew I'd retreat to my own space with him gone.

There's a soft knock on the door, and then it creaks open.

"You awake, love?" Magne keeps his voice low. He knows I don't wake up instantly like he does. I wonder what he would do if I was sound asleep. Probably crawl into bed beside me and drift off himself. He's got to be exhausted after last night, and even if he wasn't the one driving, today has not exactly been stress-free either.

"Mmm hmm," I say. I open my eyes. Most of the light has gone from the sky, but my fox eyes see him clearly as he comes in. He *does* look tired. Just about done in. "Did you get a chance to eat?"

"We got burgers from a drive-through place."

He sits on the edge of the bed and I scoot closer so I can put my head on his leg.

"Great big cheeseburgers."

"I'm gonna have to ask you to go stink up your own bathroom if you ate dairy."

He snorts a laugh. "You sure do know how to romance a guy." He strokes my hair with one hand, over and over. "I took a Lactaid," he says. "I'm not as dumb as I look."

We're both lactose intolerant, me probably because of my part-Asian ancestry, and him because of an unfortunate glitch of genetics. I know exactly what cheese would do to his digestive system without a dose of enzyme pills.

"First," I say, stretching like a cat as he strokes my hair, "I don't think you're dumb. And second, I don't think you *look* dumb."

"And how *do* I look, then?" His hand moves from my hair to my shoulder, follows the curve of my body to my hip.

"I want to say, 'devastatingly sexy'," I say, "but mostly you just look wiped."

He sighs and lays back on the bed. "I *am* wiped. I can't remember the last time I was this tired. And I need a shower."

I wriggle around so I'm lying next to him, and rest my head on his shoulder. "You smell fine to me."

"Stick your nose in my armpit, and you might change your mind."

"What was that you were saying about romance?" I poke him with my index finger, but gently.

He chuckles and rolls onto his side so we're nose to nose. Then he just looks at me.

Finally, I say, "You should get some sleep, Mags. I need your decidedly non-stupid brain sharp tomorrow. I have no idea what questions to ask, or how to ask them."

"I have one or two pointed inquiries in mind," he says, and slides his hand up under my shirt to stroke my bare back. "And I have something else in mind before sleep."

"Are you sure you can stay awake long enough?"

Instead of answering, he kisses me, not hard like before he left, but firmly. Not demanding, but asking. I kiss him back, harder, and he responds in kind, pushing my mouth open with his, sliding his tongue next to mine, until the kiss is half teeth clicking together and I don't want him to ever stop.

I press against, him, yank at his t-shirt until he strips it off, and then mine, and I press my naked skin against his and press my mouth on his mouth again. I might – finally – have my fox hormones and sex magic under control, but he makes me so *hungry*.

And hell, I've never been especially attracted to hirsute men – like body hair is definitely not something I'd put on my "desired in a lover" list – but feeling the way his hair and skin slide against me, that's the number one most delicious thing I've ever felt, and incredibly erotic. Highly recommended. Seventeen out of ten, would do again.

"Su," he says, and my name sounds like a prayer. I pull his mouth to me again and he rumbles a growly sound deep in his throat.

His hand slides down my back and next thing I know, my yoga pants are halfway off and I'm fumbling with the buttons of his fly.

I'm growling too by the time we're both naked – half in frustration and half in desire, and he growls right back. And bites my earlobe, just a nip. And kisses and nibbles his way down my neck, across my shoulder, over my collarbone. He finds a nipple and teases it with his tongue and I'm pretty sure my attempt to say his name comes out as a moan.

His lips and tongue trace burning trails down my ribs and across my belly, and then he's nudging my legs apart to taste the insides of my thighs. And then his tongue finds my center and I know this time the sounds I'm making have no words as I feel the wave of pleasure build and build and finally release.

And still I want more. I pull him back up to me, kiss him hard, and dig under the pillow for a condom. I want to flip him on his back and climb on top, but I sense that he needs to be in control after so much of the last few days has been out of control, so instead I wrap my legs around him pull him closer, on top of me.

When he slides into me, he closes his eyes and growls again.

"Magne," I say, finally able to make coherent speech. He opens his eyes and I want to drown in their depths. "I want you," I say, and pull him deeper with my legs. I put a hand on each side of his face, make him look at me and he plunges in and slides out. I see the moment he climaxes as his eyes narrow and his jaw clenches. A moan that sounds at least half growl claws its way out of his throat, and then he relaxes.

"Su," he says, breathless and sounding a little astonished. He rolls off of me, tucks me close against his side, strokes my hair, kisses my temple. "I've wanted you for so long," he whispers.

"I'm all yours, love," I say.

"And I'm all yours."

"Get some sleep," I tell him. "You can have that shower when you wake up."

And he pulls the blankets up over both of us and is almost instantly asleep, like all it took was for me to give him permission to rest.

It's early morning again, when I wake. Twilight, which my fox nature loves best. "Crepuscular," is what they call it, when creatures are most active at dawn and dusk.

Magne's already awake, but lying still like he didn't want to wake me until I was ready.

Did I mention how much I love this man?

As soon as I stir and rub my eyes he gets up, puts on the kettle, and disappears into the bathroom. I really like that I don't have to pretend not to enjoy the view of his naked backside anymore. I hear the shower start up a moment later.

I lounge in bed while he showers, watch lazily as he emerges from the bathroom wrapped in a pale blue towel – none of my towels match – and pours hot water over coffee grounds in the French press.

He smiles and sits on the edge of the bed to watch me watching him. I reach out one arm and run my hand down his back. He closes his eyes and makes a purr-like rumble.

"I'll tell you one thing about being hairy," he says. "It makes me really sensitive to touch."

I brush my hand over his upper arm, so lightly it's just touching his arm hair and not his skin.

"Mmm. It's like having whiskers all over my body." Then he looks at me, and his eyes seem even darker than usual.

"We don't have to be at the carnival until two," I say, and wiggle my eyebrows.

"Coffee's getting cold," he says, but leans into my touch instead of moving to get up.

"We'll make more."

"You mean *I'll* make more." But he's still smiling.

"Of the two of us, you do make the best java." I roll so I can reach his chest with my other hand, trail it over his belly and pause at the edge of the towel. I look up at him and he's still watching me, smile gone but eyes burning. I grab the towel and tug, roll over to get closer and find him already hard. So I slide my mouth over him and try not to grin – not that I *could* grin in this position – as his breathing goes ragged. And I don't stop till he moans, and arches his back, and I taste him, warm and bitter and salty, on my tongue.

This time, I do push him down on his back and climb on top of him, but of course he's spent, so he pulls me down to lie next to him, slides his hands over my skin like he wants to caress every part of the surface of me, and finally slips his fingers between my legs. And it's my turn to moan and arch and relax in satisfaction.

"I'm gonna need another shower," he says into my hair.

"Just assume you're always going to need another shower."

"You're insatiable," he says, and I can hear the smile in his voice.

"It's all your fault," I say, curling closer.

"I'm happy to take the blame for that," he says. "My love."

"My love," I repeat. "You are, you know."

"I think I've figured that out, finally."

"Any chance of a fresh pot of coffee?"

"For you? Eh, maybe." But he's laughing and he gets up to go to the kitchen area completely naked, and as far as I can tell, completely happy to *be* naked. Like I said, shameless.

But I'm not going to complain.

Finally, dressed, caffeinated, and mostly not smelling like we just spent the morning in bed pleasuring each other, we decide we should head to Wonder Island early so we can consult with Wolfram before we have to meet John.

I can't think of the last time I felt so contented, so happy to just exist. Probably sometime after spending a similar morning (or more likely, night) with Evgeny. And *that* thought makes me feel briefly guilty. I mean, it was his decision to break up… Well, it was mutual, but it was his issues that made it necessary. And he was the one who found a new lover almost right away, while I kept telling myself the feelings I had for Magne couldn't be real.

I shake the guilt off and enjoy the late spring sun on my face and the company of my werewolf lover. The river is dazzling and the sky bright and even though I'm nervous about the coming "interview," the day feels full of potential.

Wolfram is there to meet us at the dock, which beats wandering around trying to find him or waiting in his tent while he does his show. When I ask how he knew we'd be on this boat, he points at a crow perched on top of a nearby garbage bin.

"Sgian told me," he says. "She seems to have taken a liking to you."

I half expect the crow to talk – I swear it looks like she's checking Magne out – but she just caws and launches herself into the air to fly off between the tents. I guess it doesn't do to have *real* magic on full display, even in as weird a place as the Wonder Island carnival.

And I wonder just when I accepted the magic *is* real, and not just mind tricks and performance-enhancing symbiotic organisms.

The three of us walk through the carnival and end up back at the bench under the tree where we spoke before.

"So how do we do this?" I say, perching on the edge of the bench. Magne sprawls on the grass at my feet, and Wolfram stands looking back towards the carnival for a moment, before sitting next to me.

"I'd like to have Dr Pradip use his memory techniques on Magne first."

"Get some use out of him before we scare him off?" Magne says.

"That, and seeing him work will give me a better idea of what we're dealing with."

"I don't like using Magne as a guinea pig," I say.

"Nor I," says Wolfram. "But I am intensely curious about what memories our young werewolf is hiding from himself."

"From myself? Why would I hide memories from myself?" Magne sits up, leans forward, and his voice is curious, like it's a new idea he hadn't considered.

"That's what I hope to find out," says Wolfram. "And you have my assurance that you – and your mind – will be perfectly safe at all times."

"How?" says Magne. I can hear the nerves in his voice, even though he keeps them well hidden. I know he doesn't at all like the idea of having his brain probed, not after all the stuff we went through with Evgeny's demon-ghost, and the vengeful witches.

"Although memory is not my specialty," Wolfram says, "I will be able to tell if Pradip tries anything. And I have an associate who *does* specialize in memory. And another who is extremely perceptive about matters related to the mind." He's got a funny little smile on his face that I can't read, like he's about to pull a harmless but amusing prank, maybe.

"When do we meet these memory specialists?"

"They'll be here shortly." Wolfram looks over at the forest, not so distant here, then turns back to me. "Once we've discovered what we are dealing with, and – I hope – learn something about Magne's past, then I propose we question your professor very thoroughly about the scope of his abilities, why he felt it necessary to meddle with *your* memories, and what he had to do with your parent's deaths."

"Sure," I say, "but how do we *do* that? How do we ask him those things without him freaking out and leaving before we get anything useful?"

I glance at Magne, and he grins his big-toothed, most unsettling grin, and says, "I could turn wolf for him. That should loosen his lips."

Wolfram laughs. "Let us hope it need not come to threats. Perhaps simply showing that we know he's up to something will be enough. If, as Su suspects, he has no real malicious intent, being interrogated might be the permission he needs to spill it all, so to speak."

"You have a higher opinion of his motives than I do," Magne says, resuming his sprawl.

"If necessary," says Wolfram, "I can force him to tell us everything, whether he wants to or not. He may be a threat to someone who has been extended the hospitality of this island –." He looks at me, head cocked slightly to one side. His voice has gone very cold and I try not to shiver.

"That makes him fair game for coercion as far as I'm concerned." Then he sighs and frowns, and the coldness evaporates. "I would much rather *not* force the issue. It goes against my nature to *make* anybody do anything."

I consider this, wondering just how much power Wolfram has, and exactly what kind of being he is. Because he seems to be so far beyond human, *other*, or anything else magical I've met that I don't even know how to classify him in my brain.

Then he says, "Ah, here are my associates."

I follow his gaze to where two enormous black birds have detached themselves from the shadow of the forest to glide across the lawn. I thought Sgian was big, but these two are each at least twice the crow's size, though similar in shape. The birds land on the path and walk towards us exactly as if they were taking a pleasant afternoon stroll.

"Magne. Su," says Wolfram, a note of formality entering his voice. "Meet Huginn and Muninn. Thought and Memory. They'll be keeping an eye on Professor John Pradip as he performs his magic."

Closer up, I see the birds' feathers are even blacker than Sgian's, but also struck through with every color of the rainbow as the sunlight hits their iridescent sheen. Their beaks are massive and they watch us with bright shiny eyes so dark brown they look black, turning their heads to see us from many angles. There's a blue sort of glow about them that might be a trick of the sun on their glossy feather coats, or might actually be a lightning-spark of something otherworldly.

"Um," I say. "Hello."

The birds both turn to me and to say their regard is disconcerting is the understatement of the century. Anyone who can look a bird like that in the eye and still claim birds aren't dinosaurs can't be playing with a full set of braincells.

Then one bird dips its head. "Hello, Daughter of Foxes." Its voice is sort of deep, scratchy, and musical, all at once.

The other bird also dips its head. "Greetings," it says.

Magne has sat up again and is staring at the birds, his attention avid. He shifts onto his knees, palms in front on him on the grass, and bows his head.

"Huginn and Muninn, " he says. "Evgeny told me he met you, but I thought he must have been hallucinating." His voice is soft with awe.

"Greetings, Son of Wolves," says one bird. Its voice is just a little higher in pitch than that of its companion.

"Hello," says the other bird. It – or he, I think, but how do you tell with a bird? – sounds amused. "You needn't bow your head, Son of Wolves. We won't take your eyes." And then it makes a noise something like a chuckle, if you can imagine a giant bird chuckling.

"I only like lambs' eyes," says the higher-pitched bird. She?

"The old man whose name you invoke in prayer isn't here to judge you, wolf," says the male bird, sounding almost gentle.

And then it twigs. Magne, though not especially religious as far as I can tell, said he and many of his packmates are Norse pagans and I realize, finally, where I've heard the names of these birds before: in a book of Germanic mythology from Papa Vamp's collection.

The two birds Wolfram calls his "associates" are none other than Odin's ravens.

Chapter Eleven

ODIN'S FUCKING ravens.

"I'm not that devout," says Magne, and grins, but there is still a whole lot of awe on his face as he watches them.

"The old man wouldn't notice, anyway," says Wolfram, so quietly even I barely catch his words, and I'm sitting right next to him. I look over at him, and the blue glow of the ravens' feathers is reflected in his eyes. Or is it independent of the birds as a light source? Are his eyes glowing?

I mean, *my* eyes glow in the dark, but only when they catch and reflect other light – the moon, maybe, or a car's headlights. I swear, just for a moment, Wolfram's eyes glow with their own inner blue light. Then he looks at me and it's gone; his eyes are back to stormy grey.

What *is* Wolfram Gottfried? Somehow, I don't think that's a question I'll have an answer to anytime soon, even if I was bold enough to ask.

Then, with a flutter of wings, Sgian shows up and perches on the back of the bench. The crow bobs her head at the two ravens, and they dip their beaks in acknowledgement.

"Your boy's arrived," she says.

"Well then, shall we get started?" Wolfram gets to his feet. "Magne, I think you should take the bench, Huginn and Muninn on each side. Su, if you would fetch our guest?"

I check my watch. Not one of the vamp council's pocketwatches, but a simple stainless one I took from an unobservant lawyer a few weeks ago. It's not two yet, but I'm not surprised John is early. I think I remember something about that, how he liked to be early to have the advantage, or something. Which is funny, because when we met at the coffee shop, he was late. Unless he had been nearby the whole time, and waited for me to go in first, so I would *seem* to have the advantage, when really I didn't.

Okay, now I'm getting paranoid.

He's not waiting by the Cabinet of Peculiarities tent, but he appears out of the crowd almost as soon as I stop to look for him.

"Su, how are you?" So he's remembered I use a different name now. That's good, I guess. His voice is full of warmth and I think at least some of it is genuine.

"I'm okay," I say.

"Just okay?" He takes my hand between both of his and I feel the slight tingle of his magic. It dies out before he even tries to push it on me. A bright "caw" makes me glance up, and a crow on the peak of the tent flicks its tail at me. A white feather in its left wing tells me it's Sgian, and that either the crow or Wolfram himself is making sure no unwanted magic occurs. Or maybe the Island has its own wards.

I just catch John's frown as I turn back from the crow.

"It's been a stressful couple of days, "I say. "But things are getting better."

His bright smile tells me he thinks I'm saying that seeing him has made my day better. I almost want to tell him what actually *has* made me happy, but that would be mean.

"Shall we walk?" I say and don't wait for him to answer before circling around the tent to wander back the way I came.

He catches up and tucks my arm in his. I decide to let it stay that way, for now. I can disappoint him later, if he seems to be trying to win me back.

"How are you?" I ask, to be polite.

"Better now," he says and looks sidelong at me to see if I notice his smile. I pretend not to.

"So this memory thing you do?" I step slightly sideways so our hips bump together. I think about using the fox magic on him, but I realize I'd be no better than he is if I did. I'll save that for a last resort. I'm not above letting him think I'm interested, though.

His breathing catches a little at the contact. I probably wouldn't have noticed, when I knew him before, except these days I'm so used to picking out such tiny details in vampires and werewolves that human reactions seem obvious.

"Mm?" He's started stroking the back of my hand, so I walk a little faster.

"I have a friend who… well, they've got a blocked memory or something, and I thought maybe you could help."

"I'm very good with blocked memories," he says. "But if it's blocked due to trauma, it can be very hard for the person, when they remember. Like being traumatized all over again."

We come around the corner. Magne's sitting in the middle of the bench, completely relaxed – in outward appearance, at least – and there's a huge raven perched on the back of the bench on each side of him. Wolfram stands off to one side, watching us approach, and Sgian glides into view to land on the lawn a little ways away with a swoosh.

"I'm not sure we should go this way," says John, an edge of nervousness in his voice. Magne *is* pretty huge, even sitting down, though of the two men waiting, it's *not* Magne who is the more dangerous.

"It's okay," I say. "These are my friends." I practically have to pull him the last few yards.

"The big lunk on the bench is Magne," I say. "My neighbor and good friend." Magne raises an eyebrow at that, but doesn't say anything. I smile and he smiles back. He keeps his teeth hidden.

"And I am Wolfram Gottfried," says Wolfram, stepping forward to shake John's hand, and probably not coincidentally forcing him to drop my arm in the process. "Proprietor of the carnival."

John looks from one to the other, then back at me, like he's wondering if he's been set up.

"Can you help Magne?" I ask, making my eyes wide and pleading. I'm not good at that sort of thing, but maybe he wants to believe I need him, because the tight set of his mouth eases.

"I…" He doesn't seem to know what to say.

"Don't mind the birds," says Wolfram. "They're tame."

Magne coughs, and I catch a glimpse of his face and see that he's trying to hide laughter. Fortunately, John's attention is on the ravens, who look at him, then away, as if they're not concerned with him at all.

"You're the one with memory difficulties?" John gives me the side-eye, though he's speaking to Magne, like he's maybe not happy I told other people about him. I get it, but I also don't care.

"Yep," says Magne. "Dunno why I can't remember what happened. My thirteenth birthday. Weird, y'know?"

I have to cover my mouth to hide my smile. Magne's whole posture, his voice, the way he speaks, seems to be aiming at projecting an air of non-threatening stupidity. And because he's big and scruffy and looks like a jock, just about anyone who doesn't know him – at least those who aren't extra-observant – would buy the whole routine. I might buy it if I didn't know him. And if I weren't used to werewolves.

"Well, that shouldn't be too difficult," John says. He makes a gesture. "May I?"

Magne shrugs. "Whatever it takes, Doc. Su did say you were a doctor…"

I almost laugh out loud this time and I swear even Wolfram is suppressing a smirk. John looks uncomfortable.

"A PhD, actually," he says. "Which *is* where the title originated. But not a medical doctor, no."

"As long as you know what you're doing."

We guessed from the fact – I'm pretty sure it wasn't put on – that John didn't know what memory of mine he brought up at the coffee shop that first time that he wouldn't actually be able to read Magne's mind. Like he should, if he's as good as he says, be able to find the block but not actually see the memories. I hope that's true, anyway, because I don't want Magne to have to share anything he doesn't want to.

John steps closer to Magne, eyeing the ravens (who ignore him) and puts his fingertips on Magne's temples.

"You were thirteen, you said?" John asks. He frowns in concentration. One of the ravens ruffles her feathers, and John glances at her, then hastily away.

"Thirteenth birthday," Magne says.

"Hmm. Are you sure it's not longer ago? How old are you?"

Magne flicks his gaze to me and I raise my eyebrows. I don't actually know how old he is, only that as a werewolf he's probably older than he looks. Or acts.

"Oh, there it is," says John.

"Can you see his memories?" I don't want to distract him, and yeah, I guess I'm harping on a bit, but I really don't want John to see anything. Magne and I have both had quite enough of other people poking into our heads for one lifetime.

"Hmm?" John's concentrating now, and answers in an absent-minded voice. "No, I can only feel the shape of them. I *could* see them, if the subject was willing and I wanted to exert a lot more energy, but it's not necessary for this work."

He frowns deeper. "This feels… traumatic. Are you sure you want me to reveal these memories?"

"I'm sure." Somehow, with just those two words, Magne has transformed from big, dumb jock to … something else entirely, but John doesn't seem to notice.

"There." John drops his hands and steps back. "With a blockage that strong, and that old, it may be some time before the memories get through, but now at least they can."

"Thank you." Magne and I speak at the same time and John looks startled.

"Anything for a friend of Su's."

Wolfram steps forward from where he's been waiting in the background, and the look on John's face suggests he forgot the other man was even there. Wolfram glances at one of the ravens – I'm pretty sure it's Huginn – and he ruffles his wings before settling again. I have the distinct impression that some kind of communication has passed between them, but I couldn't say how or what.

"I must admit, I am most curious about this skill of yours," Wolfram says. "I have some skill in things of the mind, but I have never encountered a gift quite like yours."

John looks both flattered and nervous.

"Please," says Magne, standing and gesturing at the bench. "Sit. Do tell us about it."

John's not short – he's got to be close to six feet – but Magne has at least four inches on him. And he's heavier, more muscley. So John takes a step back, away from Magne and away from the bench.

Huginn leaps into to air, and then Muninn, and I'm impressed that John is able to stop himself from cringing away. He just takes another step back, looks at me. "Su?"

Huginn circles us and lands on Magne's shoulder. He hides his startlement quickly. Hell, he looks magnificent. Like a Viking.

I step closer to John, touch his shoulder. "It's okay, "I say. "He looks scary, but he's really a marshmallow."

Magne sticks his tongue out at me, and I stick mine out at him. John looks from one to the other of us, like he's wondering what he's wandered into.

Then Muninn circles around from where she's been gliding overhead and lands on Wolfram's shoulder. And the man might be short – really short – but right now he looks like a Viking, too. He looks… bigger somehow. Not taller, but more substantial. Filled with power and really freaking intimidating. I think he may be giving us the barest glimpse of who – or *what* – he is.

John stares for the space of several heartbeats – human heartbeats – then he sits on the bench. Taking pity on him, I seat myself beside him and take one of his hands in mine. I guess Wolfram decided he didn't want to wait for John to confess. Or maybe he read something in John that I couldn't see.

"You are safe here," Wolfram says, his voice seeming deeper than before. I feel it vibrate through me and I'm really glad Magne and I are together now, because it's both terrifying and deeply sexy. "At least as long as you prove not to be a threat."

"I… I'm not a threat," says John. "I just teach political science and help people with memory issues."

"Including manufacturing memories?" asks Wolfram. His glamour or whatever that was fades – or maybe he puts the glamor back *on* – and he seems more like his ordinary self, but the memory of that power remains and I realize his eyes have that faint blue glow again.

"No… I –"

"Do not lie to me. Not here on my own ground, boy." Wolfram's eyes flash, the light from his left eye almost stabbing out at John.

"No. I mean. I was trying to help." He looks at me. I think he's just realized I know what he tried to do, that I've told my friends, and no one is happy with him.

"You were trying to help me by making me think we were more to each other than we actually were?" I suddenly don't want to be nice anymore. I drop his hand and get up, go to stand beside Magne on the side that's not serving as a perch for a giant bird.

Magne touches my back, and when I smile up at him, he puts his arms around me and pulls me closer. I lean against him, and look back at John.

"I – we *were* close," he says, keeping his voice remarkably calm, considering he has two powerful men staring at him – one literally looming over him. A powerful woman, too, but he has no idea how I've changed. "I *loved* you," he says. "I thought you felt the same."

"I think you better just spill the whole thing," says Magne. "I, for one, don't relish standing here being intimidating all day."

John's mouth twitches like he might, almost, smile. "You love her, don't you?" he says. "Then you'll understand. They wanted me to keep her out of the way, and after… I thought she'd be safer if we weren't together."

"I *do* love her," says Magne. "And that's why I'm going to ask you one more time to voluntarily tell us what the fuck you were up to because she has specifically requested I don't hurt you, and I'd hate to disappoint her."

I poke him in the ribs, where John can't see, because I think he's enjoying playing the brute far too much. But he is good at it. He's also taken John's attention off of Wolfram, who's the one he really needs to worry about.

So when Wolfram's suddenly right next to him, John can't help but jump. Wolfram puts a hand on his arm. "You *are* safe here, son. For now, at least. And if you need sanctuary or protection, I may be able to help. But first you need to be honest with us. Tell us why you were tampering with Su's memories and what you know about her parents' deaths."

John's face goes pale. "I had nothing to do with that," he says. "I didn't know. But… they had, they *still* have, my mother. If I say anything, they'll kill her."

"There are very few people who would dare harm the family of someone under my protection. Your best chance of rescuing your mother and clearing your own name is to tell us everything you know."

"I don't know *who* they are, though," John says. "I don't even now how to contact them."

"Talk," growls Magne, and he shows his teeth, lets the wolf become visible on his face so he looks utterly inhuman. And hell, *I* still find him undeniably hot.

John's shoulders slump in defeat and I feel bad for him again. And he tells us how he was approached by a man – tall, pale, and very unemotional, he says (and I'd bet a large sum of money on vampire) – who offered him a small fortune to keep me distracted until they told him otherwise. He refused, he says, because it was unethical. Later, the man returned and showed John a video – his mother, tied up and terrified, with the thin man standing next to her, holding a knife to her throat.

So John agreed, as long as it didn't mean hurting anyone. He kept me busy with extra tuition, long walks to discuss topics we'd gone over in class, and when my parents disappeared, he seduced me.

At first, he said, it was enjoyable, but not emotional. But then he fell in love with me. So when the man and an associate appeared again, a little over a year later, and told him he could stop distracting me, he felt it was safer for me to break things off entirely.

He'd tried, he says, to keep tabs on me, to make sure I was safe. But then I disappeared. He had feared the men had disposed of me as he believed they had my parents, and my sister. His mother was never returned to him, though they sent him anonymous videos from time to time, to let him know she was alive. They told him they would keep her in case they needed him again.

And they had. Just before I left for Germany, they said he should look for a way to start distracting me again. That I was too nosy, and they'd have to kill me if he couldn't keep me out of the way. That he should practice his memory art to make me forget I'd ever had a family that disappeared. When I didn't readily respond to his advances, he hit on the idea of convincing me that our affair had been more significant than it actually had been, that we'd been madly in love and thinking of spending our lives together. Then, he thought, I'd be more open to being with him again and he could protect me.

And if altering my memories worked, he could try to change my memories of my family as the men suggested.

"She *has* protection," says Magne.

I poke him, this time where everyone can see. "*She*," I say, "doesn't need protection."

"And why were your business cards in Mr and Mrs Fuchs' possession? And in the girl's?" Wolfram's eyes aren't glowing anymore, but a person would be foolish to discount him. I don't think John is that kind of foolish.

"I talked to them," John says. "Just before they disappeared. I got the idea from the pale man that they were in danger. I hoped… I don't know… that the man would let me make them forget whatever it was they knew that made them a target."

"What made you think they knew something?" Wolfram moves closer and John shifts uneasily on the bench.

"Just something the man said. 'We'll pry what they know out of their heads first.' Something like that."

"And you assumed that meant they knew too much?" Wolfram's got one black eyebrow raised.

"Sounds to me like they knew something the men wanted to learn, not something they shouldn't," Magne says.

John slumps against the back of the bench. "Oh. Yes, that makes more sense."

"Well," says Wolfram, clapping his hands together. Suddenly it feels like all the tension is gone and we can all relax. "Dr Pradip, you can return safely home. Act like you had a wonderful time and all is going according to plan, and no one will be the wiser."

"But what if I was followed?"

"No one could follow you here if I did not allow it." A touch of power creeps back into his voice.

"Su. Magne. I think perhaps you two should stay a little longer." He puts a hand on each of our arms and draws us away from John a little. His voice lowers and he says, "I rather think it's time I introduced you to the House."

Chapter Twelve

JOHN IS RELUCTANT to leave despite Wolfram's assurances that he can't have been followed, and that he'll see if he can help find John's mother.

Finally, John marches up to Magne, draws himself up to his full height, and says, "If you hurt her, I'll hurt you." It takes guts, I'll give him that.

"I'd say the same to you," Magne says, looking down at John and raising an eyebrow. "But it's too late for that, isn't it?"

John's nostrils flare and a muscle clenches in his jaw. "I did what I thought I needed to to protect her."

I'm about to remind them that I'm standing right here and can take of myself, thank you very much, but Magne kind of beats me to it. "You never thought to ask if she wanted to be protected that way? If she wanted your protection at all? You never thought she might like to know you *met* the men you think killed her parents? You just thought you'd change her memories and everything would be okay. No one needs that kind of help. And if Su didn't ask you to meddle, you had no business meddling."

"At least I tried," says John. "At least if she was with me, she'd be happy."

I can't help a big snort at that, but no one seems to be paying any attention to me, just talking about me. Even the birds are looking back and forth between the two men.

"Are you saying I don't make her happy?" Magne's voice is mild, and he doesn't look the least bit threatened, but I can tell he *is* getting irritated.

"She's an intelligent woman. She needs someone with a brain to make her happy."

Magne smiles, showing a lot of teeth and no dimples. "When you get a second away from stroking your own ego," he says, "you're welcome to investigate my academic credentials. My name is Magne Thorvaldson, and I believe there was an article in the alumni magazine at GVU that you might find enlightening."

"And this will tell me what?"

Magne shrugs. "That I have a brain."

I desperately want to get out my phone and check the Great Valley University website, but I resist. Time enough later. "All right, look," I say instead, shoving each of them on the shoulder so they'll stop talking about me like I'm not here. "I'd tell you to lay them out on the table and measure…" I pause for effect, and they both stop glaring at each other to look at me, John in surprise and Magne in amusement. "But I already know who wins that contest."

John's eyes widen even more and I can see a blush creep up his neck to his face. Magne looks like he's trying not to laugh.

"John," I say. "Thank you for your help. I promise we'll try to figure out a way to help your mom." I touch his arm gently, then take Magne's hand. "And you," I say, "stop being growly already. He told us everything he knows."

Then Wolfram, trying to hide a smirk, leads John back towards the carnival.

Magne says, "So who would win?"

"What?" I say.

"The biggest dick contest?" He's grinning still, but now both dimples are visible and I want very much to kiss him. So I do.

When he finally pulls away, he says, "It's him, isn't it? He looks like a guy who's got a huge one hidden in his pants."

I can't help laughing. "You're an idiot," I say. "You really are."

"But an educated idiot," he says, and tugs at a strand of my hair.

I'm about to ask him about said education, and the article he told John to look up, but Wolfram returns, raven still clinging to his shoulder, and leads us towards the big stone building where I met the Leanan Sidhe, Máiréad. I'm starting to feel left out, being the only one without a huge black bird using me as a perch, when Sgian swoops over to join us, and chooses me to land on.

Just as Wolfram opens the door to let us in, I lean over and whisper to Magne, "It's you, of course."

"What's me?" he answers, just as quietly.

"Not that it matters in any way," I say, "because it's what you do with it that counts." I nip his shoulder. "But you'd win the measuring contest."

Wolfram turns around with raised eyebrows as Magne's laughter echoes into and through the old building.

The House is more or less as I remember from my last visit: long hallways of empty stone, widely-spaced wooden doors without any indication of where they lead, lots of echoes but not a single cobweb or dustbunny.

As Wolfram steps through the door, patterns light up on the walls, spreading a dim blue illumination around us, following him as he leads the way. I can't say for sure that they're the same patterns as last time, but they appear to me to be the same type – knots and animal figures like you'd see on old Germanic and Viking artifacts. It's beautiful. And eerie.

Almost as one, Huginn and Muninn launch from Magne and Wolfram's shoulders and glide ahead of us, farther into the building. The lights appear in the walls, following them, and when they're far enough ahead, the glow following Wolfram and that following the ravens separate, and then the birds round a corner, or fly too far ahead, or ascend or descend a stair, or who knows what, and birds and light all vanish in the distance.

Sgian stays put on my shoulder and I feel her claws dig into my skin.

I turn to watch Magne and he's looking at the patterns that shift and move and brighten and darken as we pass. His mouth is half open in wonder and every now and then a smile tugs at the corners of his lips. His hand in mine tightens and he turns to look at me. "This is amazing," he says, his voice hushed. "Ev tried to describe it, but this is…" He trails off, like he doesn't know what words to use. I totally get it. I'm not even going to try.

"It can also be a frightening place, if it wants to be," says Wolfram, pausing before a door that looks no different from any of the others we passed. "But I think the House likes you. Both of you."

Then he opens the door and the blue glow vanishes as daylight streams in. I assume we've come out at the same courtyard where I met the faery woman, and it certainly looks the same, but when we get outside I can see it's not. This one has only the one door leading in, where the other had several. And instead of a statue of Odin in the fountain, there is a tree. Or a statue of a tree.

It's so perfectly carved that it looks like it could come to life at any moment. It looks like it *is* alive, except the squirrel on its trunk and the snake coiled in its roots are unmoving, and the whole is a uniform stony grey instead of living browns and greens.

Wolfram closes the door behind us, then leads us to the tree statue. "Very few are allowed to come here," he says.

"Evgeny was here," Magne says. "He told me about the tree." He puts a hand out like he wants to touch the statue, but he doesn't.

"Indeed," says Wolfram. "I didn't intend for him to come here, but his demon tried to make him flee, and the House led him to this courtyard."

"Why?" asks Magne. "He said the ravens and the wolves chased him here."

The ravens are gone, I realize, though Sgian still clings to my shoulder. I peer up at the sky, but there are only a few fluffy clouds there, and no sign of the birds.

"Perhaps to give him strength for his ordeal," Wolfram says. His voice is thoughtful. Then he smiles. "I do not think Yggdrasil would object if you touched it."

"Yggdrasil?" says Magne, surprise in his voice. He takes a step towards the statue.

"Not the World Tree itself, of course," says Wolfram. "Merely a seedling. But it is the heart of the House, as the House is the heart of

Wonder Island."

Magne lays a hand gently, reverently almost, on the tree and snatches it back suddenly as the carved squirrel chatters at him. As soon as he removes his hand, it is just a statue again.

"I forgot," he says. "Ev told me about the squirrel." Wolfram chuckles.

"Can I?' I say. I hesitate to ask; it seems almost blasphemy to touch a statue that becomes alive and then stone again. But I'm not very religious, and hell, I'm here, aren't I?

Wolfram nods. "You may."

I put my hand on the stone bark and smile as the squirrel and the snake come to life. Even the tree feels like bark and wood, despite that it looks like stone. Magne puts his hand next to mine and we stand that way for a long moment.

"Wow," I say, when we somehow agree without words that it's time to step away from the tree. The snake and squirrel go still as if they had never moved, and tree looks like a carved statue again.

"I'm starting to think there's a *lot* more to this place than I thought," Magne says.

"Just starting?" I say.

Wolfram nods, but says nothing. I guess he's not ready to give away the island's secrets and I feel privileged that we've been allowed to see as much as we have. And nervous. *Why* have we been allowed to learn so much?

Wolfram sits at the base of the tree, and when he leans against its trunk, I expect it to come alive again, but it remains a statue as he relaxes and stretches out his legs. I sit cross-legged in front of him, and Magne sits next to me, also cross-legged, as if he feels his usual sprawl would be too informal for a place like this.

"I brought you here," Wolfram says, "because I think the Island is extending an invitation to the both of you. To what end, I don't know, but if we're going to learn anything more today, it will be here."

"How will we learn anything?" Magne asks.

Wolfram shrugs and spreads his hands. "I don't know. The House, the Island, it speaks differently for everyone. Those who can hear it. *Communicates*, I should say. For most it's a sort of knowing, for others, it is a voice, and for some, visions. But Wonder Island has not enlightened me as to its interest in you two. It might wish to communicate directly instead."

For a while we just sit, like we're waiting for something to happen, but nothing does. Sgian hops off my shoulder and walks around on the ground, poking among the paving stones.

Then Magne says, "You asked me, before, if I might have been born a werewolf."

Wolfram nods. "I did. That doesn't seem enough to give the Island a special interest in an otherwise ordinary *otherly* werewolf, however extraordinary a person you might be. But I couldn't think what else it might be."

"I was so sure I was made a wolf when I turned thirteen. Because my dad wanted me to… I don't know, be better." He tugs at one of the laces on his boot that's come loose, then carefully re-ties it.

"I couldn't remember clearly," he says. "But now I do."

"So John's mind stuff worked," I say. I put a hand on his knee, squeeze. He gives me a lopsided smile.

"It did. Now it feels like I never forgot at all, but I get why I didn't want to remember."

"You don't have to share anything you don't want to," Wolfram says, his voice gentle. "There was no cost for my help in this."

"I know," Magne says. "And that's why I *do* want to tell you." He pulls in a long breath then lets it out slowly. "You were right. My parents are both werewolves, of course, and I guess that rare thing happened where I was passed the symbiont along with all those nutrients and whatnot, before I was born.

"It was years before I developed a full wolf shape, but I wasn't very old when I could make claws and run on all fours without too much difficulty." He holds out his hand and twitches his fingers and his claws extend, long and sharp. Then he flexes and they slide back into the ends of his fingers.

"So why did you think you were thirteen?" I ask, taking his hand and holding it in both of my own. "And why do you have scars, if not from being made a were?" I trace my finger along a thin white line that runs from his wrist up the inside of his forearm and he shivers.

He looks away from both of us, into the distance.

"Stop if it's too painful," says Wolfram. "There is all the time in the world to investigate this mystery."

I don't think he means the mystery of Magne's past though, it least not entirely.

Magne shakes his head. "On my thirteenth birthday, a bunch of cousins and other kids from pack families were at the farm, eating cake and goofing off. We decided to play hide-and-seek. I was the only one of the kids who was a wolf already – the others were still too young to have been made – and I was really good at hiding. I guess most of the other kids gave up and went back to the house for more cake. But one boy kept looking, and eventually he found me."

Magne's voice is quiet and even, but a note of sadness has crept into the whiskey-and-smoke tones. "His name was Sam and he had turned fifteen the month before. I remember going to his birthday party. He found me in the hayloft, and he grabbed me, and…"

He takes a long breath again, pulls his gaze from far away to look at me, to meet my eyes. The muscles in his face, in his whole body, are tense. Then he looks down at our joined hands.

"He kissed me," he says, softly. "I'd never kissed another boy before. Shit, I hadn't even kissed a *girl* yet. But I knew boys weren't supposed to kiss other boys, that it was supposed to be terribly wrong. Evil, Dad said. I expected the world to change or the ground to swallow us or something.

"But it was just a kiss, and I didn't stop him." He looks back at me and his face is bleak. "And that's how Bjarni found us."

"Oh, Magne," I say. I'm pretty sure I can see where this is going, and my heart aches for him.

"Dad took us to the Elders for judgment," Magne says. "Sam had kissed me, so it was decided that I had the right to punish him for his transgression."

He stops again, stares down at our hands.

"Mags," I say, but I don't know how to finish that sentence.

"He was a nice kid," Magne says. "I didn't want him punished. I knew the Elders said what he did was wrong, but it didn't *feel* wrong. Nothing terrible happened. Nothing changed. But Dad was furious. He used a lot of nasty words, ugly slang for gay men, shit like that. I didn't understand half of what he said.

"The Elders decided that since I refused retribution, I was complicit. That I had to be punished, too. You already know what my pack does to queer folks."

"Holy shit," I say.

He gives me the half-hearted, lop-sided smile. "The sentence was that we should both be hunted. If we survived the night, we'd be allowed to remain in the pack, assuming we mended our ways." He laughs, but there is no merriment in it.

"Sam… didn't live very long. His family had been shamed, and they made sure he didn't have a chance, that he couldn't fight back and maybe get made a wolf by accident."

"And you lived," I say.

His mouth twitches but he doesn't quite manage a smile this time. "That was when Dad told Mum that if I lived, maybe I'd turn out to be a son he could be proud of. I think he was hoping I wouldn't make it."

I want to put my arms around him, but he's hunched in on himself, so I don't. I just squeeze his hands a little harder.

"At least I know now why I don't have a lot of close friends in my own damn pack," he says. Then sighs deep. "I almost didn't make it through the night. I probably should have died. But that symbiont I got from Mum made me stronger than wolves years older than me. Somehow, I didn't die when they tore me apart." He pulls his hands gently from mine, and lifts the hem of his t-shirt. There's a trio of scars there, jagged across his belly, that are bigger and nastier than any of the others, though the years have turned them fainter than they might be and the symbiont has healed them better than if he'd been human. I almost asked him about them, when we were lying in bed after sex, but then he'd distracted me and I'd forgotten.

He looks down at the pale zigzags across his belly, then drops his shirt back over hem "I should have died when Thorstein disemboweled me. When they left me for dead in the forest. But I didn't."

He takes my hands again. "I've never known fear like that night I spent, trying to hold my own intestines in, shivering so hard at the cold I thought I'd break all my teeth, too weak from blood loss to even cry. But somehow, the symbiont healed me enough that by morning I was able to crawl under a fallen tree for shelter. I lay there for days before I had the strength to drag myself home.

"I was too afraid to go into the house, so I stole some of Mum's chickens from the coop, and some eggs, and hid out in one of the barns where we stored machinery that didn't get used too often. My sister found me there and went running for Mum. I thought Dad would kill me for real if he found me. Or tell Thorstein to kill me. But he didn't. He just looked at me. Then he said, 'No son of mine will fuck another man. You want to keep living, you remember that.' Then he walked away. Nothing I ever did after that was good enough." His smile this time is a bit stronger, and a bit more real.

"I left home when I was eighteen. As soon as I saved enough money for a beat-up truck and a damage deposit on a shitty apartment in Great Valley. I worked at a garage, learned how to detail cars, then how to fix cars, and then how to restore them. I saved up enough to go to school, and then I got scholarships. Dad didn't come to my graduation. None of them."

"How many graduations did you have?" I'm starting to think I hardly know my best friend – my lover – at all.

"Three," he says. "And then I got a scholarship for post-grad, but it was for a university overseas." He laughs, self-deprecatingly. "Wolves are social. We don't like to be far from our families, and I guess even if my connection to my pack was distant at best, I didn't want to be that far away from them."

Wolfram has been sitting quietly, listening, but now he tilts his head as if he's listening to something the rest of us can't hear. He smiles, then looks back at Magne. "There are other packs to run with, son."

"There are other packs to run with."

Chapter Thirteen

WOLFRAM CLIMBS TO his feet. "I'm needed at the carnival. You're welcome to stay as long as you like, but I don't advise staying after dark. Sgian can help you find your way out when you're ready."

"You bet, boss," says the crow, then she resumes poking around between the stones.

Wolfram starts for the door, then pauses, comes back, and grips Magne's shoulder. "I fail to understand how a man could be anything but proud to have you as a son." Then he walks quickly away and out the door.

I scoot closer to Magne and lean against him. He frees one of his hands from mine so he can put his arm over my shoulders.

"You *are* pretty amazing," I say.

"There is one thing I haven't told you." His voice is serious.

"There's *more?*" I pull away just far enough to see his face. He meets my eyes, then looks away, watching Sgian stalk a bug across the courtyard.

"Not more memories," he says. "Just something... not so nice I never told you. Something I probably should have told you." He touches his belly where the jagged scars are, and I put my hand over his. "This just... reminded me."

He looks back at me again. "I don't want to bring up bad memories for you. It's why I never told you. But I want you to know what kind of person I really am. You should, in case… Well, you should know."

"I know what kind of person you are," I say. But do I really? There is a lot about him I still haven't learned.

He shakes his head. "Good *and* bad." And I remember Evgeny telling me once he wanted to tell me the bad things that happened to him as well as the happy things, so I could truly understand him. This is the same thing, I guess.

"You're the best person I've ever met."

He smiles and kisses my forehead.

Then I say, "But you can tell me anything. It's not going to change how I feel about you."

He bumps his forehead against mine. "When we found the werewolf who… hurt you," he says.

"He raped me," I say, my voice carefully neutral. "You can say it."

His brown eyes are soft when he meets my look. No pity, just love. "The werewolf who raped you," he says, but he says it softly, like maybe it will hurt less. "I told you he'd be put to death for what he did."

"Yeah," I say. "I felt like I should feel bad about that. But I don't."

"You shouldn't," he says. Then, "I told you I'd see to it personally."

"I figured that meant you'd make sure he was, you know, killed. That it was done for sure."

"No," he says, his voice almost a whisper. "I meant I'd kill him myself."

"Oh," I say. I'm not sure how I feel about that. I mean, I knew the guy was going to die. But Magne… he might like punching things. He might sometimes like punching *people*, if they deserve it. But I guess I never imagined him killing anyone. And back then, we were only just becoming friends. Ev and I were only newly together.

"And I did." He doesn't look at me now. "I hunted him, and when I found him, I cut him. I hurt him. And I split him open from throat to crotch. I watched him try to stuff his guts back inside his body, but unlike me, he couldn't. And when he was taking too long to die, I broke his neck, and left him in the forest to rot." He leans away from me. "And now I wonder if I'm no better than my pack. Than my father."

He snorts. "Dad actually said 'Good job,' when I reported back to the Elders." Now he does look at me and his face is bleak. "He's never said

'Good job' to me before, for anything."

He waits for me to respond, just sits quietly, more still than he usually is. Waiting for me to pass judgement or something. When I don't answer, he says, "I did to him what my family did to me, only I made it permanent."

I put my hand on the side of his face and he closes his eyes. I'm pretty sure I feel him tremble, just a bit, but he's almost as good as a vampire at being still.

"You *are* better than them," I say. "You killed a dangerous criminal. Your family tried to kill two innocent kids. They sentence people to death for loving the wrong person."

"In their eyes, those people, those kids, were criminals, too."

"They're wrong. Queer people aren't criminals for not being straight."

"I know, love," he says. "I know." He puts his hand over mine and turns his face to press his lips against my palm.

"You're a good person," I say. "A good man. And Wolfram's right; your dad should be *proud* of who you are."

"I'd do it again, Su," he says. "If someone else hurt you, I'd tear them apart. And I'd watch them die slowly." He says it so matter-of-factly that it should leave me cold. My lover is a killer. But Evgeny was a worse killer, or better I guess, depending on your point of view. Ev once snapped another vampire's neck just for *threatening* to hurt me.

And maybe it should bother me that Magne killed that other werewolf in such a brutal fashion. But it doesn't. It only makes me love him more.

So I press closer to him, till I'm almost in his lap, and then I turn his face to mine and kiss him. For a moment, he almost seems to want to pull away, but then he makes a sound that's half sob and pulls me into his arms, into his lap and kisses me so fiercely our teeth bang together.

When we pull apart, we're both breathing hard. "Sorry," I say. "You can't scare me away, wolf." He smiles, and one dimple appears.

"Good," he says, and it sounds like a sigh of relief.

"You guys want me to leave for a bit?" says Sgian, and we turn to see her strutting across the stones towards us. "'Cause I can do that. Not sure the tree would appreciate any lewdness, though."

"We're not going to get lewd, cheeky bird," I say. "And no, you don't have to leave."

"We can behave," says Magne. Then his eyes abruptly lose focus and his face goes blank. A few seconds later he blinks, and says, "Oh. Wow."

"What?"

"That was... odd."

"What?" I say, louder.

"I think the House just, uh, communicated," he says.

"It did? What did it say?"

"It didn't *say* anything, it just kind of... made me feel welcome."

"I didn't feel anything."

"It felt like...." He laughs. "It felt like my mum hugging me."

"Hunh." Okay, yeah, I'm envious. I want to talk to this sort-of-sentient, spirit-of-the-island, ancient stone building. But it's silent for me. Until it's not.

And okay, there are no words. No feelings, even. Just images. Foxes running and leaping and playing in the deep forest. And that's it. But I think it's a welcome of sorts. I think it's telling me I can visit the forest here, and run as a fox. That I can belong here.

I try to describe it to Magne, but I don't think I do a very good job. Creative writing – storytelling – was never my strong suit.

"That's pretty amazing," he says. "I wonder what it means."

"This old heap likes to be cryptic," says Sgian. "Even the dwarf can't usually communicate clearly with it, and if anyone should be able to, it's him."

We sit a while longer, enjoying the afternoon sun, but nothing else happens except Magne's stomach growls. Really loud.

"I didn't have lunch," he says.

"Whose fault is that?"

"Yours, as I recall." His grin widens and the second dimple appears.

"Oh," I say. "Right." I get to my feet and pull Magne up after me. "Pick up Thai on the way home? My treat."

"Mother. Fucker." Magne swears all the time, but that's one he reserves for when really foul language is called for. At first, I don't know what he's swearing at, but then I see it.

There's a long line of scratch marks – five parallel lines of scratches – all down the side of his truck, from front bumper to rear. Magne's stopped in the middle of the street, staring. Then he hands me the bags of takeaway and stalks – actually *stalks* – up to his truck where it sits parked at the curb, otherwise shiny and clean and in pristine condition for a truck of its vintage.

As he runs his hand along the scratches, echoing the motion that must have made them, I realize what I'm actually looking at. A werewolf – a very *large* werewolf – drew heavy claws down the side of the vehicle, cutting through paint to score deep into the metal.

Then I smell it. Urine. A werewolf also pissed on the rear driver's side tire. There's a dark puddle under it.

"Fucking asshat dickhole fucker," Magne says. Then he straightens up and sighs. "It's going to take a crapload of work to fix this."

"Who?" I say.

"My asshole brothers," he answers. "This," he gestures at the scratches, "is Thorstein's artistry. The puddle under my tire is Bjarni. He's too much of a coward to do any actual damage."

"They were *here*?"

He shrugs. "It's not hard to find out where I live. Mum has the address."

"And she just *told* them?"

"They're my brothers. Of course she told them."

"But…?"

He sighs, then takes the takeout bags back and leads the way to the door. "She loves my dad," he says, like that explains everything.

"But he…"

"He's the love of her life. And he loves her. And he's her pack leader, and *I'm* the one who broke laws. Probably."

"But…"

"I know." He's stopped again, staring, and I have to step around him to see the thick brown envelope stuck in the building door. It has Magne's name written in a flowing, tidy script on the front. Mom writing if I ever saw any.

"Your dad knows you were helping people escape."

"He does. Apparently."

"He might have sent your brothers to take you back."

"He probably did. Luckily we weren't home."

"They'll be back."

"Maybe. But their intent won't be to hurt me. Not much, anyway."

"Maybe?"

"I suspect that is the back up plan to get me back to the farm." He gestures at the envelope with his chin.

"To what, go home voluntarily?"

"The farm isn't home anymore. *This* is home," he says. "And yes, they'll assume I'd go voluntarily, until I don't. The pack – *family* – is everything to wolves. It's why it's so hard for people to leave, even if it means they'll die for falling in love with the wrong person." Then he hands me the bags again, pulls the envelope out of the door, and unlocks it.

We go to his place, where he drops the envelope on the coffee table and goes to get plates and bowls and cutlery. The whole time we're eating I keep glancing over at the envelope, while Magne ignores it. What could his mom have sent that would make him want to go back? To return voluntarily to face whatever terrible punishment they'll decide on?

Finally, he says, "Stop shooting pointed glances and go open it."

"Are you sure?"

"You already know my darkest secrets. Another boy kissed me when I was thirteen and I didn't hate it. And I gutted a man who hurt you."

So I push my plate aside, slide off my stool, and sit on the edge of the couch. I stare at the envelope long enough that Magne says, "Open it, already."

When I peel the flap open and tip the envelope onto the table, a pile of photographs slides out. Everything from eight by tens to those tiny little prints they used to make in the seventies. I spread them out and pick one up at random. It's a little boy, shaggy brown hair falling in his dark eyes, holding up a fish on a string and grinning so wide his face must ache. He's got a dimple in each cheek.

The next one I pick up is of a big, muscular blond man with braids in his long hair and beard, holding a tiny baby with a shock of brown hair.

The baby is staring up at the man and clenches a beard braid in one chubby fist.

I pick up another. A little boy, six or seven years old, sitting on the back of a different blond man. The guy is huge, but he's smiling indulgently as he kneels on all fours to play horse for the boy.

Then another with the boy sitting on the bearded blond man's shoulders, with the huge man standing to one side, smiling, and a shorter, slightly darker-haired man standing on the other side, grinning and dimpled. He looks so much like Magne looks now it's disconcerting. The boy clutches the man's hair in both fists, and smiles at the camera. One front tooth is missing and his canines are too big.

I realize what this is, and I don't know why it took so long to sink in. These are all photographs of Magne as a child. He can't be older than twelve in any of them, but in most of them, he's even younger. He was a happy little boy, and it's obvious that his older brothers adored him. They carry him, swing him from their arms, help him with a baseball bat, let him climb all over them. Even his father, never quite smiling, seems affectionate, and there are several photos of him holding the child Magne, or carrying him on his back, or resting a hand on his shoulder.

I sniff and realize I've got a tear trickling its way down one cheek. It's heartbreaking that this sweet, happy child will soon be hurt so badly by the same people who love him.

Magne leans over the back of the couch to put his arms around me.

"Mags," I say. "You were a cute kid."

"I was, wasn't I?"

"Is this supposed to make you feel… bad?"

He kisses the side of my face, where the tear was. "It's supposed to remind me of what things were like when I followed the rules and we were one big happy family."

"I don't see any pictures of you with your mom. Or your sister."

"No. Mum wants to remind me of how things were when all the menfolk got along. I still get along with Mum and Hilde, so she probably didn't think she needed to remind me."

"Your brothers aren't her sons, though, right?"

"No. Thorstein and Bjarni are from Dad's first wife. She was human, and she died a long time ago. He married Mum and they had Hilde. That was supposed to be it. An heir, a backup, and a girl to spoil. But Mum wanted another kid. She didn't tell Dad until she couldn't hide it anymore."

"But he loved you."

He shrugs. "Maybe. I mean look at me." He points to the photo of the grinning kid with the fish. "How could anyone resist such cuteness?"

He's got my arms trapped so I bonk his forehead with mine and he laughs.

"What are you going to do?"

"Not go back to the farm," he says. "Everything changed when…" He kisses my cheek again. "And even if it hadn't changed, I hope I'd have figured out I couldn't stay, anyway. I think my cousin Siobhan would have made me realize what kind of people they were, if I hadn't managed to figure it out on my own."

I pick up the photo with Magne on his father's shoulders, brothers looking on fondly. He sighs into my hair.

"Shit," he says.

"Are you okay?"

"Not really. I hoped… I hoped at least Mum would be on my side. But of course she'd side with Dad. She's always been too in love with him to see what he is. And that's the real curse of the werewolf."

"What is?"

He's quiet for a moment, then he says, "When we fall in love, real love, it's for life. If one partner dies, sometimes the other finds new love, but as long as both are alive, it's for keeps."

"What about dating?" I think about Cara, and I don't think he's still in love with her. He says neither of them was in love.

"We can date, fool around, whatever. But once it's real love, mutual love, we're doomed."

"How do you know, though? Is it like fairy tales, or those young adult novels that were so popular."

"Insta-love?" There's laughter in his voice. "Maybe. Something like that. But usually it takes time to develop. The symbiont… connects, somehow. You just know." He nuzzles my neck, and I wonder if he's trying to distract me.

"What if one partner is a werewolf," I say, almost whispering, "and the other isn't? Like lots of weres have human partners, don't they?"

"Supposedly, the human partner feels it too, though not as strongly."

"Which is why Bonnie could leave her werewolf husband."

"That, and her love for her son is stronger." He kisses my neck again, sighs. "But the wolf in the equation is doomed until the human partner dies. So her husband won't be able to move on, even if she does." He chuckles. "Doooomed."

I twist around to look at him head on. "Mags, are you…?" I can't finish the sentence.

He straightens up and stretches. "I need to go for a run, love. I need to think. Or to *not* think."

I stand up, intercept him before he gets to the door. For a moment he won't look at me. Then he takes my shoulders in his big hands and looks down into my eyes. His are bright and deep and lovely.

"I love you, Su," he says. "I'm in love with you. Completely. And yes. That's why I had to be sure it was me you wanted. So when I gave in, you wouldn't break my heart permanently."

"If I'd… if we'd… and you thought it was real but then I left…?"

"I'd still be lost," he says. "But to be honest, I think I might have been lost a long time ago."

"I love you," I say. "Holy fuck do I love you."

"Good," he says, and gives me a long kiss with lots of tongue before pulling slowly away. "Hold that thought, love. I really do need to run until I'm so tired my brain can't torment me with thoughts."

Chapter Fourteen

WHEN MAGNE LEAVES, I put away our dinner things, then pause over the photographs. I look for a long time at the one with his dad and his brothers. Then I slide the lot back into the envelope, tuck the flap in, and leave it face down on the coffee table so he doesn't even have to see his mother's handwriting if he doesn't want to. I think about shoving it into a drawer where he won't see it at all, but it's not my place, not my decision to make.

In my loft, I change into sweats and a t-shirt and let my tail show. Then I stretch and begin to work through those kung fu moves from my angry teenage days. Whenever I need calm or focus, or even just reassurance that I'm not totally incompetent, I turn to that same simple routine.

And just when I'm working up to top speed, spinning and kicking and finding calm in movement, there's a loud scratching, buffeting sound from the wall of windows and I stumble to a halt.

A black shape is visible beyond the glass, battering against it. It's gotten dark and all I can see is a moving silhouette against the dim light from the street. But as my heartbeat skips, I realize I know that shape. It's a big crow.

I hurry to the window by the fire escape and crank it open. It doesn't open nearly as far as it's supposed to – something in the hinge doesn't work properly. But Evgeny once managed to squeeze through it – how, I still don't know – and if he can fit, so can Sgian.

She clings to the edge and shimmies herself in through the gap. "Magne," she croaks.

"He's not here," I say. "He went for a run."

"He's in trouble," she says, her voice harsher than usual and her breathing quick. Do birds pant? Because she sounds like she's trying to catch her breath. "Magne met his brothers in the woods. It's not good."

"How? He said he was going for a run." Is it terrible that my first assumption was that Magne lied about where he was going? It is, isn't it?

"They ambushed him." Sgian hops from the narrow window ledge to the back of the couch. "I was checking up on your professor. On my way home I decided to take a detour over the woods. Talk to some friends of mine. I heard fighting. I came straight here."

For way too long I stare at her and try to process what she's telling me. Why can't my brain work quickly when I need it to?

"Oh shit," I say. "Can you lead me there?" And then I'm stuffing my feet into boots, finding my jacket, my keys, my phone. Out on the street I glance around and there's no one. I hope there isn't anyone looking out their window, either. I step into the relative shadow of the side street, and then I'm a fox, running headlong after a black shadow in the sky. And I'm faster than any natural fox, maybe even faster than Evgeny in his most powerful vamped-out state. I'm a small furry wind streaking down the street to the park, then deep under the trees.

If anyone is loitering at the Wonder Island dock or taking an evening stroll along the boardwalk they see me only as a reddish streak in the shadows, there and gone.

Then we're past the city and into the deep woods. Old growth along the river, moss and brush, old drystone fences where the land was cleared a very long time ago.

I stop when Sgian swoops down out of the trees and lands in front of me. "We're close," she says, and I can hear them, sticks snapping, brush crackling, the grunting of male bodies connecting in painful ways. They breathe heavily, but none of them growls or yells. That makes it worse somehow.

I crouch and slowly let my fox senses – my *magic* fox senses – extend into the forest around me. I can feel everything, but I look for the brightest sparks that mean sentience. There directly before me is the bright, crackling spark of Sgian, both crow and not crow. I can almost see her other shape, her *sidhe*-self she lost to Odin as punishment for theft.

"I'll get help," she says, and she's gone before I can answer, brightness winging away over the trees towards the river and Wonder Island.

And there's Magne, a steady glow not so bright as Sgian, but rich and deep green with a flicker of blue magic that I've never seen in a werewolf before, never seen in *him* before. I wonder if that's what Wolfram saw, that made him start asking questions about Magne's past. He's moving very fast, in a deadly sort of dance with two other werewolf glows. And there are two others nearby, one circling, the other still. Three of those others are standard steady werewolf glows, like Magne's without the blue crackle. The other, the one that seems to be most often clashing with Magne, has a strange unfocussed quality, a crackle of sickly yellow, and an intensity I can't read. It doesn't feel good, though.

I let my fox-senses fade and return to normal vision. Four other werewolves. So not just his brothers. One he could handle alone. Two or even three we could take together, but *four*? I don't know.

I creep slowly forward through the brush to the clear area, near the bank of a small stream, where they fight. The ground is torn up by werewolf claws, and the streambank is a muddy mess from their feet. Just as I creep close enough to see the combatants, a deep male voice bellows, "Enough!" and they all stop. I can hear their breathing, three of them deep, ragged, and quick. Two are measured and even.

Magne stands to one side of the clearing, mostly human, only claws and a muzzle full of teeth to show he's a werewolf. He's naked and magnificent, bleeding from half a dozen wounds. None of them look too serious, though, and one or two are even closing and scabbing over as I watch.

On the other side of a clearing are his brothers. One's half-wolf, which might be as far as he can change – I have no idea how old he is or what his capabilities might be. He's huge, and shirtless, and even more scratched up than Magne, but wears loose sweatpants that allow him to move even partly wolfed out. The other brother, the smaller one who looked so much like Magne in the photographs, is in full wolf-shape, and if I wasn't so worried for Magne, I'd be impressed by his musculature and his dark-gold fur. Just over the stream is a woman, human but for extended claws. She's wearing jeans and t-shirt and she looks an awful lot like Magne, too, but blonde. His older sister, if I had to guess.

And then, watching them all is the man I assume bellowed for them to stop. He looks like he did in the photo where Magne sat on his shoulders, dressed like a farmer in jeans and a plaid shirt. His beard and hair are longer, and maybe a touch greyer, and they now have beads tied into their braids. He's barefoot and his arms are crossed, and even fully human-shaped, he looks like a werewolf. Magne's dad is even more impressive in real life, and if I didn't know what kind of a person he was, I might think he's hot.

"Hilde," says Magne's dad. "Go back to the truck. You weren't meant to see this, and if I find out which of your brothers let you hide under the tarp –" and here he looks sidelong at the shorter, darker-haired brother "– I'll have his wolf skin for my wall."

"Don't hurt him," she says.

"We're here to bring him home," Magne's dad answers. "How much that will hurt is up to him."

"Dad, don't. Just… let him go."

He ignores her. "Bjarni." The shorter brother looks away from Magne to his dad. They all bear a distinct family resemblance, but this brother looks most like Magne of all of them, even wolfed-out as he is. "Take your sister back to the truck and wait for us."

"But Dad –"

"Go."

Bjarni shrugs and moves so fast I'm startled. He's changed back to human shape, scooped his sister up, and tossed her over his shoulder before she can even react. Then he's gone into the trees.

The other brother, the huge one, Thorstein, is still but his eyes are restless, constantly darting back and forth between his father and Magne. I extend my fox senses a bit, watch Bjarni and Hilde move away from us, and then turn to Thorstein. As I suspected, he's the one with the wavering, sick yellow tinged, oddly intense glow. It's like there's something wrong with him. Drugs, maybe? I don't think so, but even when I let my senses fade again, I can feel it. His body doesn't move, but his eyes never stop. His breathing has an odd hitch, and his wolfish teeth are shiny and wet. He's taller than even Magne, but he hunches over like a cheap movie monster so he just looks big instead of tall.

"Son," says their father. Thorstein jerks his focus away from Magne to look at him, but he's looking at his youngest son. "Come home. Your family needs you."

"You drag me in front of the Elders and you won't have me home very long." Now that he's got his breath back, Magne is so still even his chest and shoulders barely move. His stillness has an entirely different quality from that of his brother, though I couldn't tell you exactly how.

"They will determine an appropriate punishment, yes," says his father. "But if you atone, if you help fix the damage you've caused, they assure me they will be lenient."

Magne doesn't answer, but he's shaking his head. Then he says, "I have nothing to atone for. People needed help. I helped them."

"You helped criminals escape. So you will now help bring them to justice. It's the only way out of this that lets you keep your family."

"I lost my family a long time ago," Magne says. His words are hard, but I can hear the sorrow in his voice. I mean, I knew the pack, the family, was important to werewolves, but I guess I didn't know *how* important. "Justice would be to leave them alone to live their lives, to stop people like you from persecuting them."

"You *will* do as I say."

I sneak a glance at Magne's brother. His face is half wolf-shaped, not unlike Magne's right now, but Thorstein's canines are not just wet, he's drooling. Like big looping, dripping, St Bernard dog drool. Bad movie effects drool. His eyes still flick back and forth between Magne and his father and something burns in them. Not hatred, but more like madness. He looks like those people at an evangelical religious revival — the ones the speak in tongues or writhe around on the ground in the ecstasy of contact with Jesus. He scares the shit out of me. Almost literally.

I want to warn Magne, in case he hasn't noticed, but I don't dare step out of my hiding place, I don't even dare call out. So I try to *think* at him. It worked, once, when I was stuck in fox shape. Before I found out I can actually talk in my normal human voice even when I'm all fox.

Magne, your brother. I think as clearly as I can and Magne twitches, just slightly, so I think he's heard me.

Then, *Stay hidden, love*, I hear faintly back. He turns his head slightly to watch his brother.

"Dad," he says, not taking his eyes off Thorstein. "You shouldn't have brought Thors with you on a full moon. You shouldn't have had him fighting."

"He's fine. He's a grown adult and can make his own decisions."

"He's sick, and he's not capable of making decisions in that state."

"He was blessed," his father says. "And if he's a little hard to manage when the wolf is on him, that's a small price to pay."

"He's going to kill someone someday. Someone who doesn't deserve it. Maybe a lot of someones. Don't you remember Granddad's story of the *berserkr* he knew? He slaughtered a whole family and most of another. It took the pack decades to recover." *Berserkr.* I don't know if Magne's using the word the same way, but berserkers were Norse and Germanic warriors, chosen by Odin to take animal form – or to go into a battle rage that made them *think* they had taken animal form. Shit. If his brother is one, that's very, very bad right now.

His father doesn't answer; he just glares.

"Or he'll end up getting himself killed. Dad, you need to get him home, get a healer to dose him with something, or lock him the fuck up."

I hear a faint splat as some of the drool slides off Thorstein's fangs and hits the leaf litter on the forest floor.

Magne's father makes an abrupt motion with one hand. "You were always the one who could calm him best. *He* needs you at home."

"You need to get him real help," says Magne. "I can't spend my life keeping my brother from turning into a raving maniac. And I would have thought you'd want more for him, since he'll take over as pack leader one day."

"You'll do as you're told," his father says. "And Thorstein won't be pack leader."

"Bjarni?" Magne sounds surprised.

"He's the only one left, isn't he?" His dad's voice is hard, a little angry. "I once thought *you* would follow me, but there's no chance of that now, not even if you atone for the rest of your life. Do you see what your selfish little crusade has wrought?"

"Selfish?" Magne sounds taken aback. But I think it's more because his father just told him he was supposed to succeed him as pack leader, not because saving people's lives at the expense of his own is selfish.

Magne's dad takes a step forward, into the stream and then across it. I gather myself, prepare to jump to Magne's aid if need be. Magne doesn't move, not even when the older man walks right up to him and puts a hand on each of his shoulders. Not even when his dad digs fingers into Magne's shoulder muscles and pokes the claws of his thumbs into the hollow above his collarbones.

"Son," Magne's dad says almost gently. "Don't fight this. Come home, take your punishment, take your place in the family. You know a wolf is nothing without his pack."

Magne holds himself carefully still. I can practically see how hard he's fighting not to give in. That messy-haired little boy who looked up to his father is still in there somewhere, and I think he's hard pressed not to react.

"I haven't belonged in the family since I left. Since *before* I left. Not since you tried to kill me."

"I tried to make you stronger. And it worked. Look at you now."

"I'm stronger because I grew up," Magne says. "Because I fought to *not* be like you, to be *nothing* like you. I almost died because of your efforts to make me less of a sissy."

"Don't push me, Magne."

"Your tame council of Elders will want my life this time."

"Not if you submit. Not if you start atoning now. Show me your throat, son."

"I won't."

I want to yell at Magne to get away, to run before his dad hurts him worse, before his brother goes into a killing rage, but I can't force any sound out.

"You will show me your throat, boy." So quickly his dad goes from *son* to *boy*.

Magne laughs, but it's a hollow sound. "You can't compel me, Dad. Even if I wasn't more than old enough to have outgrown it. I wasn't made by the pack. There's nothing of you in me except half your DNA."

I know vampires can make their progeny do what they're told, at least until they outgrow the need for an older vamp's protection, so I guess it makes sense that werewolves can, too. But Magne was born a werewolf, so he only has his mom's symbiont, so only she'd be able to compel him, assuming he hadn't outgrown it.

"Not with my voice, perhaps," Magne's father says. He tightens his grip on Magne's shoulders. I can see his fingers dig deep into the muscle, where his claws break the skin and thin trails of blood seep out.

Magne still doesn't move. Even his face is completely still. His eyes, though, are full of emotion: pain, sadness, regret. It hurts just to look at him. He doesn't even flinch when his dad shifts his grip to dig his thumbs into the muscles behind Magne's collarbone, as his claws pierce the skin and slide into flesh.

His dad's frown deepens and his nostrils flare. "Show me your throat. Get on your damn knees and beg me to let you back into this family."

"No." Magne's voice is calm and even.

His dad abruptly jams his thumbs deep into muscle, and I watch in horror as his knuckles disappear with a wet rending sound. He's snarling now. "Submit, or you lose this chance for good."

"I won't, Dad," Magne says, sounding tired. "You're everything I refuse to be."

"Then you're no son of mine." His dad tears his hands away, sending an arc of blood spattering to each side. Drops patter onto the leaves right in front of my nose, and Magne staggers, catches himself, and doesn't otherwise react.

"Tell Mum I love her," he says. "And Hilde. And tell Bjarni to fuck himself."

His dad turns and walks away. "Deal with him," he says.

As if awakened from a trance, Thorstein's head snaps up and he focusses narrowed eyes on Magne, no longer shifting his gaze back and forth to his dad. A chilling howl, wolflike but somehow more monstrous, tears from his throat.

I leap at the same time Thorstein does, but I never reach him. A huge paw flattens me to the ground before I even get airborne and Thorstein slams into Magne. Too late, Magne discovers his arms are disabled, and all he can do is turn his shoulder to meet his brother's attack.

"Be still, little cousin," says a deep, scratchy voice next to my ear when I struggle out from under the paw. "We'll deal with this." Then the weight is gone and a huge grey wolf with faint blue lights clinging to the edge of its fur steps away to confront Magne's father. A second wolf, similarly traced with blue light, is crouched between Magne and his brother.

I ignore the instruction and take human shape so I can crawl to Magne where he's struggling to get up, help him to his knees.

"Thorgrim Thorvaldson," says the wolf, the one that stopped me from hurling myself between Magne and his berserker brother.

Magne's father turns to look, and stares.

"You should not bring a *berserkr* anywhere but to a battle in his condition," says the other wolf in a voice just a little lower than the other.

"This *is* a battle," says Magne's dad, but he's looking from one wolf to the other in confusion and awe. I don't think he even notices me.

Magne also stares at the wolves. "Geri and Freki," he says softly. He looks just like he looked when he first met Huginn and Muninn.

"Odin's wolves," says Magne's dad, voice also low. "My son is chosen of Odin."

"Which son?" says one of the wolves, and there is – I think – humor in his voice.

"The Allfather doesn't recruit *berserkrs* anymore," says the other wolf.

"Your elder sons needs the help of a *seithr* priestess," says the first.

"You're wrong."

The lighter voiced wolf steps closer to Magne's dad and I swear it gets bigger, until it makes the werewolf seem small. "You will tell Odin's wolves that Odin is wrong?"

"No, I meant…"

"This boy is ours now," says the other wolf, looming over Thorstein as he moves to get up, but looking at Magne. The *berserkr* changes his mind and scurries backwards, closer to his father, on all fours.

"He is under the old man's protection, now." I have no idea if the wolf means Odin or Wolfram when he says 'old man,' and I'm starting to wonder if it really makes a difference.

"The Allfather would never take Magne," says Thorgrim. Thorstein watches his father. He looks a little more sane now. At least he's stopped drooling.

One of the wolves laughs. The other says, "You presume to know what the Allfather thinks?'

The first says, "And you assume we're talking about Odin and not the dwarf who runs Wonder Island." She sounds amused.

"He runs with our pack now," says the other wolf.

"He has no more need of yours."

Both wolves advance slowly, stiff-legged, and father and son back away.

"Leave this place," says one wolf.

"This boy is no longer under your jurisdiction. You disowned him, and we claim him."

The two blond men hesitate and the wolves continue to advance. Finally, Magne's dad takes his oldest son by the arm, bows his head to the wolves, and they turn and walk away into the trees.

One wolf follows, melting into the shadows until all I can see is a faint blue glow, and then nothing.

The other turns back briefly and says, "Get this cub home, little cousin. He will need warmth and food and rest. We will make certain these werewolves are gone." And then she, too, disappears into the shadows and is gone.

"Holy shit," says Magne.

"I guess Sgian really meant it when she said she was going for help."

"Oh fuck," Magne says then, right before he passes out and falls over.

Chapter Fifteen

H E'S ONLY OUT for a minute, but that's one minute that nearly gives me a heart attack.

"Ow," he says when his eyes flutter open.

"Fuck, Mags, don't do that to me." I start to put his arm around my shoulders when he flinches. I'm really hurting him. Like, whatever damage his dad did might be even worse than it looks.

"I'll try not to," he says. "But I can't guarantee success." Between us, we manage to get him standing.

"I don't think you're in any condition to walk home," I say.

"Also," he says. "I'm slightly naked."

"Don't joke. This is serious."

"That's the best time to joke." He kisses the top of my head. "And it's a good thing I drove."

"How far is the parking lot?"

"Not far." Of course, "not far" to a werewolf is actually kind of far to a normal person. He starts walking, taking long steps I have to scramble to keep up with. I can tell it's bravado, though. I can see the light tremble in his muscles. He's tough, and he's a werewolf, but even the strongest manly man can succumb to shock. Not to mention hypothermia. It's a mild night, but it's not summer yet, and Magne's not in wolf shape.

"Mags," I say, and he pauses to look at me.

"Can you move better on four legs?"

He looks like he's considering it, even tries flexing an arm. Then he shakes his head. "Dad knows the best way to disable a wolf is to take out at least two limbs." He gestures with his hands. He can bend his wrists and elbows okay – though I can tell even that hurts – but when he tries to lift his arms, to rotate his shoulders, his wounds seep blood and his face goes pale.

He shakes his head again. "That's not going to work."

So we keep walking and soon his steps get slower, less sure. I wrap an arm around his waist to help steady him, but even then he falls. When I go to help him stand, he says, "Let me rest a minute." So I sit close to him, wishing I could keep him warm, but he's got so much surface area it's a hopeless attempt.

After a while, he struggles to his feet again and we keep going. I hold him tighter this time, make him take slower, more careful steps. It'll take longer, but falling is hurting him more than time will.

Eventually, I see the gravel parking lot through the trees. His truck is there, gleaming pale blue and white under a lamp post, and I hope his brothers didn't decide to vandalize it more. Or worse, disable it completely. But it looks okay, except all four tires are sitting in puddles that smell like Bjarni was marking his territory again.

"Asshole," Magne mutters.

"So, we have another problem," I say, when we pause to fish the spare key from the wheel well.

"What's one more?" says Magne.

"I can't drive stick," I say.

He laughs. I don't get the joke, but soon he's laughing so hard he can hardly stand. "Ow, ow, ow," he says. "Even laughing hurts."

"What's so funny?" I unlock the door and Magne's clothes are piled on the passenger seat. I look at them, then at him, and wonder how the hell I'm going to get the one on the other.

"'Drive stick' is a euphemism," he says, and I guess I look confused, because he adds, "for sex with men." He starts to laugh again, though I think he's trying not to. "In that sense, you're very, very good at driving stick."

"Oh shut up, you pig," I say, swatting his arm – but gently. "Asshole."

"I love you."

"Hmm," I say, pretending not to notice. There's a blanket under the truck seat and I pull it out. It appears to be clean. "You're going to have to wear this, because I don't have the patience to figure out how to get you dressed *and* figure out how to drive your truck."

"I'll drive, love," he says. He takes the blanket, carefully, and wraps it around his waist like a bath towel.

"That's not going to keep you warm."

"No, but it'll keep me decent. The heater can keep me warm." He slides into the driver's seat and says, "You might have to start her for me."

"How are you going to drive if you can't even start the engine?" I climb into the passenger seat and lean across. He pushes in the clutch with one bare foot and I turn the key. He takes good care of this old truck and it starts easily, settling down to a deep rumble. I don't know much about cars, but the engine sounds really good.

"I can drive blindfolded and tied up," he says. "Farm boy, remember. I've been driving since I could see over the dash."

"Well, let's not try that," I say. "Let's just get you home alive."

"Sure thing," he says. Then he pushes the shifter into reverse – I see him wince as he does, but he doesn't make any noise – and backs out of the parking space. I can see the effort it takes him to make each shift, and the even bigger effort to steer around sharp corners, but he doesn't complain, he just stares grimly at the road and drives.

"As soon as I'm healed," he says, "I'm teaching you to drive standard."

"Deal," I say.

There aren't any stop lights until we reach the city, and Magne chooses a route that takes us through downtown instead of along the river – this time of night, the city itself is nearly deserted, but the river boardwalk will still be populated by evening strollers.

When we do hit a red light, he says, "Can you see anyone coming?"

"From where?"

"Anywhere." He's gritting his teeth and his eyes are narrowed, like he's having trouble focusing. Worse, he's starting to shiver.

"No," I say. "It's clear." And he runs the light. He does it twice more before we reach our street. He's shaking so hard I'm afraid he's going to run us into a lamppost, but he manages to pull over in front of our building, shove the truck into first, yank on the emergency brake, and even turn the key so the truck goes quiet.

I help him out of the seat and his skin is cold. He's colder than vampire cold and as we stumble up to the front door, his teeth start chattering. He clenches his jaw and they stop, but it makes him shiver harder. I get him into the elevator and curse the slow industrial lift as we grind slowly upward, but there's no way he could handle the stairs.

He sighs as we step into his apartment. "I can't wait to get into bed. I'm so tired." He sounds half asleep already. "In fact, maybe I'll just lie down here." He starts to slide out of my arms onto the floor.

"Fuck," I say. "No." Somehow I keep him standing. "I think you're hypothermic."

"Mmm." He starts to slide again.

"Say awake, Magne," I say, dragging him upright as best I can. "Don't you fucking go to sleep." I push and pull until I get him moving again, towards the bathroom.

"You swore at me," he says, sounding dopey. "I'm sorry for whatever terrible thing I did. I won't do it again."

"Shut up," I say. "Just stay awake."

In the bathroom, I prop him half-sitting on the side of the giant bathtub, then put the plug in and turn the water on, as hot as I think he can stand it.

"I'm too tired for a bath," he protests weakly. "I'm not that dirty."

I ignore him and tug the blanket free of his waist and wrap it around his shoulders instead. "Okay, buddy," I say. "Into the tub."

"Yes, Mum," he says. For a moment, I think he's teasing me for being motherly, but then I realize he's probably hallucinating.

People hallucinate when they have hypothermia, right? Hell, I hope I'm remembering that stuff I read on the internet and a hot bath will warm him up. And not make things worse.

I manage to get him into the tub, one leg at a time, and let him slide down the slanted back until he's sitting in the hot water.

"You still awake?" I say.

"Uh hunh. If I fall asleep in the bath, will I drown?"

"Yes," I say. "So don't fall asleep."

"Okay."

"Good. I'll be right back."

I don't want to leave him, but I also want to get him a hot drink, like warming him up from the inside would be a good idea. So I hurry to the kitchen, put on the fancy kettle that heats water in about two seconds flat, and drop a teabag into a mug. I add a big dollop of bourbon. Then I take a swig right from the bottle.

Finally, hot beverage in hand, I go back to the bathroom.

The tub is nearly half full, up to his waist and creeping up his chest. "You still awake, Mags?"

For a moment he doesn't answer and I'm about to fling the tea aside and start shaking him. Then he opens his eyes and says, "I'm awake, love. Still alive, too."

I kneel down, put the tea mug in the soap dish, and adjust the blanket around his shoulders so it won't get soaked. I make sure the water isn't too hot, then lift the mug to his mouth and make him sip. I make him keep drinking until the mug is empty.

He leans back with a sigh and I pull the blanket off and turn off the taps so he can sink into the water.

"Well," he says. "That wasn't the best night of my life." Then he rolls his head on the side of the tub to look at me, and smiles until one dimple shows. "But it wasn't the worst, either."

"I'm sorry, Mags."

"What, for saving my ass? I forgive you."

"No, dumbass. For… your dad."

"It doesn't make any difference. I wasn't his son anymore, anyway."

"But he said –"

"Don't," he says, but gently. "I don't care what he said or didn't say. I haven't had much of a family for decades. Now I have a little less of one, that's all."

Then he closes his eyes and slides into the tub to dunk his head under the water. When he surfaces, he looks at me again. "But I do have you, love."

"I'm your family, Magne." I smooth his hair back from his face, feel the warmth returning to his skin, and finally relax, at least a little. His shoulders are still seeping blood into the bath water.

"Yeah, you are," he says. His eyes are bright. "I'd trade all of them for you any day."

I lean closer and kiss him, just lightly because I don't want to hurt him, but he responds to fiercely I don't stop. I poke my tongue into his mouth and he groans softly.

"I wish I felt well enough to follow that with something more," he says. "But I can't sweep you off your feet when I can barely move my arms."

"We should get you bandaged up," I say. "And then I think it's probably safe for you to sleep. Do you know any doctors who take werewolf patients?"

"I think their doors will be closed to me now," he says. "All the nearby ones, anyway."

"Shit."

"Disinfect me, tape me back together, bandage me. The symbiont will take care of the rest."

"Are you sure?" I get the first aid kit and a bottle of isopropyl alcohol from the cabinet.

He shrugs, and winces. "It always has before." He looks at his belly. "Even when my guts were literally on the wrong side of my abdominal wall."

He hisses when I pour the alcohol over and into the deep punctures over his collarbone. The rest of his wounds are shallow enough I'm not too concerned. I get a towel and rub his hair mostly dry, then gently dry his shoulders and chest so I can bandage him. A couple of steri-strips on each wound seem to hold them closed okay, so I tape a square of gauze over each one and hope they don't bleed though too quickly.

He's recovered enough that once he's bandaged and dry he's able to make his own way to the bedroom. I curl up naked next to him, to share my body heat in case he isn't warm enough yet, then I pull the blankets over us both.

"I was really looking forward to getting you naked in bed when I got back from my run," he says. "This really isn't what I had in mind."

I push myself up so I'm half sitting. "Really?" I say, wiggling my eyebrows. "What if you just lie there and I do all the work?" Because hell, even injured, even damaged and in more than one kind of pain, he's dead sexy.

One side of his mouth quirks. "I couldn't ask you to do that." He's trying very hard not to smile and it's not working.

"You can pay me back later." I lean over him to dig a condom out of the nightstand and swing one leg over to sit astride him. I start by kissing him, long and slow, and when I hear his breathing speed up, I start to work my way down, kissing his chest and his belly, tracing the shapes of his muscles with my tongue. He slides his hands over my thighs, my butt, as much of my skin as he can reach without having to move his arms too much. I respond by sliding the damp place between my legs over his hardness, again and again until he's panting.

And it turns out he's pretty skilled even with a restricted range of motion, because when I take him inside me, it's not only his pleasure, but mine, that has us both crying out.

Sometime much later than night, I wake to Magne struggling out of bed.

"Gotta pee, sweetheart?" I say, still half asleep.

"I'm cold," he says. I must really not be very awake, because I don't think much of it. It doesn't occur to me that unlike vampires, werewolves run hot. They rarely get cold, except when they've been running around naked too long.

So I just get out of bed, help him put on sweats and a long-sleeved t-shirt and snuggle back in with him. It's not till morning that I realize something is wrong.

It's barely light when I wake again, more alert this time, because early morning is fox time. I come fully awake when I realize how restless Magne is. He's tossing and turning so much I'm worried he's going to pull the steri-strips off.

"Magne." When I touch his shoulder, I can feel the heat through his shirt. He's too hot. Way too hot. He's sweating and his shirt is soaked though.

He opens his eyes and they look dry and red. "I don't feel too great," he says. "I might skip breakfast." He tries to smile. Then he suddenly lunges for the side of the bed, slips and falls, and I'm up and by his side so fast I make my own head spin.

"Gotta puke," he says, and tries to get up. His arms won't hold him, but I wrap my arms around his waist and pull and somehow we get him upright. He doesn't make it to the bathroom. Passing the kitchen, he abruptly veers to one side to lean over the sink and half-digested Thai takeaway spurts out of his mouth.

I keep my arms around him, holding him up, my face pressed to his back. I feel his muscles strain as he heaves, over and over until nothing else comes up.

Then I reach over and turn on the tap. Get a glass so he can drink some water. Rinse vomit down the drain.

He leans against the counter, head hanging over the sink, like it's too much effort to move. I put my hand on his forehead, like it'll somehow tell me more clearly that he's feverish, as if his soaked shirt and hot skin haven't already made that clear.

"Mags, you're burning up."

He lifts his head weakly. "Something smells wrong," he says. And now that he mentions it, I can smell it even over the acrid smell of sick. Infection.

I look at his chest. The wounds above his collarbone have leaked dark red through his beige t-shirt, right through the bandages. And not just red, but a poisonous greeny-yellow fluid, too. That's what smells. I carefully place my hand over them and the heat is worse.

"How – ?" I say. But it doesn't matter how. Whether his dad had something on his claws, or dirt got in the wounds, or who knows what, Magne's wounds are infected, and bad. And he's feverish and throwing up.

He leans over the sink again, heaves, but only water comes up. Foam. He pants from the effort.

Hell, what do I do? I can't take him to the emergency room. I don't know any doctors. If I'd needed a doctor, I'd have asked Magne, and that route is closed. Or I'd have asked Liam, but Liam's dead. Evgeny? No, not

Ev. Ev's not coming back.

So that leaves Wolfram. Again.

I kiss Magne's forehead, feel the heat coming off him, and go looking for my phone. As I look, I pull yesterday's clothes back on. I find Magne's phone before I find mine, and as I wake it up, I hope Wolfram doesn't mind being awakened at… I check the time… seven in the morning. He doesn't seem like a morning person. Too bad.

I dial and wait. And wait. It goes to voicemail. "Fuck." I pace, undecided, and then dial again with the same result.

On the third try, Wolfram's voice answers, sleepy and irritated. "This better be an emergency, Magne."

"It's Su. And yes. Yes, I do think it's an emergency."

Chapter Sixteen

Once again, I find myself half-dragging Magne to his truck, only this time, he's *really* in no condition to drive. He's barely conscious and when he does wake enough to take a few steps on his own, he keeps having to stop to retch. Nothing is left in him to come up, which is good.

I hope it's good.

I found a plastic washbasin in the kitchen and brought it along, and when I've got Magne loaded in the passenger seat and belted in I put it in his lap. I don't think he'd be too happy if something *did* come up and he got vomit all over his lovingly-restored cab.

Then I get behind the wheel, buckle the lap belt, and shove the clutch in. The seat's too far back, but I don't know how to move it and I'm too anxious anyway, so I loosen the belt and slide to the edge of the seat. I turn the key, and nothing happens.

"Shit," I say.

"Foot to the floor." Magne says, so quietly I'm not sure what he says at first.

"What?" I look at my feet.

"Here," he says, and reaches forward to push down on my knee. I shove the clutch harder and it moves a little. He slumps back in his seat. "Try it now."

I turn the key again and this time the engine turns over immediately and settles into a deep rumble.

"Okay," I say. "I can do this. How hard can it be?" I glance over at Magne and his eyes are closed. His breathing is shallow and harsh. "Fuck."

I wrestle with the stick and get it back into first, then ease off on the clutch and on with the gas at the same time. The engine roars and I grit my teeth and just keep going. The truck lurches but doesn't stall, and then we're pulling away from the curb.

"Second," says Magne. I thought he had passed out, and really, he doesn't exactly sound awake.

I hesitate.

"Straight back," he says, voice hardly audible over the engine. "Clutch in first." If I didn't have super fox woman hearing, I probably wouldn't have known he said anything.

I push the clutch in, shift to second, and the shifter slides to where it should be way more smoothly than I thought it would. We lurch again when I let out the clutch, but we're still moving.

"Good thing the dock is downhill," I say, but Magne doesn't respond. He stays quiet while I struggle with third gear and take the corner onto River Road way too fast.

I'm pretty sure I should be shifting again – don't most cars have at least four gears? – but there's nowhere else I can see to shift to, except reverse. I'm too scared to look at the diagram on the shift knob for more than a quick glance, so I just keep going until we get to the Wonder Island ferry parking lot. Then I push the clutch in and take the corner in neutral and coast into the spot closest to the loading ramp. It's marked "Reserved," but I don't care. I'll pay the ticket if I have to. I'll pay a hundred tickets.

I turn off the engine and put on the emergency brake and take a deep breath. I didn't kill us. I didn't irreparably damage Magne's truck.

He stirs feebly on the seat next to me. "Park in first, love," he says, so I push in the clutch and shove the stick to first. I'm kind of afraid to take my foot off the clutch, but of course the engine's not running, so nothing happens. "I knew you could do it," Magne says. He sounds like he's in pain. His eyes are closed and he's a sort of greenish color in the early morning sun.

A tap on my window makes me jump, and I reach for the knob to crank it open. A tall, skinny guy in a tailcoat is standing there, a top hat under his arm. He hands me a bright green square of cardboard.

"Put this on your dash so the guys don't tow you," he says. I look at the card. "Director's Guest," it says. I put it on the dash and fumble with my seatbelt.

"Boat's just docking now, ma'am," Mr Tailcoat says.

"Can you help me with him?"

"I'll try."

The guy doesn't look like much except skinny but he's surprisingly strong and actually takes most of Magne's weight. I grab Magne's clothes from last night off the seat and shove them under my arm and then put my other arm around Magne.

It's slow going, and we almost drop him more than once, but by the time we get to the ramp, the boat has docked and a giant of a man is stepping off.

And I really do mean giant. Like, this guy would make Magne's brother Thorstein look dainty. He's also extremely ugly, with a big nose that looks like it's been mashed flat many times and bulging eyes, but there's something about him that makes me immediately want to trust him. I bet animals and small children love him.

"I'm Troll," he says. I resist the urge to ask if that's a name or a description. "Guessing you're Su. The fox girl." He sticks out his hand.

"Mr Troll," I say. "Thank you." I watch as my hand disappears in his grip. He shakes my hand very gently.

"Just Troll. No mister. Now let's get this boy to t'island." And he scoops Magne up in his arms like he's a small child and not a full-grown — and not at all small — werewolf. The boat starts to move almost before the ramp is pulled up behind us. Troll waits by the rail with Magne in his arms and I perch awkwardly on a bench nearby.

No one speaks, but it doesn't feel weird. Like, I don't talk a lot, but I always feel like I *should*, like people get weirded out if I'm just quiet. Evgeny, Alex, Magne never made me feel that way, though, and neither does Troll.

I'm on edge because I'm afraid for Magne, but not having that added social anxiety is nice. Not having to pretend to be conversational makes the trip across the river that much easier, and under other circumstances it might have been enjoyable.

Troll's stepping up to the ramp before I even realize we've arrived and strides off up the hill as soon as it's safe. I have to trot to keep up.

The carnival isn't open yet, but there's a lot of activity and lots of curious glances. I expect hostility, but everyone who meets my eye gives me a friendly nod or an encouraging smile, and not a single person appears unfriendly.

Wolfram's sister is waiting for us at the door of the staff building. "The guest suite, please, Troll," she says. "Wolfram and Bethy are waiting." She puts a hand on Magne's forehead as Troll passes and murmurs something that sounds like, "Hang on, little brother." To me, she says, "Try not to worry; he'll be in good hands." I nod and attempt to smile, then hurry to catch up with Troll.

I don't know how many flights of stairs we trudge up – or *I* trudge; Troll doesn't seem even a tiny bit winded – but it seems endless. Finally, we come out in a hall and there's an open door in the middle of it and Wolfram is there. He ushers us in, has Troll put Magne on a huge bed at the far end of the room under an even more huge window. "Thanks," he says.

"Not a problem," says Troll. He pats the top of my head, musses my hair like I'm a little kid, then leaves.

When I turn back, a short, strong-looking woman in a long green tunic is bending over Magne and shaking her head.

"Tell us what happened," Wolfram says, so I recount, probably in more detail than necessary, the events of last night. I include the vandalization of Magne's truck and the photographs, and – blushing fiercely – the fact that we had sex, not because I think it's relevant, but because I don't know *what's* relevant and I don't want to miss anything.

While I talk, the healer strips Magne's shirt off, ignoring his surprised hiss of pain, and peels away the bandages.

"Well, fuck," she says, and Wolfram looks taken aback, like maybe he doesn't hear her swear much.

"Is it bad?" I ask. I sit on the other side of the bed. I want to take

Magne's hand, to touch him so I can feel that he's still alive, but I don't want to get in the way.

"It's not good," she says. "Not good at all."

She pokes one of the wounds and yellowish pus leaks out. Magne moans but doesn't open his eyes.

"I need to clean the infection out," the healer says. She looks at me, then at Wolfram. "I'll need both of you. It's going to hurt very much."

Wolfram nods. "Tell me what to do."

"Sit him up," she says. It takes all three of us to get him there and keep him there because Magne doesn't – can't – help at all.

Bethy points to Wolfram. "Get behind him. Hold him around the torso, and try to keep his arms pinned if you can."

Wolfram does as he's told. "My arms aren't long enough," he says. "He's a rather strapping lad."

"Just keep him upright. And you –" she turns to me, "– sit next to him, talk to him. If he comes to, get him to look at you. Tell him to focus on you, not on the pain."

I take Magne's head in my hands, one palm on each side of his face, support it so it's not lolling forward onto his chest, and his eyes blink open.

"Hey buddy," I say.

He looks at me, squints, blinks. I think he's having trouble focusing his eyes. "Su?"

"You know it," I say.

He tries to smile.

"Hang in there, Mags," I say. "Everything's going to be okay."

He licks his lips. His voice sounds like he needs a glass of water. "Why do I get the impression things are going to get worse before they get better? And how come I can't move?"

"Wolfram's holding you still. Can't have you knocking out the healer while she's trying to help you."

He shifts slightly, like he's testing Wolfram's grip. "Old man sure is strong," he says, in that raspy, desperately tired voice.

"The old man is right here," says Wolfram.

"I know." Now Magne does manage a smile, a brief and fleeting one.

The healer comes back with a steaming basin and a pile of cloths.

Magne watches her. "This is going to hurt, isn't it?"

"Quite possibly more than anything else you've felt before."

"Worse than having your intestines ripped out by your favorite brother?"

Bethy's eyes widen but she says, "I expect it might."

"Oh, well. I'm always up for a new experience." Then she reaches out and presses a thumb on each side of one of the infected wounds. Pus gushes out and Magne's eyes roll back and I think his dead weight is going to be too much. But we hold him.

"Good," says the healer, turning her head from the stench of the infection seeping out of Magne's chest. "I was hoping he'd pass out."

When she's got as much out of the wounds as she can, Wolfram and I ease Magne back down on the bed so she can apply a poultice that smells almost as bad as the infection.

"Let him sleep," she says. "Go get something to eat. I'll send someone if you're needed." It takes a minute for me to realize she's talking to both of us conscious people.

I kiss Magne's sweaty forehead – he's still burning with fever – and reluctantly follow Wolfram out the door.

"I've had breakfast sent up to the roof," Wolfram says, taking my hand to lead me to the stairs. "There isn't much else we can do for now."

I can't eat much, and end up just shredding some very nice pastries with my fingers. The tea is good, though, and I'm on my second cup when Wolfram says, "What did you say Geri and Freki told Thorgrim?"

At first I can't remember who Thorgrim is. Right, Magne's dad. Last night already seems so far away and the panicky feeling in my guts is distracting. Finally I dredge the words out of my memory, more or less.

"They said they claimed him. Magne. That Magne runs with their pack now."

"Interesting." I glance up at Wolfram and he's staring out over the forest. "I would have thought they'd consult me before making such a declaration. If I had to guess, I'd say it's just as much that the House, the Island itself, has laid claim to our Magne."

By the way he says "our Magne," I'd guess myself that the House isn't the only one. I think Wolfram really is starting to see Magne as a son. I wonder if he ever had any kids of his own, and if so, where they are.

"When Sgian first led me to him," I say, "he was fighting his brothers. I used my… well I have this way I can extend my senses, sort of, to feel the forest and all the life in it. I have to concentrate, so I can't really manage it while I'm moving."

Wolfram doesn't turn from the view, but I can tell he's listening.

"I stopped before I reached them, so I could see what I was walking into. One of his brothers… he didn't look right."

Now he does look at me. "How?"

"I see living things as glowing. Werewolves are steady lights, not super bright, but deep, kind of. And Magne's brother looked… out of focus. And way too intense, with this sickly yellow sort of crackle. Like he might suddenly flare up and burn out."

Wolfram's voice is soft. "I had heard one of Thorgrim Thorvaldson's sons was a *berserkr*. They used to say *berserkrs* were chosen by Wotan, but now, well, the gods don't take much interest in the middle realm these days."

"And yet Odin's wolves came to our rescue last night."

"So they did."

"You sent them?"

He nods and stares back out over the trees, looking thoughtful. "And how did Magne look, to your expanded senses?"

I find myself blushing, with no reason for it. "He looked strong and steady. Deep and rich." Wolfram turns back to me again, something in his grey eyes intensely curious.

"Green. His glow was green like the deep forest. But there was a flickering, crackly blue light in the heart of him." I look right into Wolfram's eyes. "It's how I see magic, when I use that way of looking."

"And this is new?" Understanding, I think, is growing in his eyes.

I nod. "The last time I saw Magne when I used my fox senses was in the winter, when we went north to confront the demon-ghost."

"And he looked like a normal werewolf."

"Stronger than his packmates, maybe, but yeah. No blue crackle."

"Something has changed him."

"You think it's this island, don't you?"

He doesn't answer, when he does speak, he says, "And how do you see me, with your fox senses?"

"I haven't looked," I say.

He regards me steadily without speaking, so I unfocus my seeing eyes, and let my senses expand. And am almost blinded by intense white light so strong I can see nothing at all in it, not even the magic that I know has to be there.

When I can see again, he's got a cheeky grin on his face.

"That wasn't nice," I say.

"I promise, I didn't know."

I narrow my eyes at him.

"I swear," he says. Then, "I do suspect the Island has something to do with the magic you see in Magne. It's why I took you to the House. I hoped it would communicate with him, with both of you, let you know what it intends."

"It just kind of welcomed us."

He sighs, then gets up and paces towards the edge of the roof where he stands and stares into space. "I think the Island wants him for purposes of its own. To belong here, to be one of its denizens."

"Is that a good thing or a bad thing?"

He shakes his head. "I don't know. The Island is not a malevolent place, nor is the House a malevolent entity. It gives us shelter and in return we keep its secrets safe, protect its borders and each other. But not all of its gifts are welcome, even if they are not ill-intended." He steps away from the edge of the roof and takes me by the shoulders. "I worry that bringing him here, while saving his life, may make him more vulnerable to whatever plan the House has for him. If it's a plan he welcomes, then all the better."

"But if it's a plan he doesn't want?"

He sighs and drops his hands. "Let us hope that is not the case."

I'm saved from having to come up with something to say to that by the arrival of the healer, Bethy, on the roof. She looks tired, and gratefully accepts a cup of tea and a chair.

"He's resting comfortably," she says. "Or as comfortably as can be."

She takes a long sip of tea.

"The infection?" asks Wolfram.

"The poultice is working. I'll have to change it a time or two more, I think, but it's drawing the infection out. I'll feel better once his fever has broken, but I've got cold cloths and ice packs on him."

"He'll be okay?" I say. I realize I have a death grip on my teacup, so I put it carefully on the table with the remains of breakfast.

She smiles. "It's not over yet, but yes, I believe he will. Thanks to your quick action in bringing him here." She takes another sip of tea and sighs in contentment. "Not that I have treated many *other* kind, but he seems very strong for a werewolf, yet he doesn't look old enough for it. For such strength." She glances at me. "How old is he, anyway?"

Wolfram looks at me, too, and I have no idea how old Magne is. I've never really even thought about it. I mean I know when his birthday is – July twenty-fifth – but not the year. I shrug, but I know I'm blushing fiercely.

"I guess it never came up."

Wolfram almost manages not to smile. "He seems the equivalent of perhaps thirty, in human terms, I'd say. For most werewolves, that would be fifty or sixty. But Magne was born a werewolf, and I have no idea how that would affect his aging."

"I've seen photos of him as a kid," I say, feeling more and more embarrassed I can't answer such a simple question about the man I'm crazy for. Is he really that much older than me? "He looked like he was growing up normally to me."

"So perhaps he *is* like other werewolves, then, and aged like a human until he reached maturity, more or less. Fifty or sixty seems about right then."

"Ten years is a big range," I say.

Wolfram doesn't hide his smile now. "Not when you live as long as a werewolf." He looks at me sidelong. "Or a fox woman."

Okay, so Magne *might* be twice my age, or he might not be. Quite. I'll just go with thirty in human terms.

"Definitely strong for his age," Bethy says. "But..." She frowns.

"What is it?" I say, fearing something awful, but wanting it all out in the open.

"His symbiont is not helping the healing as much as I would have thought, especially considering his unusual strength. It never should have allowed the infection to get so bad, and the infection should not have progressed so rapidly."

"Something is fighting his symbiont?" Wolfram asks. He meets my eyes and I see his worry.

"I don't like to speculate without accurate testing, but I think something is not only fighting his symbiont, it's eliminating it."

Chapter Seventeen

I FOLLOW THE healer back down when she finishes her tea, and when she goes to make a fresh poultice she hands me a bowl of cold water with a cloth floating in it.

"Any bare skin," she says. And I must look stunned because she has to add, "To help cool him off," before I realize she's telling me to sponge the water on Magne's hot skin. To keep the fever from cooking him alive.

I perch on the bed and set the bowl on the nightstand. I realize, as I'm wiping cool water onto Magne's face, that having something to do, some action instead of just sitting and waiting, is calming me. I don't feel quite so crazy with worry.

He makes a noise in his throat but doesn't wake, so I keep sponging him, moving down his neck to his chest. It's a weird feeling, this completely intimate but not at all sexual action. I could sit here and do this forever, if it weren't for the fact that he's desperately ill.

"Is it okay if I move his arms?" I ask when Bethy comes back with fresh herbs to spread on the wounds.

She raises an eyebrow.

"I thought, the cool water. Because armpits get hot." I'm feeling really dumb, but then she smiles and nods.

"Let me help." She gets the dressings changed and helps me gently lift

Magne's arms away from his sides so I can trickle cool water into his armpits.

He sighs and Bethy's smile grows.

"Yes, I do think that's helped." She lifts his head just enough to pull out the icepack under his neck. "I'll go fetch a new one," she says. "Keep sponging. It's making a difference."

When she leaves, I pull the sheet down to keep wiping cool water on Magne. Bethy put a towel over his nether bits for modesty (as if Magne *has* any modesty) and I decide to keep him covered. Best not to get distracted.

I carry on with his legs, and hell, I've pretty much kissed and licked and sucked on every part of this man's body, but somehow I feel like I'm learning the shape of him all over again. And he's beautiful. Not angelic, unearthly, like Evgeny. But grounded, wild, like a forest is beautiful. Even his hairiness can't diminish his beauty like I once thought it did.

I reach his feet, wipe cool water onto his soles and start working my way back up again. When I reach his belly, I glance up and his eyes are open.

"Hey," I say.

"Hey love." He licks his lips. "Can I have some water?"

There's a glass with a straw in it next the bowl on the nightstand. It's full, but tepid. Maybe it's best not to give him cold water, anyway. You're not supposed to give really cold water to sick people, anyway. I think. I hold it for him and he sips. Not much, but even that effort seems to tire him. I put the glass down and lay the wet cloth over his forehead.

"That feels nice." His voice sounds a little less raspy, at least. I touch his cheek and he doesn't react, so I guess he's asleep again. Or unconscious.

I hear Bethy come back but I don't turn from watching Magne sleep.

"Troll wants to talk to you," she says.

"What for?"

She tucks the fresh ice pack under Magne's neck, then removes the cloth from his face to press the back of her hand to his forehead.

"Fever seems to have gone down a bit. Not enough, but some." She wets the cloth again and returns it to Magne's forehead, pulls it down to cover his eyes. "He didn't say, but you'll find him in the menagerie. Best not keep him waiting."

I don't move and she looks up at me. "Your wolf is going to be fine," she says. "I admit I was worried, but he's doing fine." I think about how she just said his fever hasn't gone down enough and wonder if she's just trying to keep me from worrying. It won't work, but all I can do now is wait, and I hate waiting.

Alex and I went to Troll's Menagerie once, when we visited Wonder Island to escape demon-induced nightmares. She felt bad for the animals, but I figured a lot of them wouldn't survive wild, so maybe it wasn't so bad.

And I have to say, the four-legged chicken seems quite happy to rule the place from her nest box in one corner. She pops out to greet me, then scurries away when she senses the fox in me. The place looks pretty much the same with its albino snakes – at least one of them with two heads – a really tiny tortoise sharing space with a really huge one (two members of the same species, the label assures me), and a tank of two-tailed fish. But I'm not here to gawk, and I don't see Troll.

There's a door at the back that's half open so I head there and sure enough, I find the huge man on the other side, sitting at a desk and poking at the keyboard of an ancient looking desktop computer. Two very large cats and one very small one are perched on various parts of his person.

"Wanted to show you a thing," he says. "If you're up for a hike."

"What thing?" One of the cats – the tiny one – climbs down from Troll's shoulder and walks across the desk to stare at me. I hold out my hand for her to sniff and to my surprise she butts my fingers with her tiny head, asking to be petted. I oblige and she begins to purr, unbelievably loud for her tiny size.

"Cat are usually nervous around me," I say, stroking her ridiculously soft fur in wonder.

"Raised around carnies and sideshow freaks," Troll says, a smile spreading over his face. And, no lie, the expression almost makes him handsome, squashed nose, pockmarks and all. "And things much stranger than a fox girl." Then he goes serious again. "The place I found your sister's things. Won't be nowt to see now the polis gone over it, but Wolfram thought you might want to see anyway."

No doubt he thought, at least partly, that it would help keep me from losing my shit while Magne's trapped in bed, unconscious.

"Yes, thank you," I say, scratching the cat under the chin. I swear her purr gets even louder. "Is it far?" The tiny cat pins my hand to the desk then walks up my arm to rub against my face.

"You want a cat?" Troll says, smiling again. "You come ask me."

"Um…" I say.

"She likes you." He stands up, displacing the other two cats, who look irritated and retreat into the outer room. He plucks the cat off of me and puts her in a basket under his desk. "It's a good hike," he says. "But I can take you a shortcut. Hour maybe."

So not quite a quick walk, but really not that far of a hike.

"South end of island," he says.

"You can walk all the way to the end of the island in an hour?" I try to picture the shape of Wonder Island as I saw it from the roof. It seemed a lot bigger than that. In fact, from there it looked a whole lot bigger than it did from the mainland shore.

Troll grins and taps the side of his nose. "Shortcut," he says. "Through t'ouse."

"The House," I say. "Of course."

The way he leads me through the stone halls shouldn't even get us to the other side of the building but when we step out the door he opens, there's the river, and we've come out beneath a ruined bridge with a little cabin tucked under what remains of its span.

"My vacation house," Troll says and chuckles. Then, "Don't look back. Unless you want to get dizzy." So of course I look back, at the door opening into the space behind the bridge supports, which is, impossibly, also the House. I'm suddenly so lightheaded I almost fall. "Told you," says Troll, as he catches me.

"Yeah," I say. There's no sign of the House from this side, save the dark stone hallway I glimpse before Troll closes the door. "Just like fucking Narnia," I say. Magne would be so proud of me for having read a book.

Troll laughs again. "Just up this way."

Just up this way takes most of an hour to walk to. I'm expecting to walk along the river bank, but most of the way the trees grow right down to the water and lean out over it. So instead we follow narrow meandering paths through the woods. I'm glad Troll is there, because if I was here by myself I'd be hopelessly lost, even with the sound of the river like a constant white noise off to my right.

Then we come out on a sort of beach and I have to stop and stare. The light sparkles on the water and the trees are still bright green in their spring finery and seem to glow. The shore is gravelly and bare, like sometimes the water washes away anything that grows. There's a huge rough-hewn chair sitting right at the end of the gravel, facing out over the water.

"There." Troll points to a place where the river, when it was higher, undercut the bank and left a ridge of bare dirt and gravel. It looks like people have been digging there. I police, I guess, looking for more clues. I can see signs of disturbance all over the area, now that I know to look. And Troll was right, natural beauty aside, there's nothing here to see.

"I'm guessing you didn't bring the police here through the house," I say, talking to cover my disappointment. I really don't know what I hoped to find, but at least I won't be tormented by thoughts that I *could* have found something no one did.

"Nope. By river. They have boats."

I sigh and pick my way over the gravel. I poke the toe of my boot into the space where the garbage bag would have been, then wander upstream to the huge chair.

"Like to sit here, sometimes," Troll says. "Never thought there was a thing there, till fox dug it up. Then I told Wolfram right off. He called polis."

"A fox?" I doubt it's a magical fox, a creature that could maybe tell me more about what I am, what I can do. But this *is* Wonder Island, so you never know.

"Mm," he says. "Used to see them over the east side fair bit. Foxes like the fae folk and the 'digenous spirits better than the likes of me and the carnival folk." He laughs. "But last few months a young kit's been hanging around. Reckon she smelled the jerky and candy and dug up your sister's things to get them." He looks out at the river. "I'm awful sorry 'bout your family," he says.

"Me too," I say. "But it's old hurt. I'm okay." Or I would be, if I knew what happened to my sister. I sit in the chair and stare upriver. I don't want to leave Magne any longer than I have to, but I also don't want to head back without finding *something*.

"What's upriver?" I ask.

Troll walks over to stand next to the chair, shades his eyes, and looks. It's like having a mountain with legs walking around. "They find your dad up that way, yeah?"

"Yeah. And Mum here on the Island."

"Down near the dock, it was," he says, softly. "Up there's park on the west side, out past the city. East side were industrial, once. Mostly abandoned, now."

I sit up. Abandoned factories sound like exactly where you might find vampires lurking, if they wanted to get out of the city. And yeah, it's a movie cliché, but vamps are pretty much one big cliché after another.

"Anything on the river? With a dock maybe?"

"Surely is," says Troll, and by his voice I think he's catching on. "Couple places. Most intact is old glass factory. Took out all the kilns and all, long time gone, but buildings all still there." He stoops and plucks something out of the gravel and hands it to me. It's a fragment of pale green glass, tumbled smooth by the river like a semi-precious stone. "Sometime find some real pretty ones," he says.

"I think I'll have to pay this factory a visit," I say.

"You be careful," he says. "Don't you go alone."

But I'm going to have to, aren't I, because Magne's in no shape to go confront murderous vampires, and Alex is in Germany. And who else would go with me?

I don't say that, though. I just say, "I'll be careful." And then I have to catch my breath, because when I turn to look back at the Island, a little pointed, furry red face with bright greenish-brown eyes is watching me from the undergrowth.

"Troll?"

"Mm?"

"Is that your young fox?"

He goes still, turns slowly, and looks where I'm looking. "'Tis," he says.

"Why's she staring at me?"

"She's curious. And you smell like a fox, some. But you don't look like one."

"Hey little fox," I say. "I see you." I let my senses expand, slowly, carefully. If this is a magic fox, maybe looking at her with my fox senses might scare her. Or she might not even notice. I haven't really figured out if those I see when I use my expanded senses are aware of being seen. I mean, most – I think – are oblivious, but some might notice.

She doesn't react when my senses reach far enough to touch her; she just keeps staring. That doesn't necessarily mean she doesn't *know*, though.

Troll is a glow not unlike Magne's, which surprises me, though I'm not sure why. He looks deep green with blue sparks, but he feels absolutely *ancient*. And I think, though I don't know how I know, that he could disappear from my seeing entirely, if he wanted to. Like ancient old vampy Karasu.

The fox is a bright spark of fire, like the *hexenfuchs* I met in Germany. Does that mean this fox is a *hexenfuchs*? I spread my awareness wider, try to catch an ordinary animal so I can compare, but I don't know if there *are* any ordinary animals on Wonder Island. I mean, there must be, right? Hell, I wouldn't really be surprised to learn that everything here is magic in some way.

But I *have* felt ordinary animals before, ordinary foxes even. What were they like? Just glows. No sparks, not much in the way of color. So she must be *hexenfuchs*.

I must make some sound, because she twitches her ears, crouches like she's about to run.

Troll makes a crooning sound deep in his throat and she relaxes.

"Sorry," I whisper. "She's a *hexenfuchs*," I say. "She's like me, a little bit."

"Is she?" says Troll. "S'pose I should've seen it. But animals are equal far as I'm concerned."

We stare, unmoving, one small fox, one fox woman, one huge man. Then the fox creeps closer, belly to the ground, ears pricked.

"Hey there, little one," Troll says, his voice a soft rumble. He slowly crouches, holds out his hand. She creeps forward a little more.

I don't move, don't speak. Animals trust Troll. Most of them don't like me. Except Troll's tiny cat. And Odin's wolves and ravens. And Sgian, but she only wears the shape of an animal. Okay, *some* animals like me. The *hexenfuchs* in Germany liked me. He appeared to me in dreamspace like a handsome human man (who looked a little too much like my dad to be sexy), and spoke to me in a human voice. Unfortunately, I was out cold when it happened, so I can't exactly replicate that here.

But maybe… when I first turned into a fox I got stuck that way, and before I learned to use my human voice, I figured out I could sort of *think* at people. First it was just Alex, which worked because she's a witch and has mental abilities of her own.

But I did it with Magne, just last night (how can that have only been last night?) as he faced down his brothers. And he had been able to *think* back, even if it was faint.

Will it startle her, though? Me suddenly communicating in a way she's not used to? What if she's the only *hexenfuchs* on the Island and doesn't know how to communicate that way?

I push more energy into my fox senses and her ears twitch. I can feel her more strongly now, her presence sharp and clear, bright with magic that's more like flame than the usual blue crackle.

Does that mean she's a different kind of being than other magical folk? But Alex is green like the plants she's so good with, so maybe I just haven't encountered very many different types of magic with my fox senses yet.

I can tell she's female, and young, not yet full grown. I can tell she's very aware of me, and curious, but nervous. She wants to creep closer to Troll, to let him scratch behind her ears and under her chin. She recognizes him as the nice man who mended a hawk's wing once, who let a family of mice live in an old blanket next to the chimney in his cottage, and who sits sometimes in the chair I'm in, staring out over the water, lost in thought.

Me, she's not sure of. She recognizes me as being like her, but my human shape, my almost human smell superimposed over my fox scent confuses her. And she doesn't like being confused.

I keep very still, let my fox senses fade, and she creeps closer to Troll again. She emerges from the brush onto the gravel, and her tail waves from side to side, the white tip like a flag. I have a tail like that. Foxes communicate with their tails as much as anything else. And I'm wearing sweats with a hole in the butt so I *can* have my tail showing. So I take a chance, let it manifest, let my eyes turn slit-pupiled.

The young fox freezes, looks at me. I wave my tail, slowly. I'm not sure how much she can see, what with me sitting in the chair.

She cocks her head, looks at me, then half-pounces forward, landing with her front half in a crouch and her butt in the air with that fluffy tail sticking straight up, just the tip twitching.

I grin. "Playful, are you?" I wave my tail again, more vigorously.

Troll stares at me, then looks back at the fox, then at me again.

"Forgot you could put on a fox tail," he says.

"A whole fox shape, too, "I say.

"Might be you could talk to her that way," he says. "Eventually she trusts you."

I grin wider and shift on the chair and all at once she's wary again, crouching, ears back, creeping backwards.

"Wait," I say. And suddenly she spins and vanishes into the forest. And I do that stupid thing where I act without thinking, and I'm running after her in fox shape, hardly hearing Troll as he calls after me.

"Don't chase her," he says. "There's things on this Island won't be friendly to you, even do you belong here."

Chapter Eighteen

SHE'S FAST, the young *hexenfuchs*, but I'm faster, even though she has the advantage of knowing the terrain. I don't really want to chase her, just to catch up to her. See if she can communicate, if she's maybe seen anyone on the Island that shouldn't be here, if she saw who brought that garbage bag of my sister's things, assuming it didn't just wash up on the shore.

So I don't *try* to catch her, just follow, and when she lets me, I run alongside her. I think she realizes, seeing my fox shape, that I don't mean her any harm. So she slows and then suddenly we're tussling, play-fighting, snapping and leaping away and I want to laugh. It's like having a little sister again.

Finally, we stop and get a drink at a tiny stream with the clearest, coldest water I've ever had, and we lounge in a patch of sunlight.

Very carefully, trying to keep my thoughts gentle, I *think* at her. *Hey, little fox, my name's Su.*

She lifts her head from her paws and looks at me.

Do you understand me? I try. I mean, *hexenfuchs* are basically just foxes with magic. I don't really know if she'll be able to understand me, because as far as I know, it requires a witch to teach a *hexenfuchs* how to take human shape. It probably takes a witch to teach them human words, too.

She cocks her head, studying me, like she's thinking.

And then again, the *hexenfuchs* I met in Germany wasn't a witch's familiar, and had more ordinary than magical fox ancestry, but he was still able to use human speech in dreamspace.

That's okay, I think at her. *I'm glad to have met you anyway.* I look around and realize I have no idea where I am, and even less idea of how to get back to the gravel riverbank or the ruined bridge. And that's assuming Troll waited for me after I ran off like an idiot. It's going to be a very long trip back to the carnival and the afternoon isn't getting any younger.

Human, she thinks, and I whip my head around so fast she scoots away from me a little.

Me? No. Hexenfuchs, like you.

She sits up, cocks her head the other way. *Fox, but not fox.*

That's right, I think. *I have a human shape and a fox shape. But I'm the same me.*

She shakes her head, scratches an ear.

I get to my feet and stretch. *Can you help me get back to Troll? To the big man?*

She stands, too. *Like the big man. He's kind.*

He's probably worried because I ran off.

Follow, she thinks, and trots away with purpose.

I sure hope she's leading me back to the river, and not deeper into the woods. I mean, I want to get to know her; maybe we can both learn more about what it means to be *hexenfuchs*. But the last thing I need is everyone out looking for me. And now that the excitement has worn off, worry for Magne is gnawing at my guts again.

Have you seen any strangers? I think at the young fox. *People who don't belong?*

She makes a motion that almost looks like a shrug, pauses to wait for me to catch up. *All strange here.*

I almost laugh, and wouldn't *that* freak her out, my human laugh coming out of my fox face? *That's true.* And anyway, we're talking about things that happened years ago. *Hexenfuchs* have longer lifespans than regular foxes, but she's young enough it still could have happened before she was born.

The landscape is just starting to maybe look like somewhere I might have been recently when a familiar black bundle of feathers drops though the branches and lands in front of me. The fox shies and scurries under a bush, but doesn't run away.

"Su!" says Sgian, her voice sounding as much like cawing as speech. She flicks her wings into place on her back and fixes me with one beady eye. "Ol' Troll-face is frantic," she says. "Thinks you're lost to the fair folk or some such." She turns her head to look at me from the other eye. "And your hunky werewolf's very unhappy papa just showed up at the dock."

"Wait, Magne's dad is *here*?" The words burst out without thinking, but the little fox just looks at me curiously.

Sgian follows my gaze. "Oh, hey kid," she says, and the fox lolls her tongue out.

"You know her?" I say.

"Sure. I don't spend all my time running messages for His Short and Mighty," Sgian says. "I've seen this one around."

She hops closer and gently pokes the end of my nose with her beak. "Wolfram said to bring you back as quickly as possible."

"Okay, lead the way. I'll be fastest in fox shape."

"No," says Sgian, "You'll be *lighter* in fox shape." Then she sort of pounces, and curls her wings around me and the whole world shifts sickeningly, and lurches, and suddenly I'm on a stone floor and I can smell Magne, and herbs, and Wolfram, and I don't dare open my eyes or I might throw up.

"Apologies for the rather dizzying mode of travel," Wolfram says. "You do get used to it eventually."

"I could do this all day," says Sgian.

"You couldn't, even if I returned your powers to you permanently," Wolfram says drily.

"Fine," Sgian says. "But I'd do it a lot. That was fucking awesome. I'd forgotten how much."

"Your help is appreciated, Sgian."

"Yes," I say, cracking one eye open. I almost say, "Thank you," but remember just in time that you're not supposed to thank the Fair Folk, and Sgian, as *sidhe*, is definitely Fair Folk, even if she is trapped in the shape of a crow. Just in time, I change it to, "Most appreciated." I open my other eye, and discover I'm back in human shape – with clothes on, fortunately, and I'm crouched on the floor of Magne's sick room. I get carefully to my feet, steadying myself with a hand on the back of a nearby chair.

"And thank you for returning," Wolfram says to me. "Sgian, would you mind letting Troll know our wayward fox is back safe?"

"Sure thing, boss." And Sgian leaps for the open window and is gone.

Wolfram looks back at me and I suddenly feel like I have to produce an explanation, like the time my dad caught me sneaking back in my bedroom window when I was sixteen. "There was a fox," I say. "A *hexenfuchs*. I didn't think, I just followed her."

He raises an eyebrow. "You needn't explain," he says. "Only keep in mind that this island can be dangerous for the unwary. Had you been human, you would not likely have made it back safely, or unchanged."

"I'll be more careful," I say, instead of the cheeky, "Good thing I'm not human," that first comes to mind. Then I remember the reason for the hasty journey. "Sgian said something about Magne's father?"

"I've had him detained at the dock, but Thea will bring him here shortly."

"What does he want? He pretty clearly disowned Magne last night. *He* caused those wounds." I gesture angrily at Magne, unconscious on the bed. At least his color looks a little better, and the sheen of sweat is gone.

"I know," Wolfram says quietly.

"He tried to *kill* Magne. To… to… he told his… Magne's brother to…" I'm so mad I can't make the words form proper sentences. I try to reach for calm, to make myself breathe like my kung fu teacher taught me, but the anger lingers and won't be soothed.

Wolfram puts a hand on my arm and my first instinct is to shove him away, but it fades as he squeezes, and instead I feel comfort. I wonder if he's using some kind of magic on me.

"I *know*, child," he says. "Be very sure I will not let him try again." He looks at Magne, lying still on the bed. Too still.

"Bethy says the fever will break soon, and he'll wake. It could be some time before he has full use of his arms. He's going to have a lot of hard work ahead."

I feel my shoulders slump. Magne's been *my* rock for so long, and now, somehow, I'm going to have to be the steady one. I sit on the edge of the bed and push Magne's damp hair off of his face. His skin is still too hot, but now it's dry instead of sweaty.

"He has to be okay," I say. When Wolfram puts an arm around my shoulders, I lean into him.

"He's strong," he says.

"He's also…" I pause.

"Vulnerable," says Wolfram. I nod. "He cares deeply, and I think this situation with his family has hurt him more than he lets on."

"Yeah," I say, trying to keep my voice from breaking on that one simple word.

"I was reluctant to even let Thorgrim off the boat," he says. "But what right do I have to keep a father from his ailing son?" I start to protest and he puts a finger against my lips. "I *know*," he says. "I know." Then he sighs. "But we also need to know what Thorgrim wants, what he intends to *do*." He makes a chopping motion with his free hand. "*Otherly* werewolves aren't much of a threat on their own, but if he should mobilize his pack against us, it would be… unpleasant."

"I don't think he'd do that. Would he? For a son he doesn't even want?"

Wolfram laughs softly, humorlessly. "I think he may have exaggerated his rejection of Magne somewhat. But let us hope you are right."

"Wait," I say, turning to look at him better. "You said *otherly* werewolves like there's another kind."

He smiles, but this time there's real amusement in the quirk of his lips. "Karasu would have us all believe his progeny are the only kind of vampires and werewolves in existence," he says.

"But he's wrong?"

"Not so much wrong as … dismissive."

I'm about to ask more when Magne stirs under my hand. When I look at him, his eyes are open, squinting against the dim light.

"Hey, buddy," I say.

His eyes shift to Wolfram. "Why is your arm around my girlfriend?"

he says.

Wolfram laughs. "I'm glad to see you returning to your old self." He pats my shoulder and drops his arm.

"I have a wicked fucking headache," Magne says.

I bite my lip, and say, "Your dad's coming."

"He what?" Magne struggles to sit up and I push him back down. It says a lot that he barely resists. I hope it doesn't mean he *can't* resist. "Fucking hell. Is he going to sic Thorstein on me again?"

I look at Wolfram, who says, "He came alone, demanding to see his son."

"Last time he saw me, he said I was no son of his. Why the fuck is he here?" He starts to cough so I get the glass of water, help him sip. He slumps back against the pillows, looking too pale.

A sharp tap at the door draws our attention. Magne tries to sit up again, and Wolfram says sharply, "Stay!"

I feel a push of magic, hear Magne's sharp intake of breath, and stare at Wolfram as he rubs his left eye.

"I'm sorry," he says. "I shouldn't have done that."

"Damn right you shouldn't," Magne says, but there's no force, no anger behind his words.

"You're too weak to get up," Wolfram says. "Let Thorgrim see what he's done to you."

"I do *not* want to be weak in front of him." Magne's teeth are clenched, and he's panting, trying to sit up again, and it's draining him. After a moment he sinks back to the bed. "Fuck," he says.

"I know, son," says Wolfram. "But you're stronger than this. Stronger than him. I know it, you know it, Su knows it."

"*He* doesn't know it."

"If he doesn't, he will soon enough. Maybe not today, but soon."

"Fuck," Magne says again, but he doesn't try to move. Instead, he closes his eyes and lets me pull the blanket up to his chin.

Wolfram goes to the door, opens it, and doesn't move out of the way. I see Thea through the opening, her eyes stormy. She does not look at all pleased to be escorting Magne's father here.

"You will not keep me from my son." I barely recognize Magne's dad's voice, it's so full of venom. The way his words echo Wolfram's from earlier makes me uneasy.

"I don't intend to," says Wolfram mildly. "But you must know, I hold you fully responsible for his current state." Then he steps aside to let Thea in, moving to block Thorgrim again with a hand to the chest. He doesn't seem bothered by the other man's considerable height advantage.

Thea steps around the bed, touches Magne's forehead gently and says, so quietly I barely hear, "Remember little brother, there are other packs to run with."

Then Wolfram steps away from the door, positioning himself on the opposite side of the bed from Thea and me, so the only way Thorgrim can approach is from the end.

Thorgrim crosses his arms and glowers at Magne. "I didn't raise you to be a weakling," he says, his voice as much snarl as it is words.

Magne looks back at him, no emotion on his face. He looks more ill than when I first landed on the floor with Sgian; I think struggling to sit up took more out of him than it should have.

"You gave a valiant effort to not have to raise me at all," Magne says, his voice hoarse. He's keeping all emotion hidden, but something lurks there; I just can't tell what it is.

"What?" Thorgrim's nostrils flare.

I step forward, ignoring Thea's warning hand on my arm. "You tried to kill him," I say.

"I tried to make him stronger." Thorgrim's voice is a growl. His blue eyes are narrowed as he looks me over. "And who are you supposed to be?" There's no missing the contempt in his voice.

"I'm Magne's friend," I say. "I'm the one who got him home after you left his brother to murder him. Again."

"Is that so?" He takes a step closer, looking down his nose at me – and though he's not as tall as Magne, he still has three or four inches on me. I feel all three of the people at my back tense, ready in case they need to leap to my defense.

"No," says Magne. "She's my girlfriend."

Thorgrim's eyes flick from me to Magne. I know the older man's a raging homophobe, but is he racist, too? I hear the bed creak and I hope

Magne's not trying to get up again.

"You had your pick of nice girls from good werewolf families," Thorgrim says. "Any one of them a good match. And you chose this…"

"Don't, Dad." Magne says.

Thorgrim doesn't finish the sentence, just looks down his nose at me again. I refuse to back down. I don't care if he's bigger, taller, older, more powerful than me. I care that he's a bully. That he hurt Magne. That he's probably the reason his other sons are assholes.

"I would like to speak to my son in private." The words come from between clenched teeth and I can tell he's used to being obeyed. He doesn't seem to know how to actually *ask* for anything.

"I have given Magne sanctuary here, Thorvaldson. He is under my protection," says Wolfram.

Thorgrim looks at Wolfram with complete disdain. "I'm not going to touch a hair on his precious weak body," he says.

Wolfram looks at Thea and she frowns, but they move away from the bed. "Don't expect us to leave the room," Wolfram says as they retreat to the living area. I'm pretty sure Wolfram, at least, has good enough hearing that he's offering privacy only in appearance.

I don't move.

"Get out of my way," Thorgrim says.

My nostrils flare. "You did this to him," I say.

"Out of my *way*." His voice has gone very calm, very quiet, very even, but his teeth grind together and I can see the flash of his wolf-like canines.

"Su," says Magne, "It's okay. Come sit by me."

"No," says Thorgrim. "I will not have some… human… listen to what I have to say to my son."

I still don't move. I can feel Wolfram and Thea watching from across the room and I know I should join them. I know they won't let Thorgrim do anything to hurt Magne. But I'm not sure I *can* move, now. My angry streak, my stubborn side, are fully awake now, and I want to hurt Thorgrim in return. I wouldn't even feel too bad killing him. And hell, that says a lot about my state of mind, I guess, since normally I wouldn't even *think* of hurting someone who wasn't trying to kill me.

I think maybe he sees some of that in my face, because he snarls, wolflike, inches from my nose.

"Move, bitch," he says.

"Make me." Yeah, I know, real original, but I'm not exactly thinking straight, you know?

And I've forgotten how fast werewolves can move, forgot that just because I can sometimes use powerful magic that werewolves – especially old, experienced werewolves – are fucking dangerous. He lashes out, hits me backhanded across the face before I even see him move.

And I'm sprawled backwards across the end of the bed, stunned, as two things happen at once.

One, I feel a surge of movement from where Magne's supposed to be tucked under the covers, and suddenly there's a wolf standing over me. And I don't mean a werewolf in wolf-like shape. I mean an actual, furry *Canis lupus*, grey wolf, four legs, teeth and all, standing over me and snarling.

And two, a Voice – and I use the capitalization deliberately – booms out, "Stop!" And everything stops.

Chapter Nineteen

I'VE FELT SOME pretty powerful magic in the short time I've known magic exists, but I've never felt anything like this.

It feels like the whole world has stopped and is waiting for Wolfram to tell it what to do next. Because it was Wolfram's voice that commanded, "Stop," and Wolfram's power that is holding us all utterly still.

For a long moment, nothing stirs at all. Then movement in the corner of my eye. Wolfram walks into my field of view to stand in front of Thorgrim, puts a hand on the other man's chest, and *moves* him, backs him up until he's against the wall.

"I allowed you to come here," Wolfram says, "Because I thought – I hoped – something might be salvaged of your relationship with your son. It seems I was wrong." He takes a step back and Thorgrim's eyes follow him, something that might be fear growing in them. "Everyone here, in this room, on this Island, is under *my* protection, and you have violated my hospitality. Feel very fortunate that I do not do worse than ban you from Wonder Island."

He stands facing Magne's dad a while longer, watching as a variety of expressions cross the other man's face. Fear is followed by anger, then respect, and some kind of understanding that has his eyes widening and his nostrils flaring.

"You," Thorgrim says.

I sure as hell wish I could see *Wolfram's* face. I wish I could see whatever Thorgrim sees that has drained all the aggression out of him.

Then Wolfram spreads his arms and blue lights flicker along the stylized wolves tattooed on them. And out of the shadows in the corners of the room step two massive grey wolves – Geri and Freki.

"Odin's wolves," says Thorgrim in a voice that's barely more than a whisper.

"You have met them before." Wolfram does not pose the sentence as a question.

"Yes." Thorgrim looks past the wolves, past Wolfram, past me to the wolf that stands over me. "I was wrong," he says. "I thought my eldest was chosen, but it was Magne."

Wolfram's voice has a dark humor in it. "*Something* has chosen him," he says. "And now he belongs to me. You no longer have any hold over him."

Thorgrim jerks his chin up, defiance overriding whatever else was driving him. "If he cannot be my heir, then I take my name from him. He is a Thorvaldson no longer."

The wolf standing over me growls softly.

"I'm sad to hear that," Wolfram says. "I don't think he wanted to lose his family so completely."

"It's done," says Thorgrim.

Wolfram nods and turns away. The wolves take his place and I don't think Thorgrim dares move.

Suddenly, *I* can move again, and Wolfram extends a hand to help me crawl out from under the wolf.

"My apologies," he says. "I should have seen that coming. Bethy will not doubt have an odorous poultice for the swelling." He touches my face where it burns and aches from Thorgrim's blow, and I swear it stings less.

"I shouldn't have been so mouthy," I say. "I was just so angry."

"As you should be."

He turns to the wolf and the look on his face shifts from regret to a fierce delight.

"Magne," he says, and the wolf looks at him. "You should be resting.

No more harm will come to Su, I promise." He puts a hand on each side of the wolf's huge grey-brown head and looks into its eyes – *his* eyes, Magne's, brown and endless. "I can't say I was expecting the House to give you this particular gift, but I can't say I'm surprised, either."

"I'm not the least bit surprised," says Thea, and Wolfram's lips curve a little.

He pushes the wolf's head down so they're forehead-to-forehead and the huge beast relaxes. "Back to bed now, son," Wolfram says, and then there's no wolf but only Magne, muscles shaking with effort, breathing in short gasps. Between us, Wolfram and I get him back under the covers, propped up on the headboard.

"Holy fuck," Magne says.

I glance over at Thorgrim, who watches, glowering. When he looks at Magne, I see fear, and wonder, and maybe even respect. But no pride for his son. No love.

"So that's it, hey, Dad," Magne says. "Guess I'll have to change all my ID." His voice sounds light, almost joking, but I can hear the heartbreak underlying it.

"Send me the bill," Thorgrim snarls.

"I don't want anything from you," Magne says. Then he looks away. "Except one thing."

"I will give you nothing."

Magne looks back at his father, and they look so much alike in that moment. "Get Thorstein help," he says. "Stop treating him like your personal one-man enforcement squad. Let him have his own life."

His father doesn't answer.

"Get him out of here," says Wolfram, and the wolves herd Thorgrim towards the door. Thea follows and closes the door behind her.

The pressure of magic eases and Wolfram staggers and has to lean on the edge of the bed. I help him to a chair and he rubs his left eye, then both eyes, then his whole face with the palms of his hands.

"Ouch," he says. "That's going to cause a nasty headache."

"Who *are* you?" I say. Or maybe I should have said *what*.

He looks up at me and his face is tired, a bit sad, and he looks ancient. "Just Wolfram Gottfried," he says, but there's a quirk at the corner of his mouth.

"Yeah, okay," I say. I sit on the edge of the bed and let the tension drain out of me.

"More immediately," Magne says, "What the fuck just happened to me?"

"The House decided it likes you," Wolfram says. "It is not a thing that is easily described, but it is magic, and very old, and has sentience of a sort." He sighs, closes his eyes, and leans back in his chair.

"I need a drink," he says.

"You and me both," says Magne.

"Make that three of us," I say, and I get up and dig out a bottle of Irish whiskey I saw Bethy stash under the counter, pour a generous amount into three glasses, and pass them around.

"Am I still a werewolf?" Magne says, after taking a long sip. He holds out a hand, tenses his muscles, frowns. I can see the effort in his face, in the trembling of his muscles. Slowly, his hand reforms, reshapes into a paw – not a real wolf paw, but an *otherly* werewolf paw, complete with long claws. He relaxes and his hand returns to its human shape.

"Bethy thinks the magic you were gifted has removed the symbiont from your blood," Wolfram says. "In that sense, no you are not a werewolf anymore."

"Fuck," says Magne. "It couldn't have asked what *I* wanted?"

"I don't think it will remove your ability to take your werewolf shape entirely, at least not right away, but it will likely be more difficult."

"Will I still heal quickly?" Magne says. "Will I age like a human now? Will –" He cuts himself off.

"I wish I had answers for you," Wolfram says. "But if you have become what I believe the House has made you, your lifespan will be even longer than an *otherly* werewolf's. Your ability to heal will have changed, but it will still be swift. Your speed and strength likely increased."

"And what, exactly, do you think the House turned me into?" Magne's voice is still light, but there's an edge to it, like he's this close to completely freaking out.

"*Varulf.*" Wolfram pronounces the word with an accent I don't recognize, something like German, but not.

"That's not the same thing?" I say.

"Werewolves were named for their superficial resemblance to *varulfr*. A werewolf is no more a varulf than he is a natural wolf."

"Then what is it?" Magne lets out his breath in a exasperated huff. I think he's scared, and it's making him irritable.

I swing my legs up onto the bed and scoot over so I'm sitting next to him, my shoulder pressed against his. He turns, tilts his head to kiss the side of my face, and I'm relieved to find his temperature feels normal.

"These are not easy concepts to explain," Wolfram says. "Not in English. You are a man who can become a wolf. A wolf who can become a man. A *real* wolf, a natural wolf, except bigger, faster, more powerful. Most of us have other magical abilities. What yours are, you will discover in time."

We sit and digest this information for a while, sipping our drinks. Then Magne says, "I'm going to need some time to process this."

"Take all the time you need," says Wolfram.

"And I guess I have to pick a new last name," Magne says.

"He can't really take your name, can he?" I say. "I mean legally?"

"I don't want his anymore." He rests his head on my shoulder, and I can feel him sagging against the pillows. "I'm also going to have to find a new job, since I expect Dad won't wait to spread the news of my banishment to the whole pack."

"I may be able to help," says Wolfram.

"You have a job for me?"

"There are always jobs on the Island. We also have interests on the mainland. Get better. Heal. Think. Then come see me and we'll find you something." He pauses and a mischievous look comes over his face. "Perhaps you could become our new strongman. I hear Mr Strong and Mr Tall are thinking of retirement."

I watch Magne's face as he's trying to decide if he's being teased or not. "Would he be Mr Strong or Mr Tall?" I ask, trying to keep my face smooth and unmarked by the grin that's trying to curl my lips.

"Both, I imagine," says Wolfram, and then we all burst out laughing.

"I don't suppose you'd have a job for me, too," I say. "I've been thinking of leaving behind my life of crime."

"I'm sure I can find something," Wolfram says. "I may also have a solution for your surname issue, Magne." He's staring at his hands now, and I swear his voice is… hesitant? He's nervous, afraid of Magne's reaction, which is weird since he just used some seriously powerful magic to stop the world. Okay, not the world, but that's what it felt like.

Magne leans forward a little. "You have a suggestion?"

Wolfram stares at his hands a moment longer, then looks up. "None of my children lived to adulthood," he says, old pain in his voice. "Eventually, I decided to stop trying. I will, now, never have a son or daughter to take my name." He stops, looks back at his hands.

"You… want me to have *your* name?" Magne's voice is carefully neutral, and even I can't tell what he thinks of the idea.

"It's only a suggestion," Wolfram says. "But I would be honored to give it to you."

Magne's forehead furrows. He looks at me and I shrug. I don't know what to tell him.

"Would that mean I'd be your…"

"My heir? My adopted son?" Wolfram looks up again, something wild and proud in his face. "Only if you want it. My legacy is not an easy one, and you might want to learn more before you decide. In the meantime, my surname is yours if you want that much." He smiles wryly. "But don't feel you must. I won't be insulted if you don't want it."

"It'll be a giant fucking pain in the ass to change my name," Magne says. "I think I'll keep using Thorvaldson for now. Just to spite Dad." His face softens. "But I'll consider your offer. Thank you."

Wolfram nods. And then something he said earlier catches up to the front of my brain and I sit up straight.

"Wait a minute," I say. Both Magne and Wolfram stare at me because I've spoken louder than I meant to. "You said, 'most of us'." I stare back at Wolfram.

"I said…"

"When you were telling Magne what a *varulf* is. You said, 'Most of us have other magic.' Does that mean you're one too?"

Wolfram's face changes entirely, and it's like the sun's come out. All the cares, the conflict, vanishes as he smiles with his lips and his eyes both. I'm pretty sure that if I looked at him with my fox sight now, I'd be blinded.

Then I feel a crackle of magic along my skin, and instead of Wolfram sitting in the chair, there's a wolf, surprisingly large, with clear grey eyes and black fur.

"I am," the wolf says, in Wolfram's human voice. "Among other things."

Later, with Magne resting and the carnival closing down for the night, Wolfram and I sip tea on the roof and stare out over the dark forest. It's full night, and the stars are brighter than they should be, so close to the city. I'm beginning to learn that this Island has a lot more to it than I ever would have suspected.

"Troll says there's an abandoned glass factory upstream," I say.

"There are many abandoned industrial buildings upstream," Wolfram says.

I shift the ice pack on my cheekbone, glad that Bethy agreed it would be more use than a smelly poultice. My face still aches, but I heal fast and the pain is fading; by morning, it will probably be just a memory.

"I thought it might be where…" I can't say, "Where my parents were murdered," so I say, "Whoever took my sister was hiding out."

Wolfram straightens up in his seat. "Damn," he says.

"What?"

"I should have sent someone years ago. But…" He trails off.

"It wasn't your concern," I say. "You turned over what you knew to the police, and for all you knew it was just some mainlanders, humans. Nothing to do with you or Wonder Island."

"True," he says. "But I wonder if my strict policy of non-involvement is so effective at keeping us safe as I always believed. Thea has been telling me for years that we can't stay isolated forever."

"I don't know," I say. "I think it's good to have a sanctuary. I bet there are a lot of people… of beings… here that wouldn't do so well in the modern world."

"Kin," he says. "We use the word kin to refer to ourselves. Or folk, sometimes."

"Kin," I say. "I like that. I… apparently I studied anthropology before." I sip my tea.

"Before your memory was taken," he says. I like the way he phrases it. Not, I *lost* my memory, but my memory was *taken*. Like it isn't my fault. Now if only I could get it back.

"Yeah," I say. "There's this concept in anthro called 'fictive kin' that I always thought was a great idea, could maybe even make the world a better place."

He smiles. "Kin based on choice or non-genetic social relationships," he says.

"Exactly," I say. I take another sip of excellent jasmine green tea. "Do you really want to adopt Magne?"

He considers, his gaze aimed over the forest, but focused on infinity. "I know it seems odd," he finally says. "I've only known him a short time. But he's everything I would want in a son of my body. So why not a fictive son?" He gives me a self-deprecating smile. "And my motives are a bit selfish, too."

"Yeah?"

"I do need an heir. I still have many years left on Middle Earth, gods willing, but I won't live forever. I need someone I trust to guard this Island as I have. I once hoped Thea would have a niece or nephew for me to train, but she tells me it will never happen."

The way he says "Middle Earth," I know he's not being a rabid Tolkien fan, but using it in the Norse-Germanic mythological sense. Midgard, where mortals live. Which make me wonder if the other realms are real.

"And would that come with Geri and Freki? Huginn and Muninn?"

He looks at me sharply, then smiles. "Among other things," he says and rubs his left eye. That seems to be his answer for when he's not ready to elaborate. "They've already accepted him, I think." I want to ask why he keeps rubbing his eye, if his use of power pains him, but I've already gotten way far away from the topic I meant to discuss.

"I'm going to go to that glass factory," I say. "I need to see if they were there."

"Of course," says Wolfram. "When?"

I like that he doesn't even try to talk me out of it, like he knows I'm determined, and maybe even trusts my ability to keep myself safe.

"Tomorrow," I say. "If there's vampires, I don't want to be there at night."

"I would ask you not to go alone," he says.

"I can't take Magne."

"No." He looks at the sky. The Milky Way is absurdly bright. "I wish I could go with you. Or send Thea. But one of the conditions of our… situation… is that we cannot leave the Island." He laughs. "Well, *I* cannot. She *dares* not."

"Too many enemies?" I guess. I'm really starting to like his cold, dangerous sister, but I can see how others could easily not.

"Just so," he says. "And Troll *won't* leave. He doesn't even like taking the boat to the mainland, even if he stays on board."

Meaning he really did do us a favor when he came across to bring Magne back. I smile. Mags really *could* find a new family here. A chosen family.

"It's okay," I says. "I'll go in fox shape. If anyone's around, they'll never even know I was there."

"I'd be happier if you had backup," Wolfram says. "I can ask Sgian if she'd be willing. She likes you."

"It's okay," I say. "I'll be fine."

"Humor an old man," he says, and I almost laugh, because however old Wolfram actually *is*, he doesn't look it. "If I offer to return her powers for the day, I doubt she'll refuse."

"Bribery?" I say. "Isn't that stooping a little low?" But I'm smiling. Hell, maybe *I* can find a new family here.

He laughs. "Whatever it takes. Besides, it will be good to remind her of what she's repenting for."

"Can you do that? Give her back her *sidhe* shape? Her magic?"

"Temporarily, yes. To make it permanent, I'm not the one she has to convince."

"So the gods are real?"

"Not in the here and now, but yes."

"All of them?"

He shrugs. "I can only speak of personal experience."

"Are you –" But I stop myself. There are some questions I can't ask yet. And some he probably wouldn't answer even if I did ask. Maybe some he *couldn't* answer.

"Tomorrow, then," I say. "I'll find out if there's anything to be found in that factory."

"You're sure it's the place?"

"No, but Troll says it's one of only a few that still had a dock seven years ago, so I think it's the most likely." I get up. "Do I need to go back to the mainland tonight?"

He looks at me in surprise. "You needn't go back to the mainland ever again, if you don't want to."

"Does that mean I'm an honorary Islander?" I smile.

He inclines his head. "Go stay with Magne," he says. "He's had a trying day and I expect your presence would be a comfort."

"Trying doesn't cover the half of it." I turn for the stairs.

"And Su?"

I pause.

"Don't tire him out. He's still got a lot of healing to do."

I refuse to turn around and acknowledge the expression I can practically hear in his voice. I just lift one hand briefly, resist the urge to make a rude gesture, and head back inside.

Chapter Twenty

MAGNE'S ASLEEP WHEN I walk in, and I almost curl up on the couch instead of climbing in next to him, because I don't want to disturb him. But he looks fragile, and I don't want him to wake up alone, so I strip off my clothes and slip under the covers.

He mumbles and reaches for me, pulling me close and spooning against my back.

After a moment he says, "You're naked."

"Yeah," I say. "They don't provide pjs at this hotel."

He snorts, then kisses the back of my neck. "I'm naked, too," he says.

"Are you? I hadn't noticed." But of course I *had* noticed.

He kisses my neck again, this time behind my ear.

"You should rest, Magne," I say. "I'm under strict orders not to tire you out."

"Whose orders?" he says, nibbling he way down to my shoulder.

"Your new dad." As soon as I say it, I realize it was the wrong thing to say. Maybe sometime in the future, parts of yesterday will seem funny, but right now, there is nothing to laugh at. Everything is still too raw. And even though Magne doesn't move, I can feel him withdrawing from me.

"Shit," I say. "I'm sorry." I roll over and even though it's dark, my fox eyes let me see his face clearly. His eyes are moist and his muscles tense.

"It's okay."

"It's not okay," I say. "I should have thought before I opened my mouth." I touch his face, stroke his cheek, his hair, and he sighs. "I'd ask if you're okay," I say. "But I can tell you're not."

"No," he says. "I'm not okay. My whole fucking world just changed in less than a day."

"Not your whole world," I say, tangling my fingers in his hair and making a fist so he has to look at me. "I'm still here, and I'm not going anywhere."

He looks into my eyes, like he's searching for something. I guess what he finds is enough, because he smiles. Just a small, fleeting one, but I see it. His face relaxes and he turns his head to press his lips to my wrist.

"I know, love," he says. "You might be the only thing keeping me from losing my shit."

"Glad to be of service," I say. I wiggle closer to get more of my skin pressed against his, stretch my neck to kiss him. "Now how else can I be of service?"

"Since you mention it," he says. "I've got an itch right between my shoulder blades that I can't reach."

I shake my head, stretch my arm around his ribcage, and scratch his back.

"Over," he says. "No, other way. Up a bit. There. Oh yeah." He moans in mock pleasure. Or maybe not so mock. "That's good."

"Dumbass," I say, but then he's kissing me and I can't say anything else because his tongue is in my mouth.

When he pulls away, he says, "Tell me how I can make your life better."

"You already have," I say. "Every day I wake up and I know you're there."

He touches my face, fingers gentle on the spot where his dad hit me. "I would have killed him," he says. "I was going for his throat when Wolfram stopped everything."

"I'm glad he did." I put my hand over his, squeeze his fingers. "You'd have hated yourself."

"I don't think I would have." But his voice isn't so certain.

"He's an asshole," I say. "A bigot, a giant piece of shit. But he's your dad, and I know you loved him once. I saw the photos. If only because it would break your mother's heart, you would have regretted killing him." I slide my hand down his arm to his elbow, up to his shoulder, and let it rest against his ribs. I can just see the glistening track of a single tear sliding down the side of his nose.

"Yeah," he says, voice thick.

"But I love you for trying." I reach down to grab his butt and pull his hips closer to mine, push my pelvis against his until I hear his breath catch. "Now," I say. "Roll over and let me show you how much."

"Maybe *you* should roll over," he says, nibbling on my earlobe.

"You're supposed to be resting," I say. "Therefore you should let me do all the work."

"I think this counts as physiotherapy."

I laugh until he stops me with his mouth, and in the end, we settle for lying on our sides, face to face. I hook one leg over his thigh to reach his hardness with my wetness, push against him till I'm gasping, then have to lean away to find my pants and my pocket, in which I've got a condom stashed – always be prepared, I say.

When he's inside me we push slowly together and pull slowly apart, letting tension and pleasure build gradually until all at once we're urgent, thrusting against each other and then, finally, going still, relaxing.

"Make a new life with me?" Magne says softly into my hair.

I don't answer for a moment, and then I say, teasing, "Magne, are you asking me to marry you?" I don't mean it, of course. At least I don't think I do.

Now it's his turn to be quiet. "I wasn't," he says finally. "But if I did, would you?"

I bite his chest because my arms are wrapped around him and I can't be bothered to move in order to poke him. "That's hardly a fair question," I say.

"Would you?" His voice is only just above a whisper.

"I've spent my life wanting to never get married," I say. "My parents were the perfect couple, happy and in love the whole time they were… How can I hope to match that?"

"Not even when you met Ev?" he says, voice still soft. "He was the love of your life."

"Not even then," I say. I tilt my head to see his face. A little moonlight has crept into the room and it reflects off his eyes, making them glow. "But as it turns out," I continue, "it's possible to have more than one love of your life."

He's breathing carefully, like he's afraid of… I don't know. Something.

"Not for me," he says. "You're it for me."

"Evgeny *was* the love of my life," I say. "But you…" I bite my lip. "You're –"

"It's okay," he says. "It's enough that you love me at all."

"No," I say. "That's the thing. He was. I never thought it was possible to be that in love with someone. To love them like if they disappear life would have no more meaning."

"Su –" His voice sounds broken.

"Magne," I say, raising my voice, because I need him to hear this. "That's what I thought. But he left me, and I'm still here. Life still has meaning. Because of you. You were – you *are* – my friend. You're my lover. And you're my beloved." I grab his face, make him look into my eyes.

"Somehow," I say. "I don't even know how, and I don't care, you're *more* the love of my life than Evgeny was. And if you ever decide you want to marry me, then I will."

He's staring at me, just staring, and I don't know what else to say. Then I see another glistening tear track, just one, then it's gone.

"I lost everything today," he says. "Except you. And somehow you make me feel like it's going to be okay."

"It *is* going to be okay," I say. "Whatever happens, it's you and me. Always."

Then he smiles. First one dimple appears, then the other. And suddenly he yawns and I laugh, and everything really *is* okay, or it will be.

I wait till morning to tell him my plan for the day, and he doesn't like it, but he doesn't try to talk me out of it, either. He once let me walk into a secret vampire research lab all by myself, and trusted that I would make it back out, and this is way less dangerous. Of course, we weren't together then. In fact, we were only just becoming friends.

Still, he knows I'm strong and capable, that I can handle myself, and his trust makes *me* believe it.

"I won't be alone," I say. "Sgian will be there, full powers temporarily restored. Worst case, I'll send her for help. *Then* you can come rescue me."

He laughs. He's still wobbly standing up, and even just going to the bathroom is an effort.

"Let's hope it doesn't come to that, because I don't think I can even manage to piss in this toilet without sitting down." His voice echoes through the open door of the bathroom. "I'm not going to be much help in a rescue situation."

I wait till he's settled in bed again, cup of strong coffee in hand, before I leave.

"Be safe, love," he says.

"Always."

Sgian and Wolfram are waiting outside, sitting on a stone bench in the shade of the building, only I don't realize it's Sgian at first. What I see is a young-looking woman with fair skin, huge eyes, and very black hair, dressed in dark jeans and t-shirt.

"Hey, foxy lady," she says in her thick Scots accent and I recognize her voice immediately.

"You look good in that shape," I say, and she grins.

"Troll will take you across the river in his rowboat," Wolfram says. "You'll have to make your own way back."

"I'll handle that, boss," says Sgian. "Now that I've got my mojo back. I could take us right there, too."

"It would tire you too much," Wolfram says. "You're out of practice and you need to be at full strength when you arrive, just in case."

"And," I add, "I figured it would be better to approach from downstream, slowly. Sneak up, in case anyone is still there.

"Right right," she says. "Stealth. I can do stealth."

"Tell that to Wotan," Wolfram says.

"Cheap shot, boss," Sgian says.

We walk to the House and through its corridors, and come out under

Troll's ruined bridge, where he waits, sitting on a stump and watching a tiny brown bird eat seeds from his enormous hand.

"Boat's up at the gravel bar," he says, when he sees us. "Figured it were better than rowing all the way round the end."

It's an hour to the boat and another to row across to the east bank of the river and find a place Troll deems suitable to land. It's not too far from the glass factory, but not so close that anyone watching would guess it was our destination. When he pushes off to row back to the Island, I take fox shape, and Sgian puts on her feathers and is a crow again, and we're just two animals in the forest.

"You sense anything?" Sgian asks.

"Not yet," I say. I extend my senses, touch minds with a bobcat, a raven, a whole flock of little birds, and hundreds, thousands of other, smaller lifeforms. I try not to notice the overwhelming number of extremely tiny living beings. That way lies madness. "Just normal forest life."

"Me too," she says. "Let's get closer."

I slip into the underbrush, and Sgian launches into the air, glides from branch to branch until we find the old chain link fence that marks the factory's property line. There are "No Trespassing" and "Warning" and "Danger" signs everywhere and I'm very aware that there could be chunks of broken glass hidden in the weeds and rubble.

We stop where the fence lies twisted and half-collapsed and I extend my senses again.

"Rats," I say.

"Like 'damn' or like small furry rodents?"

I refuse to laugh at Sgian's terrible joke. "The second one," I say. "Mice, too. An owl in the rafters."

"Skunk was here," Sgian says. "Gone now, though."

"Good," I say. "I could do without getting sprayed." We're speaking quietly, but it still makes me nervous. "Can you communicate… not out loud?"

Like this? she asks, and I think she might be laughing at me.

Like that, I reply. I step carefully past the fence. I don't feel or hear or see anything out of place. Nothing that shouldn't be here, but I know some beings can hide themselves, even from extra-human senses. Karasu doesn't show in my fox senses, except as a sort of negative. The Witch of the Wald hid by directing my senses away from her until I moved away instead of towards her house.

I let my nose guide me instead, and my eyes, and I pick my way across the sunny open area in front of the big factory building. Sgian glides overhead.

Over here, she thinks at me, and I look to where she's landed in a broken-open window. *You can climb up on the roof.*

There was a sort on entryway with a roof to shelter it from the weather that has fallen down on one side, making a ramp I can jump up to. I meet her at the window and see there's a catwalk running around the perimeter of the building inside. It looks unstable, but my fox shape is light and it hardly trembles as I hop through the window onto it.

Sgian glides in after me, swoops towards the floor, and lands with a flourish in her *sidhe* form, human-like but not human.

Show off, I think at her. I find a rickety stairway and follow her down, taking my human shape at the bottom. It will be easier to look for clues, and easier to understand what I'm looking at. Too long in fox shape, and I start to think like a fox.

"Smell that?" Sgian says, voice pitched low so as not to carry.

I pull in air, sort through the scents. "Human," I say. "Fresh?"

She considers. "Not very. Not here in this room. But nearby, something fresher, maybe."

I wonder about her sense of smell, which seems to be even better than mine. It must be part of her *sidhe* nature, or an aspect of her magic, because crows don't have that keen of a nose. Or much of a sense of taste. Easier to live off carrion, I guess, if you don't have to taste the rot.

She walks back and forth across the huge, gutted space of the factory, sniffing. I take the perimeter, inhaling slowly and carefully through my nose.

"Here," I say. "This way." We slip outside through a doorway missing its door and head around the building, moving quietly, carefully. There's another door, an entrance to a second, smaller building. It's cracked open and I smell a human. And a vampire. Maybe more than one. The human smells close, but I can't tell if the vampire scent is old or new. I mean, it can't be years old, if I can still smell it, but it could be minutes or hours or days.

"One human," says Sgian, so quiet it's barely a breath.

"Vamp?" I breathe back.

She holds up one finger, then another, and a third.

Shit. "Recent?"

She cocks her head. "Listen."

I do, focusing on the other side of the door. At first, I hear nothing, Then quietly, muffled, movement. A slight echo. Weeping? I look at Sgian.

"There's our human," she says.

I extend my senses again, see nothing but insects and spiders. But then I feel a space below floor level. A basement. And there's the human. Female, older, a slight blue spark of magic, like John's. His mother?

I see a nest of rats, spiders, silverfish, tiny things. I don't see any vampires.

"Vamps?" I ask.

Sgian shrugs. "Nothing fresher than a few days. Unless it's a very old one."

"Okay," I say. "Shall we?"

She mock-bows, gestures for me to go first. I ease open the door and it swings smoothly, hinges oiled not too long ago. Definitely more recent than seven years.

This feels like a trap, but there doesn't seem to be anyone here other than one human. I take a deep breath, hold it, and step through the door. Sgian lets me take a few steps in before following.

Straight ahead there's a corridor, and to the right, a door marked "Basement." It's locked. I want to swear. I can pick locks. Simple ones, anyway, but I didn't think to bring my lockpicks.

Sgian grins and motions for me to step aside. She feels in her hair and comes out with three slender, shining devices, like my lockpicks but much more elegant-looking. And I'd swear the metal is too blue to be steel.

Of course, the fair folk, of which the *sidhe* could be considered a subdivision, aren't supposed to like iron, and I suppose steel counts too, being mostly iron. I wonder how Sgian feels about being in this factory with so much old rusted steel around, so many cast iron remnants. She hasn't said anything, but maybe it's a delayed reaction. Or maybe that bit of folklore is like vampires and garlic – which is to say, bullshit.

While I'm puzzling over *sidhe* and iron, Sgian's picked the lock and the door swings open. We edge through and look. Concrete stairs leading down, damp walls on both sides, darkness at the bottom – but not complete darkness. A bit of light comes in from somewhere, and it's plenty for me to see by.

"Can you see?" I ask Sgian.

"Eyes like a cat," she answers.

I nod and she lets me take the lead again so I slowly creep down, one step at a time. If we're going to find a nest of vampires, it'll be here, at the bottom of a dark stairway. Let's just hope my fox senses were right, and there's nothing more here than rats and spiders and one human woman.

At the bottom of the stairs, there's a short corridor, then it turns sharply and opens into a big room. Not as big as the factory building, but not small. A grate in the ceiling at one side filters daylight in so it's dim but not dark. It smells damp, like mildew and rat shit.

I hear the movement again, the weeping. Words. Human words, but not in a language I know.

Sgian points, and under the dappled light of the grate is a stack of crates and pallets, half rotten, but piled into a sort of partition. Beyond that, soft sounds of movement.

We walk quietly, side by side, checking left and right but the rest of the room is empty space and there is nothing else there but rusting bolts and mysterious fittings where machinery once stood.

We round the side of the pile of old wood and there she is. She stares at us, terror on her face, but also resignation. I feel a push of magic, not strong, but determined, and I block it automatically – finally, my fox woman powers working like they're supposed to.

"Hey now, none of that," says Sgian, and the magic stops abruptly. "I don't know what you think memory magic is going to do to help you anyway."

Memory magic?

"Mrs Pradip?" I say and the woman looks at me. She must be in her sixties, but fear and captivity have made her look older. "I'm a friend of John's," I say. "We've come to take you home."

Chapter Twenty-One

JOHN'S MOTHER STARES up at me, and it's then that I notice the shackle on her wrist, chaining her to an old fixture on the concrete wall.

"Sgian, can you pick that lock?" I point at the cuff around the woman's wrist.

"John?" the woman says, and looks around wildly. "Is he here? He must not come here!"

"It's okay," I say. "He's not here. He doesn't even know *we're* here."

I help her to her feet, or try to. She's weak and can't seem to stay upright. Finally I give up and crouch next to her.

"You must leave me," she says. "The terrible men will come back, and if I am not here, they will go after him." She leans forward, whispers, "They are scientists, doctors."

"Why do you say that?"

There's a clank as Sgian drops the now-open manacle and the woman starts. She whispers again. "They take my blood. For experiments."

I look at Sgian and she looks back at me. I don't know what she knows about the vampire group I took out last year, but she must know something, because she says, "I thought you killed that guy."

"I didn't," I say. "The other vampires did. But maybe someone else took over. We freed all the captives but didn't touch the facility. Maybe this is them starting over."

"Here?" Sgian gestures around us. "There's nothing here."

I sigh. "I don't know. Maybe this is a decoy."

"In which case, we probably shouldn't linger."

I look at the woman's wrist where the manacle was, to check that she's okay, and I suddenly feel cold. There are scars on her wrists, like a suicide victim might have only not so deep. Most of them are healed, but some are fresher, and one is only newly scabbed over.

"How did they take your blood?" I say. "With a needle? An IV?"

"A knife," she says. "They cut me and caught it in a bottle." She covers her wrist with her other hand, but I see old cuts on that arm, too.

I look back at Sgian. "My parents…" I say. "They had cuts like that."

"Then we *really* shouldn't linger," she replies.

"Can you get her back to Wonder Island?" I stand and stretch. "I want to have a quick look around. Then I'll go back the way we came. Swim across."

She shakes her head. "I can take her, but it's not a good idea to show up uninvited and alone on the east side of the island."

"I'll head for the gravel bar, then, on the south end."

She shakes her head again. "I don't like it. Don't stay too long, Su. Wolfram will have my magic for good if you get hurt. And your werewolf will eat me for lunch."

I smile. I suspect Sgian is more than a match for Magne, even if he was in top form, and even if she has been stuck as a crow for who knows how long. "I'll be careful."

The woman looks back and forth between us as we talk. "No," she finally says. "You must leave me."

"Nobody's leaving you," says Sgian. "Do you think your son would be happy if he knew we found you and left you here? He'd come looking for you himself. I don't even know him, but I could see that much when we met." She leans over the woman, taking her hand gently. "Besides, I bet Wolfram will offer sanctuary for you *and* your son, if need be."

"Do you think?" I say softly. "They're human."

Sgian shrugs. "Some of the carnies aren't anything more than human with a bit of magic. But if you have a better idea, I'd like to hear it. But later, when we're the hell away from here." Then she turns to Mrs Pradip, lifts her arm, and they're gone in a swirl of black feathers.

I have a quick scout around the basement, but there's nothing else to see, and even the rotting crates are empty. So I head back up the stairs. At the top I glance out the door and see the sun high in the sky still. Lots of time before dark.

I send my fox senses out ahead of me, down the dark hall, and try to feel out the shape of the room beyond and whatever might be in it. Nothing. Insects and spiders and nothing bigger. Not even a mouse.

My nose doesn't tell me much more. The vampire smell gets stronger as I step carefully down the hall and around the corner, but it doesn't seem any more recent. No more than a couple of days, I think.

It's almost as dark in here as it was in the basement. A single grimy window lets in a little light and there's an electrical buzzing from the corner and the sudden rattle of an ancient compressor that makes me jump. The electricity is on, which is weird, and there's an old dirty white refrigerator on the far side of the room. Between me and it there's a hefty sort of table.

I freeze mid-step on my way around the table to the fridge, caught by a familiar smell. Or a familiar *sort* of smell, anyway. Grave dirt and damp. And I realize the table is not a table at all, but a coffin on trestles. A very plain, simple box which is why I didn't see it for what it was at first. I inhale deep through my nose, even though the last thing I want is a deep whiff of whatever's in there.

Grave dirt, damp, vampire. Only the damp smells fresh. Or not *fresh*, but you know what I mean.

I edge carefully around the coffin. I need to see what's in that fridge. Then I'll get the hell out of here.

Hardly daring to breathe for fear of making noise – even though if there's a vamp in that box it's been there for more than a day or two and that might mean it's not coming out soon. But it being daytime won't stop it if it does come out – if there's anything in there at all – because not enough sunlight is getting through the window to do more than make a vampire a little bit uncomfortable.

I reach the fridge – it's an early 80s model (and don't ask me how I know that) with a faux wood panel and an ice maker in the narrower of the two side-by-side doors. The left door opens easily – the seal's gone and this thing must be drawing a shit ton of electricity to keep it cold with the amount of air that's got to be leaking out. There's nothing there but some desiccated ice cubes in a plastic tray.

The right door is harder to open. Something sticky and dark has spilled and hardened on one edge and it's glued the door shut. I try to tell myself it's jelly or wine, but who am I kidding? I can smell that it's blood. I yank and the door comes open with a horrible peeling sound. I look over at the coffin. No movement, no old horror movie creak of the lid opening.

Inside the fridge, along with a lot of mildew, are mason jars full of deep red liquid. A lot of it has congealed, and none of it is labelled. I inhale cautiously, even though I already know what it is, can already smell it. And it's not like I even mind the smell of blood – my fox nature even kind of likes it. But I don't relish inhaling mildew spores. I mean, I don't know if that's bad, but it probably isn't good. And I really don't like the smell.

And yeah, it's definitely blood. I start to reach out, to touch a jar, because maybe some of that belonged to my parents, my sister even. But I stop myself. I don't have the kind of senses that could tell me much more than if the blood is probably human, and I can tell that already from the smell. So I pull my hand away and accidentally brush my bare wrist on the sticky edge of the door.

"Yuck," I mutter, and shut the door. I try to wipe the old blood off on the surface of the fridge and leave a rusty smear on the dirty white. I turn around and try to make myself think. There's nothing else here. No other buildings to search and if there were ever any cupboards or closets they were stripped out long ago.

So what do I have? John's mother, who might be able to tell us something about her captors. A fridge full of congealed blood that I have no intention of disturbing. The faint scent of vampires – at least three, if Sgian's nose is any good. And one coffin.

And hell, I'm going to have to open it, aren't I?

I'm not a big horror movie fan, but Magne loves them – the cheesier the better – so I've seen quite a few. And I know opening the vampire's coffin is a Bad Idea in capital letters. Then again, so is leaving *without* looking. So I walk slowly and carefully over to the box, slip my favorite silver-tipped stake out of its holster in the small of my back, and put my hand on the lid.

Then I stand there, trying to gather up enough courage to actually open the thing. I mean, I can handle a vampire. I've taken out a few even though the idea of killing a thinking, sentient being leaves me very uneasy. But if they try to kill me, I try to kill them back. This place is really getting to me. The blood in the fridge, John's mom chained in the basement. None of it makes sense and that makes me the most nervous of all.

Finally, I make myself take slow, careful breaths, just like my kung fu teacher taught me. Let the bad thoughts flow around my center of calm until I'm completely still, inside and out.

Then I flip the lid off the coffin and shift into a fighting stance.

The coffin is empty.

Well, not *entirely* empty. There's a layer of dirt on the bottom – and I'd bet good money it came from whatever country the vampire who sleeps here came from. And if he's old, it probably came from the cemetery he was buried in, before he was Reborn a vamp.

And there's a little rectangle of pale cardboard. I lift it out of the coffin and almost laugh out loud. John fucking Pradip's business card. I let it fall from my fingers and its flat shape catches the air, flutters to one side of the box where it lands on edge and then slides flat, next to something shiny so nearly buried in the dirt that I almost didn't see it.

I really don't want to touch some skanky old vampire's grave dirt, but I guess I don't have a choice if I want to see what the shiny thing is. I touch it with one finger. Cold metal. I work it free, wipe the dirt off with my thumb, and almost laugh again.

Of course. A pocketwatch. I don't need to flip it open to know it'll have cut outs in the face that show the inner workings. And I don't need to pry off the back to know I'll find a line or two of pompous-sounding Latin engraved there, parts of a sort of poem or vampire manifesto.

I put the watch in my pocket. I can wait till I'm back to check, to compare it to the other watches that have been turning up on the vampires we've disposed of since I first met Evgeny.

There's nothing left to see here unless I stumble over something in the weedy yard. I really wish I knew where the vampire who usually occupies this coffin is hiding out, and where his two or more cronies are (and I say "he" because for reasons I've never figured out, most vamps are male, and also white, but that's something to ponder another day).

I walk carefully back down the hall and pause to peer out the door. There's an eagle high in the sky – I can just make out its white head and tail against the darker body feathers – something shifting in the weeds across the yard that a quick check with my fox senses tells me is a mink – and nothing else but bugs and other small creatures.

I slip out the door and I'm about to take fox shape when I change my mind, and head for the water instead of the woods. Fox shape is safer, but I'm a lot taller in human shape and that'll help me see... well, whatever there turns out to see.

The dock is as rotted as the pallets and crates in the basement, so I walk carefully, picking my way across the solidest-looking boards. Looking directly across the river, I see forest, and then as then land rises, the city. There's the former-warehouse district where my apartment is, and farther up are more residential areas.

To the right, the boardwalk and more manicured park areas are visible, and then the downtown core of Riverbend. Farther right still, the dark bulk of Wonder Island blocks my view of the rest of the mainland, but I know that if I could see more, I'd see thicker and thicker forest, and then finally the farms and ranches of the Bottomlands. If it was dark, I could probably make out the cityglow from farther-off Great Valley.

From here, the Island looks entirely wild, its inhabited north end out of sight behind dense trees. I pick up a rotten chunk of wood and toss it out into the river, watch as it bobs slowly to the surface, so old it barely floats. The current catches it and pulls it out towards mid-stream. It's too small to really see where it ends up, but when I lose sight of it, it's heading directly towards the tip of Wonder Island.

I'd be willing to bet that if I could follow its journey, that chunk of wood would wash up somewhere on the Island. At the gravel bar, maybe, or if it was caught in a stronger current, it might fetch up farther north where a curve in the shoreline forms a little cove where the ferry docks.

A body thrown in the river here would wash up on Wonder Island.

I toss another chunk of wood, this time just dropping it in to the water below instead of throwing it out into the current. It catches in an eddy then slips away, hugging the shoreline. I have no doubt it will wash up on the riverbank, not too far north of here, and not too far south of the Island.

My parents were kept here, just like Mrs Pradip. Chained and drained, and finally throat-cut and discarded. But why? Why them? Why Kit? And why not me? Why keep me distracted instead of using me?

There are too many whys. Too many unknowns, and even though I found where my parents were murdered, I don't have any more answers than I had this morning. Than I had seven years ago.

"Shit," I say out loud. Too loud. I hear a noise that turns me cold.

Movement, creeping, scuffling closer to shore, under the dock. I really, really hope it's an animal.

More scuffling, from the part of the bank that supports the pilings for the dock, from deep in the shadow of the undercut bank.

I send out my senses and realize the riverbank blocked this area from my awareness when I was looking from the other side of the factory. I mean, I probably *could* have seen here, but I didn't think to look. Now, I find two presences and a void. Vampires. Two vampires plus a third so old I don't really even see him.

I remind myself that they can't come after me in daylight. If they step out here where I am, the sun will incinerate any exposed skin and burn so hot only a few insignificant fragments and a handful of ashes will be left.

Still, I should have been more careful. Now I'll have to pass over them to get back to dry land. And the thought of them reaching up to grab for me between the rotten boards of the dock is very, very not pleasant.

Fuck, fuck, fuck. I can't claim to be the smartest girl in class, so I probably make the wrong choice, but I decide to go with bravado. To let them know I know they're there. Maybe it'll mean they flee and we won't be able to find out who they are. But even if I pretend not to know they're there, they're not likely to stay put once they find out we rescued John's mother.

So I say, loud, "I know you're there."

More rustling and scuffing. "Best you leave, little girl," says a voice. Male, as I suspected. English accent, but fading, so he's probably been here a long time.

"This is a dangerous place," says another voice, also male, with an even more faded English accent. "That dock could collapse at any moment."

The old vampire, the one I only suspect is there, who can hide his presence, and who *really* makes me nervous, doesn't speak. But I feel a familiar aura of fear, worn like a cloak but mostly – currently – hidden. And I know that fear could at any minute blossom into abject terror that could – literally – make me piss myself. I know this from experience and I'm not keen to experience it again.

Involuntarily, I take a few steps back. Hell, it can't be. Can it? Karasu? Here? Or it could be a different ancient vampire, right? Like, he's not the only one in existence. I don't think.

I take another step back, forgetting where I am, forgetting I'm standing near the end of a rotten dock, precariously balanced on crumbling pilings over a very fast, very cold river.

I just have time to take fox shape before I'm falling off the end of the dock. And then I hit the frigid water.

I wouldn't have thought a river could retain memories, seeing as it's constantly moving and changing its water. Or maybe its the old blood I brushed against with my arm earlier, or the magic John's mother pushed at me. But somehow when I hit the water, I'm also hit with a memory. But even though it's a memory of being a fox in the river, it's not *my* memory.

It starts when I lose my balance, really, so maybe it really isn't the river at all. When I lose my balance it's like I'm suddenly watching a split-screen movie – or more like I'm *living* a split screen movie. Or one of those video games where two players share the same computer monitor, one on each half.

On one side of the screen, I'm me, and on the other side, I'm a little girl wearing a sparkly t-shirt.

On the me side, I lose my balance, shift into fox shape, and plunge into the river.

On the little girl side, I'm running down the dock, full tilt, terrified, and then I'm a fox tangled in my human clothes and I struggle free and leap. And plunge into the water.

On the me side, I claw my way to the surface, turn to face downstream, try to aim for Wonder Island's southern tip from which I at least sort of know my way home, and I start swimming.

On the girl side, I relax and float, let the current take me, and watch my captors on the dock slowly recede, yelling after me. And I almost drown when terror and confusion overwhelm me.

As me, I swim until I'm exhausted, claw my way up the gravel bank, and lie panting next to Troll's huge chair.

As her, I paddle desperately to keep afloat, hit the shore back feet first, and scramble up the bank to lie panting next to a huge chair then scurry for the undergrowth as crackling branches and heavy footsteps warm me of the approach of a man the right size to fill the chair. I try to run, but I'm too weak and the man doesn't threaten me. He just watches, speaks soothingly until I creep towards his feet and then he dries me off as best he can with a handkerchief from his pocket. And he feeds me half the sandwich that was wrapped in the cloth.

The memory skips and I'm lying on the gravel watching a garbage bag float to shore. Each time I see it again, it's more and more buried in the bank. And one day, for no reason I can figure, I feel the desperate need to dig it out. The gravel hurts my feet as I dig, but I find it, tear it open, and pull out a piece of cloth that smells familiar and I don't know why. Then I forget the bag and chase a butterfly into the trees.

And the memory is gone as suddenly as it started, leaving me no clue as to where it came from or why it came to me.

But I do know one thing: Kit is alive.

Chapter Twenty-Two

MY LITTLE SISTER is alive.

Okay, she's trapped in the shape of a fox, but she's alive!

I drag myself to my feet, reach out with my fox senses and am overwhelmed by the life around me. I mean, every forest has a staggering amount of life in it; the trick is not to look too closely, too deeply.

But this forest! Almost everything I turn my attention to has a crackle of magic to it and I don't know how long I just sit there, staring about me in wonderment.

Then I shake my head and concentrate. *Little fox*, I think. *Kit? Can you hear me?* I don't get a reply, but I can't sense her nearby, so I don't really expect to. And I guess I don't *have* to see her right away. I know she's alive, and probably safer here as a fox than she would be as a human on the mainland.

And I *should* get back, let everyone know I'm safe. And maybe Wolfram can help me find Kit, or Sgian. And then I have to sit down, to laugh until I'm stretched out on the gravel, silly fox tongue hanging way out.

Because that day I met the little fox and chased her into the woods and Sgian came looking for me, the crow had said – I thought –"Hey, kid," to the fox. Thinking back now, I'm pretty sure she actually said, "Hey, *Kit*."

Which means Sgian knew all along. Except she didn't connect a magic fox with a human name to my missing sister.

Kristine Mei Fuchs, I think as loud as I can. *I'm your sister, Panya Su. Come find me. Find Troll, the big man. Or the crow, Sgian.* I stand up again. *I love you, beastie.*

Then I turn my weary legs downriver, try to follow along the paths Troll used when he first brought me out here. I'm pretty sure I'm at least heading in the right general direction.

I stop when I hear crashing in the bush and then a voice.

"Were you this loud when you were an *otherly* werewolf, little brother?" Thea. And there's only one person besides Wolfram she'd call "little brother." Magne.

The only answer is a low, and I think half-hearted, growl.

Then Wolfram's voice. "He's still not recovered, Thea. You can't expect perfection. Besides, his werewolf shape was a little bit different from his *varulf* shape."

I turn towards the voices, finding a burst of speed from somewhere, and hurtle out into the dappled sunlight of a broader path than the one I was attempting to follow. I run right into a huge, furry, grey-brown body.

"Magne," I say, changing to my human shape to throw my arms around him.

He grunts, and huffs, and almost falls over.

"You're a wolf again," I say, and I can't keep the happiness out of my voice. I'm giddy from learning my sister is alive, and giddy from Magne just being here.

I cling to him a moment, bury my face in his thick fur, and then I remember we're not alone. I sit back and see two other wolves, big and black and grey-eyed. They both shift as I watch, and then Wolfram and Thea are standing there.

"He's been practicing," says Thea. "Because he would not – like a good boy – stay in bed to rest."

The wolf shudders under my hands and then it's Magne, stark naked and apparently unaware of the fact. He pulls me close. "You were drowning," he says.

I hug him, stroke his hair, and feel the trembling in his muscles.

"You forgot clothes," says Thea. "Again."

"I'm still getting the hang of that," Magne mumbles into my hair.

"As it turns out," says Wolfram, "One of Magne's new magics is to know when you're in danger." He looks at me, head cocked. "But you appear to be fine."

"One of his other new magics," Thea says, looking down her nose at Wolfram, "Is the ability to get my brother out of the carnival and into wolf shape." Her voice is dry. "Magne kept saying you were drowning and insisted on coming out here to find you."

"I *did* fall in the river," I admit. "And I was – I am – pretty tired. But I'm okay now."

I grab Magne's face and grin at him. "And my sister's alive!"

He looks into my eyes and smiles. "That's fantastic, love. Do you know where she is?"

"Here," I say. And I tell them all about the vampires, and the rotten dock, and how I somehow re-lived one of Kit's memories when I fell in the river.

"She's a fox," I say. "*Hexenfuchs*, but I'm pretty sure she's trapped in fox shape."

"Perhaps," says Wolfram, "She isn't so much trapped, as hiding."

"Then why didn't she take human shape when I found her, or at least tell me who she was?"

"She may have been hiding so long she no longer remembers. I suspect you know what it's like staying in animal shape too long. You begin to forget there ever was another way of being."

"We have to help her," I say.

"Consider this," says Wolfram carefully. "She's safe here, and hidden. It may be best to let her remain as she is until we have figured out the mystery behind the vampires who killed your parents."

"Maybe," I say, reluctantly. "But you can't expect me to just pretend I haven't found her."

"Of course not." Wolfram smiles gently. "You may visit her whenever you like. Just let her remember in her own time, on her own terms. Don't push her or she may retreat even more. Let her continue to feel safe here."

And I get what he's saying. He's right, of course, and it's not that different from what I was already thinking myself. But dammit, I want to see my little sister again, to see how she's grown and changed in her human shape.

"I might suggest," says Thea, softly, which is unusual enough we all look at her. "That even after she learns her human self again, Wonder Island might be the best place for her to remain."

"But –" I say, and she waves her hand to stop me.

"She lived seven years as a human child, and seven years as a fox. Whatever else she may be, she is a creature of magic, and a wild thing, a feral child. The human world will be an unfamiliar and perhaps unwelcoming place. Remaining on Wonder Island will let her choose what she wants to be, without any pressure."

Magne strokes my hair and when I look at him, he smiles, but doesn't offer an opinion.

"Yeah," I say. "You're right. I hate to admit it, but you're right. She's safe here."

"Safe from witches who do love a fox familiar," Magne says then. "I seem to remember you telling me *hexenfuchs* make the best familiars of all."

I poke him. "Why are you so smart?"

He shrugs. "Can't be genetic." A brief look of hurt – there and gone again – crosses his face and I know he's thinking of his dad, his brothers.

"Okay," I say. "You're all right. But I'm going to spend a lot of time here, getting to know her again."

"Of course," says Wolfram. "And that leads to the job I have for you, should you want it." He looks at Magne. "But first let's find this wolf some pants."

It turns out Wolfram and Thea got together with most of Wonder Island's council – Karasu not included since it's daytime and that turned out to be a good thing once I told Wolfram about the ancient vampire I sensed at the glass factory. And anyway, Karasu's a "outside advisor" to the council and not an Islander at all, so no one cared that he wasn't there.

They all agreed that the several-years-old washing up of bodies, added to the new possibilities of hostile werewolves and vampires, indicates a need for better security.

The carnies would handle things at the dock and the carnival, and Troll would look after staff quarters and the House, as they had been doing. But Wolfram nominated Magne and me to handle security for the wilder parts of the Island, in association with the people and creatures who live there, of course. I guess the council members figured a *varulf* and a *hexenfuchs* would be perfect for the job, capable of covering a lot of ground, but also able to confront humans in human shape when necessary.

Wolfram was careful to point out that we'd be protecting the Islanders from outsiders, but also protecting outsiders from the Island.

So long as Magne could remember to manifest clothes when shifting back from wolf shape to human.

It would also give Magne a chance to work more closely with Wolfram, to see what he'd be taking up or turning down when he made his decision about being Wolfram's heir. He'd meet all the kin and folk of the Island, learn diplomacy, all that.

"It wasn't that long ago," Magne says, when Wolfram pauses for a reaction, "that I was certain there was no such thing as magic, that werewolves like me were just a result of a perfectly explicable symbiotic organism."

"As far as you were concerned," Wolfram answers, "that was the whole of it."

"Will we have to live on Wonder Island?" I ask. Because as much as I like it here, I don't really want to live here. Someday, maybe, but not now. Hell, I don't even want to give up my loft to move in with Magne and he only lives downstairs. And we spend most of our time together now, anyway.

"I actually think it would be best if you didn't," Wolfram says. "I'd also like you both to liaise with mainlanders. It's long past time we improved diplomatic relations with kin who choose not to live here."

"And humans with magic," I say, thinking of John.

Wolfram nods. "*Others*, as well."

I look at Magne and he looks at me. I raise my eyebrows.

"I was hoping there'd be more building involved," Magne says.

Wolfram laughs. "There is always maintenance on the Island. And renovations. You're more than welcome to work on that, too."

"I'm not great with people," I say.

Wolfram smiles at that. "I think you're better than you know. Everyone you've met on my Island trusts you right away. *I* did."

"Su's friends are loyal," Magne says.

"Well, as long as there's still lots of time for leisurely pursuits," I say. "Did you know Magne paints?"

Wolfram looks at Magne with interest.

"Yeah, I paint a mean fence," Magne says. "Walls, too."

"You know that's not what I meant."

He just looks at me.

"That time Ev had to stay in your spare room, I saw how you had it set up as a studio. I wanted to look through your shelf full of sketchbooks, but Ev wouldn't let me. He said it would be an invasion of privacy." I pretend to pout. "But I did sneak a look at what was on your easel. It was really good."

One dimple appears. "I do like to draw," he says.

Later, when we're back home in Magne's living room, I poke him until he grabs my hands, laughing.

"I'm not going to make you show me your art," I say. "But I'd really love to see it."

"I mostly just draw comics. It's not something I've shared with many people," he says. "Except…"

"Except?"

"I showed Dad once. I don't think I need to tell you his opinion of art."

"For sissies, if I had to guess," I say. "And a waste of time for someone who was going to grow up to be a werewolf and a farmer."

"I thought he was going to hit me. But he just took my sketchbook and threw it in the fireplace. Which was, I might add, lit and burning some well-seasoned hardwood logs at the time."

"How old were you?" I ask softly. I put my arms around him and he tucks my head against his chest.

"Nine or ten," he says. "I mean, I was a kid, my drawing sucked, but it hurt."

"What did you do?'

"The next day, when Dad was out in the woodlot, Thorstein came home with a big bag from the art supply store in Great Valley. He handed it to me and said, 'Don't fucking let him see it this time.' And then he just walked away."

I look up at his face and his gaze is far away. "What was in the bag?"

"Sketchbooks, tracing paper, pencils of so many kinds I didn't even know what to use them all for. Ink and pens, watercolors and brushes. Everything a kid would need to figure out what kind of art he wanted to make." His voice is quiet, his eyes sad.

"I'm so sorry, Mags."

He glances down at me. "For what?"

"He was your big brother. He loved you so much."

"Yeah, until he tried to kill me." He steps away, hand on his belly where the old scars are.

I don't let him walk away, but follow him, embrace him from behind when he leans on the kitchen counter to stare out the window. "You know that was probably your father," I say.

"What I can't figure out," he says, putting his hand over mine where it lays on his chest. "Is how Dad got Thors to attack me."

"He wasn't in his right mind," I say. "Isn't that basically what it means to be a berserker? To go into an unstoppable killing rage?"

"That's just it, though. When Thors was at his worst, Dad would lock him in the basement of the farmhouse. Unless he needed somebody… dealt with. I guess he still does that." He squeezes my hand. "Ever since I can remember, I'd steal the key, sneak down there. Hell, when I was eight I taught myself to use the keycutter. Dad bought it at an auction because Bjarni was always losing the tractor keys. I made my own key so I wouldn't have to steal Dad's.

"I'd sneak down there every full moon, when the *berserkrgang* was worst, to sit with Thors. There he'd be, half wolfed out and barely conscious of who he was, and I'd creep down the stairs with a plate of sandwiches and two huge chocolate milkshakes.

"He'd curl up on the mattress on the floor and I'd lean against him, and we'd eat cheese and roast beef and suck fucking milkshakes up with straws – and if you've ever seen a werewolf try to use a straw…

"I'd read to him. *Archie* comics, and *Swamp Thing*. He really liked *Swamp Thing*. When I got a bit older, I'd read him whatever fantasy author I was into, or Stephen King.

"Dad never knew, and Mum never told him. Even Bjarni kept his fat mouth shut."

He turns away from the window and wraps his arms around me again.

"And Thors never once attacked me. Sometimes I'd go down there with my sandwiches and milkshakes – I wasn't lactose intolerant yet – and he'd be raving, clawing the walls, completely out of his mind, and he'd see me and just… stop. He'd go still and lay down and I'd read to him."

"He loved you even when he didn't know who he was," I say.

Magne clears his throat. "Yeah. So when I was… When they hunted me, to punish me as the Elders decided, I was more afraid of Dad and Bjarni, because I knew Thors would never hurt me."

He buries his face against my hair and breathes against the top of my head for a few breaths.

"Bjarni caught me," he says. "Clawed me up good." He holds out his arms, where the thin, pale tracery of scars is visible in the fading daylight.

"He did all that?" I know his whole body is covered with those pale lines.

"Most of it. Some of it was from later. I got in a lot of fights after that." He turns his arms over to look at the scars on the other side, then wraps them around me again. "I thought Dad would… I don't think I really thought he'd kill me, just hurt me bad, so I'd learn my lesson, whatever the fuck that was supposed to be."

"To do as you're told? To be what they wanted you to be?"

"Yeah, maybe. Anyway, Dad never laid a hand on me. Not that night. Instead, he brought Thorstein."

"You don't have to tell me this, Mags. I know what happened."

He shakes his head. "The worst part wasn't even watching my own guts spill out onto the ground, like butchering a pig. It was seeing the look in Thorstein's eyes. I mean, he wasn't *there*. He didn't know me; he just saw a body to be torn open at Dad's direction."

He stops and his nostrils flare, his jaw clenches. I stroke his tense back muscles and I'm not even sure he feels it.

"Having it be Thorstein that ripped me open was really what almost killed me. I didn't even *want* to live after that."

He clears his throat again.

"I'm glad you did live," I say.

"I guess I'm just too stubborn to die." Then he's quiet, just holding me.

"After that," he says. "I was afraid of him. Of Thorstein, who had always protected me, who had never been violent towards me before, even when he was at his worst. *That's* what I most hate my dad for.

"And Thors… he never apologized. He wouldn't even look at me, tried never to be anywhere near me. I wanted to ask him why, but from that day until I turned eighteen and walked out of my father's house for good, he hardly said two sentences in a row to me. He still hasn't."

I listen to his heartbeat, then I say, "Maybe he couldn't forgive himself."

"Yeah, maybe," he says. "It sure seems like he let Bjarni turn him into an asshole, though. You saw what he did to my truck."

"I also saw that when your dad told him to deal with you, he hit you like a freight train, but he didn't use either his claws or his teeth."

"Mmm." He kisses the top of my head, then unwinds his arms and pours good bourbon into a couple of glasses and heads for the couch. He sprawls, I sit, and we both take thoughtful sips.

After a minute, I notice he's staring at the wall with an odd smile on his face, so I look at what he's looking at.

"When did you get that?" I say, trying not to sound horrified. Between two tall bookcases and over a glass-fronted cabinet full of leather-bound volumes there's a painting in a fancy silver-gilt frame. It's a howling wolf and full moon in that unfortunate airbrush style that was popular in the 1980s for decorating the sides of vans.

It might be the worst example of its kind I've ever seen, though to be honest, I haven't made a point of looking at airbrush pictures, or depictions of howling wolves. Except the ones on Magne's boxers, and then it's not the wolves on the fabric I'm looking at, but the wolf *inside* the fabric.

"Like it?" he says. "A buddy of mine painted it. I just got it back from the framer's before the proverbial shit hit the equally proverbial fan." He's holding very still, which means he's trying to keep me from seeing how he feels.

And *that* means he either really wants me to like it and is afraid that I won't, or else he's trying not to laugh.

"Um," I say, tilting my head as if it will somehow lessen the painting's awfulness. "The framing looks expensive." Okay, *that* was a dumb thing to say under any circumstances.

He snorts. "I had it done before Dad decided to banish me and make sure no werewolf in Riverbend will ever hire me again."

I look at him, and even though his mouth is still he can't stop his eyes from crinkling at the corners. He is laughing. Or trying not to.

"I mean," I say, attempting to sound like I haven't figured out his game. "It's *your* place. You're the one who needs to like it."

"You *don't* like it," he says, sounding crushed. Sounding *fake* crushed. His eyes are crinkling even more and he can no longer entirely control the upward quirk at the corner of his mouth. Both dimples are showing, even though he's almost managing to keep the rest of his face from smiling.

"It's fucking awful," I finally say, and his laughter bursts out. He falls back against the cushions, his glass of bourbon balanced on his stomach, held in place by one hand.

"Your face!" he says. "You were trying so hard to figure out if I was serious before you said anything that might hurt my feelings." His whole body is shaking with laughter now, and I can't help but join in.

"You're an asshole," I tell him.

"Yes, but you love me anyway."

"Lucky for you."

He stops laughing then, takes a sip of his drink, and says, "It *is* lucky for me."

"Flatterer."

"Only because it's true."

"Hrumph." I sip my drink to hide my smile. As annoying as it is to be pranked, I'm glad he's able to laugh. And I have to admit, he's been building this one up for a long time, and never once let on it was a joke until now.

"Are you really going to leave it hanging there?" I say.

He leans forward to put his glass on the coffee table.

"Matt's going to hang it in his shop."

"The guy who painted it?"

"Yeah."

"Wait, is that the guy who does pinstriping?"

"Yep."

"Tell him to stick to pinstriping."

He chuckles, strokes a hand down my back, and says, "No, I'm not going to keep it on the wall." Then he points to a brown-paper-wrapped package leaning against the cabinet. "That's what's actually going to hang there."

"What is it?"

"Open it." He's got a mischievous look on his face again, but it's a different kind of mischief. And he looks... apprehensive?

I look at him for a moment longer, and though the laughter is gone from his face, there's something else that makes him smile softly, makes his eyes glow.

Soft expressions look good on his strong, hard face. I want to kiss him, but instead I get up, pick up the package, and lay it on the coffee table.

I kneel across from where he sits, look up at him.

"Open it," he says.

"I'm almost afraid to, now."

"No more jokes, I promise."

So I peel off the tape and fold back the paper. This painting is also framed in silver-gilt, but it looks tasteful instead of tacky. And the picture. I stare at it a long time.

It's me. It's a portrait of me, just my face, my hair a stylized swirl around the paper and tangled in my hair, a fox. The watercolor paint is luminous and even though I recognize my face, this me is far more beautiful than the me I see in the mirror every morning. I look for a signature. Then I look up at Magne.

He looks... I don't know, hopeful? Nervous?

"Do you like it?" he says.

"*You* painted this."

"Yeah."

"You painted *me*."

"I hope you don't mind," he says, voice gone uncertain, which is in no way normal for him.

"Holy fuck, Magne. It's so good. *You're* so good."

"The woman who framed it wants me to have a show in her gallery."

I forget to close my mouth and just stare at him. He's looked away from me and is concentrating on his own hands. Then I remember to close my mouth, only to open it again and say – not even sure if sound is going to come out – "There's only one thing wrong with it."

"Oh?" He says this softly, and turns his gaze to the painting, searching to see the flaw before I can point it out.

"You made me way more beautiful that I really am."

He smiles and shakes his head, meeting my eyes with his. "I don't think I made you beautiful enough, love." He reaches across the table to take my hand. "I tried to paint you exactly how I see you."

And then I kiss him, because what am I going to say to that? And I climb over the table and into his lap, and have my way with him, right there on the couch.

CHOSEN of GODS

read on for a preview of the *Wolves of Autumn* series

Chapter One

A werewolf walks into an art gallery. Sounds like the set up for a real groaner of a joke, no? Well, there's groaning, all right, but not much of a joke.

I'm supposed to be re-hanging the gallery, but instead I'm trying to decide how to frame the latest painting I took on consignment when a guy walks in with a portfolio under his arm and I have to work *really* hard not to stare.

Because I gotta tell you, this dude is worth looking at. Tall, seriously built, strong jaw, killer cheekbones, and dark hair that should look unkempt but instead looks like he just rolled out of bed after giving you the fuck of your life. Every movement is relaxed but efficient, sending his muscles sliding under his skin and my libido soaring.

He looks at me and smiles, and fuck me, he's got a dimple in his cheek. And deep brown eyes I could stare into all day.

"Hello!" I say, putting on my helpful gallery owner voice. *Do not drool, Raine*, I tell myself.

"Hey," he says. "I'm told you're the best framing shop in town." His voice is deep and smoky, like really, really expensive whiskey, and makes me shiver like whiskey does, too. I mean, I don't actually, physically shiver, but I feel that voice from the top of my head and the tips of my toes right to my crotch.

"We do our best," I say, walking over to the design table and patting its top. "Let's see what you've brought me."

"Okay, but don't laugh," he says, but he's grinning, and shit, he's got *two* dimples. He opens the portfolio and pulls out a canvas board, lays it on the table, bottom towards me. Automatically, I spin it around so the bottom faces him to make it easier for him to choose a frame. I'm used to looking at art upside-down. And then I *do* look at it.

And I barely manage not to laugh. "I never laugh at anyone's art," I say. I think I manage to get it out with a straight face and an even voice.

"At least not to their face," he says, which is of course exactly what I was thinking, and I can hear the amusement in his voice. I glance up, and his eyes are crinkling at the corners.

Fuck. I love a guy who smiles with his eyes as much as his mouth. And speaking of mouths, this guy's got a wide one, built for grinning. And kissing. And other things.

So the painting he's deposited on my design table is a wolf. A howling wolf against a full moon. Painted with an airbrush. It's one of the tackiest things I've ever seen. It *might* be tackier if it was painted on black velvet.

"So," I say. "Any thoughts on how you want to frame this? Black? Bright colours? Fancy? Plain?"

"Completely over the fucking top," he says. Then, "Sorry. I spend too much time on construction sites."

Okay, construction worker. Not exactly intellectual or artistic. But a good honest job. Pays well. Not that I'm interested in anything long-term. Or even medium-term. I like to take home strays, give them something good to eat, and send them on their way. I sneak a look at his hands, and they're clean. No dirt under the fingernails is a good sign. Or maybe it's a sign he's got someone to keep them clean *for*. His hands are also calloused and muscular. Clever-looking, if a bit hairy-knuckled.

"No shit," I say, and he laughs. "I went to art school and dated a chef. I can handle swearing." I lean on the table and contemplate the painting. "If you want over the top, I'd start with a linen liner. No. Black silk. And an ornate gilded frame. But maybe silver rather than gold, because of all the cool tones in the painting."

"I like the sound of that." I look at his face again and he still looks like he's trying to hold back laughter.

"Is it for a gift, or for yourself?" I say, reaching for a sample of the fanciest silver-gilt frame we carry, and grabbing a wide silk-covered liner and arranging them on one corner of the painting.

"It's for a joke," he says.

I raise my eyebrows. "Custom framing is expensive," I say. "Might be a bit pricey for a joke."

"It's been a while since I had something framed, but I have an idea," he says. "And when my girlfriend sees this, the look on her face is going to be worth whatever it costs."

"Ah, gift for the girlfriend." Damn. I try not to let my disappointment show. But they do say all the hot ones are taken. Or is that all the good ones are taken and the hot ones are assholes? I always get those mixed up.

"She thinks I have terrible taste in art," he says. "That I actually, unironically love the airbrush howling wolf shit."

"But you don't." This guy seems nice, too. Even if he was single he probably wouldn't act like a dog, which is kind of what you need when you want to take a guy home for a good lay and nothing more.

"I think it's amusing. Crap, but amusing. I got a buddy who pinstripes and airbrushes cars to paint this for me. He's going to hang it in his shop once the joke's over."

Then he glances up at movement outside the window. "Hang on," he says. "I parked in a fifteen and a spot out front just opened up. I'll be right back."

I watch him walk to the door, and holy hell, that ass! Firm and muscular and his jeans fit so perfectly I can imagine what his butt looks like naked. I fan myself with the stack of work orders.

My colleague Katie pops her head out of the back room. I wondered how long it would take for her to react to the sexy as fuck male voice and make an appearance. She whistles, low and long, after the door closes. "Tell me he has a brother," she says.

"He has a girlfriend, but I'll report back on the sibling situation."

"Excellent," she says, and vanishes again.

I look back to the window and an absolutely pristine Chevy C-10 pickup, blue with white roof, gotta be a 1970, pulls up at the curb. I can feel the rumble of the big engine more than I can hear it. And smokin' hot airbrush wolf dude gets out and heads back into the store. Even his fucking ride is hot.

"So you found a nice woman who'll put up with your idea of a great joke, hunh, cowboy?" I say, and immediately bite my tongue. It's a good thing I'm half-owner of this place, or I'd have been fired a long time ago for being cheeky. Thirty-seven and still as mouthy as when I was seventeen.

But he smiles and his face goes soft, by which I can tell he's completely in love with her, whomever the lucky woman is. Okay, for real no chance with this morsel. Damn.

"She's a saint," he says. "And a goddess." Then he opens the portfolio and pulls out another piece. As the sun through the window hits it from behind I recognize the watermark on the paper. Top quality, and very expensive, watercolour paper. "This is what I'm really going to hang on the wall, after she sees the wolf."

He hesitates, then puts the paper on the table, over the hideous airbrushed piece. He handles it by the edges, like he knows his way around art on paper. So okay, maybe I misjudged him. Big, muscley construction guy doesn't necessarily mean unrefined, right?

I lean over and look at the paper, and then I have to turn it to face me so I can *really* look at it.

"Wow," I say. It's a watercolour, rich, but restrained. Whoever did this knows how to handle a brush, knows when to add a hint of darker outline to bring out a shape, and when to let the white of the paper do the work. "Let me guess," I say. "Your girlfriend?" It's a stunning portrait of a woman with a fox. She's fucking gorgeous, but shown in a way that looks like she's unaware of being observed. Her river of black hair – painted without even a touch of black paint – swirls around the paper, and her eyes are the same amber as those of the fox.

"Yeah," he says. I glance up and I swear he's blushing under his day or two's worth of facial scruff.

"This might sound weird, seeing as it's a painting of your girlfriend, but who's the artist? I'd love to get a print. Maybe carry their work in the gallery."

"Oh," he says. "It's mine."

"Your work?"

"Yeah."

"Fuck me," I say (see, mouthy). "You're really good."

He's staring at the painting, but he looks up at me, surprise in his wide – fucking gorgeous – brown eyes. "Thanks," he says.

"You ever want to have a show, let me know. We're always looking for new artists."

"I mostly draw comics," he says.

"No shit."

He shrugs. "I was thinking about putting them up online, maybe crowdfund to print a paperback."

So we do a design for the beautiful watercolour – just as extravagant as the wolf, but it looks elegant instead of overdone – and when I give him the quote he doesn't even flinch, and this is one of the highest-priced jobs I've done in a while.

I write his name and number on the work order. "Magne Thorvaldson. Very Scandinavian."

"Norwegian," he says. "My dad and my brothers were born in Norway."

"You have brothers?" I can't help the note of interest that creeps into my voice. In fact, I might even encourage it.

"I'd offer to introduce you," he says, "but they're both assholes."

"Don't all brothers say that about each other?"

He shrugs.

"Older or younger?" I ask and a smirk tugs up one corner of his mouth.

"Older," he says. "But really, total dogs, both of them."

"I like dogs." I look him right in the eye as I say it, and one of his eyebrows quirks up. And "older" is the right answer, because he looks thirty, maybe thirty-five, which is on the young side for my current tastes.

"Who's a dog?" That's Katie again. I'm surprised she stayed out back as long as she did, with Mr Sexy Voice out here. As usual, she's dressed to the hilt in the perfect retro outfit: fifties-style red-dyed hair, makeup, dress, shoes, and all. Even her pointy bra is period-appropriate. I don't miss the appreciative look Magne gives her, but I also don't miss that there's not a trace of lust in it.

Katie makes me feel underdressed in my comfy linen trousers and flowy top, with my dark hair gathered into a simple bun at the nape of my neck. She turns heads everywhere, and to tell the truth, we bonded over drinks and tales of past conquests before we ever realized we both loved art and dreamed of opening a gallery. We even sometimes make bets on who gets a particular tasty specimen of manhood into bed first. We enable each other, is what I'm saying, which is great for our friendship, but maybe not so good for the condition of the hearts of the kinder men we've collected.

Unlucky for her, another customer comes in before she gets her answer, and she has to go be helpful instead of flirting with Mr Tall, Dark, and Taken.

"Your brothers like art, too?" I ask.

"Not that I'm aware of."

"Are they as… tall as you?" I say, 'cause he's gotta be well over six feet and my five-foot-four ass has to look way up to meet his eyes. Not that I've ever shied away from climbing a tall man.

"Thors is taller," he says. "Bjarni is… not."

"Taller?" I say, looking him up and down. It hardly seems possible.

"Taller."

"And how tall is not?"

"Only five eleven."

"That's not so short."

"Not according to Bjarni, whose baby brother bests him by five inches."

"And how much taller is taller?"

"Six ten." He seems very amused by my questioning, and leans one hip against the counter, like he figures I'm going to keep him there a while.

"Holy fuck."

"He's also very… burly."

"Is that a euphemism for fat? 'Cause that's not a deal breaker." I mean, if he's half as good looking as this specimen, I don't care. I'm an equal-opportunity slut.

"No, it's a euphemism muscles on top of muscles."

"More than you?"

His mouth twitches and a dimple appears then vanishes. "More. But really, my brothers are assholes."

"Irredeemable assholes?"

"There might be hope for Thors. Bjarni's been a dick for a very long time and I don't think he plans to change. I'm pretty sure he *likes* being an asshole."

"So can I get his number?"

"Bjarni?"

"The other one. Thors?"

"Thorstein," he says, and frowns. Something soft and pained crosses his face and is gone. "He's had some pretty bad mental health issues." Regret, that's what I'm seeing.

"Still," I say. "Not necessarily a dealbreaker. What kind of issues? And does he look anything like you?" I'm trying not to come right out and tell this guy he's hot right to his face. Maybe he already knows. But he strikes me as a guy who's comfortable in his body, in his own skin, who likes his physical self but really isn't concerned with what other people think. And that's just extra hot, you know?

"There's a family resemblance," Magne says. "Thors is taller, bigger, blonder, and has no interest in much other than taking over the family farm from my parents."

"Farmboy, hey?" I say. "I like animals."

"Bjarni is shorter, not quite as blond, and has similar ambitions, except for the part that's actually hard work."

I shrug. "I wasn't thinking of proposing marriage. But honestly, this Bjarni sounds like Katie's type. She likes assholes." I point my chin to where my colleague is showing an older lady the selection of signed reproductions we just started carrying. And it's true. You fuck an asshole, you don't have to worry about him hanging around too long after.

"And you like dogs," he says, his lips curving. Understanding has crossed his face, that I'm only interested in a good time. Then he shrugs and pulls out his phone. "I'll text them, but I can't guarantee a response. We don't get along."

He doesn't hide the screen as he types, and I see the message before he sends it.

Hey asshole. Excellent Framing on Station Street has a couple of very lovely women who are for some inexplicable reason interested in meeting my brothers. Try not to be a dick.

Texts in full sentences. With big words. And checks to make sure everything is spelled correctly before sending. A bit weird, but okay.

His phone buzzes and he glances at the screen and then turns it so I can see better.

fuck u shitstain, it says. I'm pretty sure I can guess which brother sent it.

"Thanks for trying," I say as I ring up his deposit.

"Bjarni's too curious for his own good," he says. "He'll be here. And Thors will probably come along to keep an eye on him."

I hand him my card and give him a wink as he leaves. I can't resist saying, "If you ever decide to leave your gorgeous girlfriend, look me up."

"Not gonna happen," he says, and his grin has a lot of teeth in it. "But I appreciate the sentiment."

I hope he's right and his brothers do show, because if I can't have that one, I want one like him.

NICO SILVER LIVES like a hermit on the edge of the woods, and haunts used bookstores like a wraith. They fully expected to be found someday as a mummified old corpse crushed under a toppled to-be-read pile, but the rise of e-books has made that somewhat less likely, though the books will always outnumber even the dustbunnies. Nico will read just about anything, including the instructions on the back of medicine bottles, but has a particular fondness for good stories with a hint of magic. They write dark, sexy urban fantasy, and sometimes dream in black and white.